CAPTURE

THE

FLAG

KATE MESSNER

SCHOLASTIC INC.

No part of this publication may be reproduced, stored in a retrieval system, or transmitted in any form or by any means, electronic, mechanical, photocopying, recording, or otherwise, without written permission of the publisher. For information regarding permission, write to Scholastic Inc., Attention: Permissions Department, 557 Broadway, New York, NY 10012.

This book was originally published in hardcover by Scholastic Press in 2012.

ISBN 978-0-545-41974-1

12 11 10 9 8 7 6 5 4 3 2 1   12 13 14 15 16 17/0

Printed in the U.S.A.   40
First paperback printing, September 2012

Title page character illustrations copyright © 2012 by Yuta Onoda
Interior illustrations copyright © 2012 by Whitney Lyle
Book design by Whitney Lyle

FOR MAL CUTAIAR — TEACHER,
HISTORIAN, AND ONE OF THE
GOOD GUYS

ONE

They never should have unlocked the door.

They never should have let them in.

The party had already gone late in a blur of red, white, and blue bunting and orchestra music and fancy gowns and thin, crispy crackers with caviar.

The tour wasn't on the schedule.

But Erma Emma Jones, the director of the Smithsonian Museum of American History, made curator Jeff Brodie unlock the chamber one last time. "We have a dignitary who's requested a private viewing," she said.

"But we've already secured the area." Brodie's brow wrinkled as if he felt personally responsible for each of the museum's 355,000 treasures of American history. "The key is way down in the lockbox."

"This *particular* dignitary made a *particularly* large

donation. He would like a tour for his group." The director looked over her glasses and handed Brodie a clipboard.

Brodie sighed. He was tired of dignitaries. He never watched the news and couldn't have cared less about all the politicians and visiting heads of state who came through the museum. But he nodded and set off toward the escalator, weaving through women in ball gowns and waiters balancing trays of tiny cream puffs.

"Excuse me." The gala was so crowded he nearly had to climb over the three kids sitting on a bench next to the bronze statue of George Washington. The freckly-faced girl hovered over a purple notebook, her pen flying back and forth across the page. The skinny boy with the messy black hair held a thick paperback and nibbled on cookies from a napkin in his lap. Next to him, a sturdier boy with short-cropped hair poked his thumbs furiously at a handheld video game. None of them looked up.

Brodie took the escalator to the basement security suite, buzzed the officer at the main desk, and entered to get the key.

"One more," he said. The officer grunted, took a bite of his meatball sub, and looked up at the bank of monitors that showed every corner of the museum. Brodie punched in his code, opened the safe, and pulled out the key card. On one monitor, he could see the final tour group, already gathered near the exhibit.

"Be back soon."

Upstairs, five men waited, all in black tuxedos. Two were stocky bodybuilder types. There was a skinny one who kept rubbing his bald head as if he'd forgotten to put on his hair, a younger one who wore sneakers with his tux, and a tall one who seemed to be in charge. His perfectly sculpted, wavy brown hair made him look as if he'd stepped out of a shampoo commercial.

"Good evening," the tall man said when Brodie arrived, "and thank you. We are so looking forward to this tour."

Brodie's eyes dropped to his clipboard. "Wait — I have four on the clearance list. Not five."

"Is that so? Because my good friend — your boss, I believe — assured me that whatever my group wanted, there would be no problem." The tall man nodded across the room, where Erma Emma Jones was hugging the orchestra director. Over his shoulder, she nodded at Brodie and flicked her hand toward the exhibit, motioning for him to get moving.

So he did.

He led the men past the charred piece of timber left behind when British troops burned the White House in 1814.

Past wall panels that told the story of the siege of Baltimore just days later.

Past a real British bombshell — one of hundreds that fell that night, blasting shrapnel into Fort McHenry.

And right up to the polished silver punch bowl molded in the shape of a bombshell and engraved with the name of Fort McHenry commander George Armistead. To the right of the punch bowl hung a portrait of Baltimore seamstress Mary Pickersgill. She had eyes that followed you wherever you went in the exhibit, right into the far, shadowy corners.

Brodie lifted the lanyard with the key card from around his neck, reached over the top of the portrait's frame, and inserted the thin rectangle of plastic into a hidden card reader.

When he pulled it out, a navy blue panel on the opposite wall slid to the side with a quiet hum, revealing a smooth steel door that looked as if it had never been touched. Not a single fingerprint smudged its cool surface.

"One moment." Brodie punched a code into a numeric keypad at the side of the door, then stepped forward and looked into an eyepiece. There was a series of high-pitched beeps, then a click from deep within the steel door's lock mechanism.

Brodie pushed it forward and stepped into a short hallway with another steel door at the opposite end. He motioned for the men to follow. "That first door has to close." It thunked shut behind them, and immediately, one of the bodybuilders began shifting back and forth on his shiny black shoes.

"Claustrophobic?" Brodie asked, smiling a little. "If we were attempting to break into the chamber, both doors would remain sealed now. The double doors form a mantrap; we'd be locked in this passageway until the police arrived." He paused. "But of course, security is well aware of our tour." Brodie punched in the code, stepped up to have his retina scanned again, and waited for the second door to open.

"In we go." He led the men into a cool, dark room. "Your eyes will adjust in a moment."

The tall man stepped toward the table, his dress shoes clacking on the concrete floor. "There she is," he whispered, and breathed in a long, deep breath, as if he could still smell the smoke from the battle drifting through the stars and stripes. "So this is the actual flag that inspired Francis Scott Key to write 'The Star-Spangled Banner.'"

"Yes, indeed."

"What a treasure. Is the preservation work complete?"

"It is, sir," Brodie said. He wished the man would step back a bit. He was breathing all over the stars.

"They won't be patching the rest?" The man gestured toward a gaping hole where one of the flag's original fifteen stars was missing.

"No, sir. At this point, the flaws are part of her history. The bits of stripes were cut away over the years and tucked into caskets by the widows of Fort McHenry's heroes. The star there" — Brodie gestured toward the hole — "was supposedly given to an important person, according to old letters. Some say it's buried with Lincoln, but we've found no evidence to support that." He took a deep breath of the room's cool, quiet air. "At any rate, it's all part of her story now. We won't be fixing anything more — just trying to prevent further damage."

One of the bodybuilders stepped forward and whispered something in the tall man's ear, just as Brodie's cell phone buzzed. The curator cringed as if the noise alone could pollute the pristine air of the room. He looked down to read a message and let out a sharp sigh. "If you'll excuse me, gentlemen, I'm being summoned to deal with an issue in our First Ladies exhibit. Officer Lahue is on his way to escort you out."

The steel door whooshed open once more, and a Smithsonian guard entered the room. "She told me to get you there, pronto," he told Brodie, reaching out for the clipboard. "I'll finish up here."

"Thanks, Paul." Brodie gave a hurried wave and left the chamber.

"All right, gentlemen. Have a last look if you will. We need to lock down for the night." Paul looked down at the clipboard. "Let's see . . . checking out a final tour group of four, correct?"

"Correct, sir," the tall man said, and turned briskly toward the door. "And thank you. It has been a rare gift to see the flag up close."

"My pleasure. All set, then?"

Four men followed Paul out of the chamber, past the silver punch bowl and the portrait of Mary Pickersgill, and she watched as they walked by the charred timber and the British bombshell and spilled back out into the reception hall, where the crowd was clapping for the orchestra's final piece, and the champagne flutes were almost empty.

The fifth man — the one whose name was never on the clipboard — had disappeared.

TWO

The three kids on the bench near Washington's statue weren't friends. If they had introduced themselves, they might have learned they were all in seventh grade, and their schools shared the same February break. They might have learned that they were all only children with busy parents and were used to entertaining themselves.

If they had talked a little longer, they may have discovered they had something even more unusual in common.

Ancestors who had crafted some of the most stunning artwork and conceived of some of the greatest inventions in history.

Relatives who had taken a secret oath, made a promise to protect the world's artifacts, and passed that promise down through generations.

Close family members who wore silver jewelry in the shape of an ancient jaguar goddess, took urgent, whispered phone calls in the middle of the night, and traveled across continents to keep those promises, no matter what.

But the kids didn't talk about any of that as they sat together at the museum, even though the night seemed to go on forever while the adults blabbed on and on.

Anna Revere-Hobbs had been too busy scribbling notes for the story about the museum reception she was going to write for her school newspaper back in Vermont. It wasn't the story she'd planned; she'd wanted to get an interview with the man her dad hoped would be the next president, but the presidential primary election season had begun, so he was too busy shaking hands all night to notice her with her notebook. Anna's mom was a TV news anchor back home, and nobody ever ignored *her* questions. What was the use being a senator's daughter if it didn't even get you the good interviews? Anna sighed. She had plenty of notes from the reception and was more than ready to go when her father said good-bye to his staffers and took her back to his Washington, DC, apartment to pack for the flight home the next day.

★　　★　　★

José McGilligan had been disappointed in the night, too. He hadn't seen his mother in three weeks. Sure, it was fantastic that she was one of the textile scientists selected for the Star-Spangled Banner restoration project. But he thought tonight they'd be just regular McGilligans again, he and his mom and dad goofing around and enjoying dinner and maybe some cake. He'd never imagined this big, elaborate thing with fish eggs and desserts that looked too fancy to eat. There wasn't a cupcake to be found. His mom was busy being congratulated, fluttering around in her evening gown and black-and-silver shoes and her favorite dangly earrings with the silver jaguars. His dad was busy being proud. José was proud, too, but after a while, he got bored and slipped his tattered paperback copy of *Harry Potter and the Goblet of Fire* from his backpack in the coatroom. He found some halfway normal cookies, wrapped them in a napkin, and parked himself on the bench, where he read all the way to the part in the graveyard before it was time to return to the hotel.

Henry Thorn didn't want to come in the first place. But his father had to go on a stupid cruise for his stupid honeymoon with stupid Bethany. So he was stuck

staying with his aunt Lucinda, who was not stupid but so smart it was painful to be around her.
She'd inflicted every museum, library, memorial, and
monument in the nation's capital upon Henry this
past week.

"Look, Henry! The original Declaration of Inde-
pendence!"

"Look, Henry! The original Bill of Rights!"

"Look, Henry! An original Vermeer portrait!"

"Look, Henry! The original Wright Brothers'
plane!"

This fancy-fest at the museum was the icing on
the cake. Aunt Lucinda made Henry wear a tie, and
she was all dressed up in a sparkly green gown, pointy
high-heeled shoes, and a silver bracelet with some big
leaping cat charm jingling all over the place. She was
in serious Look-Henry mode, too.

"Look, Henry! The original ruby slippers from *The
Wizard of Oz!*"

"Look, Henry! One of Abraham Lincoln's original
black top hats!"

Henry liked Aunt Lucinda; he really did. And he
knew she was just keeping him busy to get his mind
off his dad's stupid wedding and his mom, who had
died of stupid cancer three years ago. But after a week,
all the "Look, Henrys" were driving Henry crazy. All
he wanted to see was an original cheeseburger and his
video game screen. At least the girl and the skinny kid

on the bench left him alone until Aunt Lucinda came to get him to go back to her apartment.

"Look, Henry!" she said on the way out. "An original gunboat from Lake Champlain! Not far from your house in Vermont."

That last "Look, Henry" bugged him more than all the rest because his house in Vermont wasn't going to be his house much longer. At the end of the school year, they were leaving Burlington's Old North End and the house where his mom used to make corn muffins on Sundays. They were leaving his middle school and the park by the lake where he took his little neighbor, Will, when he was babysitting, and they were moving to stupid Boston with stupid Bethany because — what great luck! — Boston University had hired his dad for a stupid teaching position.

"Look, Henry!" Aunt Lucinda said. "One of the cannonballs that sunk the boat is still lodged in the side of it!"

Henry looked at the cannonball and then looked at his watch. Tomorrow, he'd be on a plane going back to where he had *originally* planned to spend his February break. Home.

By midnight, Anna was asleep on her dad's pullout sofa.

José was asleep in his hotel room.

Henry was under his blanket in the guest bedroom of Aunt Lucinda's apartment, determined to make it to Level 9 before he slept.

And in the hermetically sealed chamber, behind two steel doors, guarded by a nineteenth-century flag maker's portrait, the bald man from the tour group crawled out from behind a large table.

He shook out his legs, careful not to move too quickly. He didn't want to raise the temperature in the room. If a spike set off the alarm at Central Security, he'd have trouble.

He stepped up to the table, hands shaking as he reached out to feel the rough woolen fabric, so threadbare and tender. He'd have to work carefully. Delicately.

Just as he was about to reach under the edge of the flag table, there was a muffled click from the direction of the entrance.

The man froze.

Footsteps.

Another click.

He slipped back into the shadows just as the second steel door opened and a woman stepped into the room.

"Well, you've had a long day now, haven't you?" Her voice was quiet, but it filled the chamber, echoing off the walls. No one answered her. "Humidity levels look good, a touch high maybe, but I think we're okay. Well, this is it, my friend. Time for me to say good-bye." Her feet — the man could see black pumps with silver bows under the table — were still. The woman sighed, her breath a whisper in the quiet room, until finally her heels clicked back to the door, and it slid shut behind her.

The man counted to one thousand. One thousand shallow breaths from behind the table. His knees creaked when he finally stood.

He stepped forward and slipped one hand under the edge of the table until he felt the first cold metal clamp that secured the flag, on its protective backing, to the display table.

Slowly, he turned the clamp until he felt its cool weight drop into his palm. He slipped it into his pocket and slid his hand along the smooth underside of the table to the next clamp.

One by one, he removed them. When his pockets were almost full, he began setting the clamps carefully on the floor instead.

When he was halfway around the table, the man looked at his watch.

12:14.

He needed to go faster. The shift changed at one, and the guard they had bribed would soon be gone, replaced by another who hadn't been paid to look the other way.

With seven minutes to spare, as he was reaching

for the final clamp, he sneezed. Darn allergies. Who knew what kind of old dust he'd stirred up just touching the flag.

The man sniffled. Another sneeze tickled his nose.

No, he thought. The noise and the moisture could set off alarms.

And he was so close.

He wrinkled his itchy nose and puckered his twitching lips.

The sneeze went away, and he unscrewed the final clamp.

Then, as if he were folding up a beach blanket, the man took a corner of the flag in his hands and pulled it across the table until it rested on the opposite corner. He folded the flag over and over on itself until it was piled up on an edge of the table, the size of an extra-large garbage bag, stuffed full.

He heaved the fragile bundle over his shoulder — he could smell its dusty age — and calmly walked out of the room.

There was no problem.

No lock.

No retina scan.

The security system was designed to keep people out. Not in.

His path to the freight elevator was clear, as he knew it would be at this hour. He punched in the code he'd memorized. The metal cage opened, and waiting, as promised, was the black case on wheels, plenty big enough for the flag.

It was almost done. With trembling fingers, he flipped the latches and lifted the lid. He eased the flag inside, tucked in the frayed, yellowing edges, and closed the lid.

The man took a deep breath and pressed the elevator's DOWN button. It was clear sailing now. He looked like just another museum employee at this event, helping with cleanup. All he had to do was stay calm, avoid suspicion.

When the freight elevator sank to the bottom level, he wheeled the case onto the smooth concrete floor of the hallway, past caterers clinking along with carts of dirty dessert plates, past the loading dock attendant drinking coffee in his glassed-in booth.

"Have a good night, now." The guard nodded and waved.

"Will do."

Whistling "Stars and Stripes Forever," the man pushed the black case up to the silver van that waited, swung open the back door, and loaded it inside.

He looked back at the loading dock and scratched his itchy nose. Had it really been that simple? A few fat snowflakes parachuted down in the floodlights as the man climbed into the passenger seat.

He slammed the door, and the van disappeared into the night.

THREE

If there had been an appropriate number of electrical outlets at Gate B-16 of the Washington, DC, airport, Anna, José, and Henry probably would have stayed strangers.

But there weren't enough outlets. Not even for a regular day. And for sure not for a day when half the flights were delayed because of a freak snowstorm that had started after midnight and grown in intensity through the morning.

Anna was tired of the kid with the video game hogging all the electricity.

"Hey! What do you think you're doing?" he yelled.

"Sorry, but I thought you'd be done by now, and I really need this outlet." She had already unplugged his game and plugged in her laptop. "I have so many ideas right now, I'm about to burst, you know?"

The boy in the University of Vermont baseball cap apparently didn't know. He glared at her as if that would make her surrender the outlet. Anna was impressed; it was a good glare, not unlike the one her math teacher gave kids who forgot their pencils. And even aside from that, this kid looked familiar.

"Hey! I know you. You were at the museum last night!" She'd noticed him on the bench next to the other kid, who had been reading a book.

What luck that he was from Vermont, too! She could interview him about the museum thing and add to her story. Anna double-clicked and opened up a word-processing document. "What's your name?" She looked up at the boy, tapping her fingers on the space bar.

"Henry Thorn. Why?"

"For my notes, obviously."

"What notes? I don't wanna be in your notes." Henry reached up and pulled his baseball cap lower over his eyes. The screen of his SuperGamePrism-5000 flickered.

"But I'm a journalist." Anna tipped her head in what she hoped was a journalistic way. He didn't need to know that the interview she was supposed to get at the museum reception had fizzled out. She still felt deflated. The reception had been fun, and she'd loved listening to Sounds for a Small Planet, that orchestra made up of musicians from all over the world. Anna had written down the names of all the different instruments and used her new mini video camera to shoot footage of the big poodle that danced along to the tunes, but she had promised her school newspaper an interview with someone famous.

Henry wasn't famous, but at least he'd be another interview. "Is there an *e* at the end of *Thorn*? Or is it just *Thorn*, like the prickles on a rosebush?"

"There's no *e*, but —" His screen flickered again. "Get your dumb laptop outta here. That was my outlet!"

"Shhh." The voice came from a pile of luggage next to them.

Anna kept typing.

Henry spun around. "Who's shushing me?"

"Sounded like that big black backpack," Anna said.

"Listen, I don't know who you think you are, squeezing in here with your fancy computer, but I need to charge this thing because I have a flight soon, and —"

"Ah! Don't count your owls before they are delivered," the backpack said.

"What does *that* mean?" Henry asked.

"It means that it's unlikely you'll be going anywhere today." A head popped up from behind the luggage pile. It sported wire-rimmed glasses and had hair that stuck out around the ears. "So you should probably settle down and relax." Then the head disappeared behind a thick book.

"Hey!" Anna said. "You were at the museum last night, too, reading on the bench!"

The boy held up a copy of *Harry Potter and the Goblet of Fire*, whose pages appeared to be on the verge of spilling out all over the terminal. The cover was worn and torn, loved to death like Anna's copy of *Harriet the Spy*. The boy grinned. "This one's my favorite."

"So what's with counting owls?" Anna tipped her head. "Is that from your book?"

The boy nodded. "From one of them. It's a quote from Albus Dumbledore. I'm quite fond of him. And all the world's great philosophers, really." He held up a black-and-white marble notebook with *Wisdom of the World* written in messy red marker on the front. "I kind of collect quotes, the way people collect baseball cards and stuff."

Henry tipped his head. "What do you *do* with them?"

"I just . . . keep them and . . . read them over, I guess." The boy shrugged.

"I see." Anna wrote that down. It wasn't how she would choose to use a good notebook, but to each his own. She flipped to a new page of notes. "Could you tell me your name and spell it, please?"

"José McGilligan. J-O-S-E . . ."

"Does the e have one of those little slashy lines over it?"

"An acute accent. Yes."

"Got it." Her fingers sounded like little bird beaks pecking at the keys.

"Dude, you don't have to tell her everything, you know." It seemed to bother Henry that José was being a good interviewee.

José shrugged. "Might as well get to know one another. We're going to be here a while." He nodded up at the arrivals and departures screen, where flight statuses were switching from delayed to canceled.

"Aw, man!" Henry stomped up to the TV screens, took off his hat, and threw it to the floor. It landed next to a big brown cowboy boot.

"Well, my good young man, that's no way to act." The cowboy boot belonged to a big man with wavy dark brown hair and a white cowboy hat with a sky blue band that stretched around the rim. Tucked under the band every few inches was a Tootsie Roll — one of the big ones that rich families gave out at Halloween. Not those little ones that are always stale.

Anna gasped. She unplugged her laptop and scurried over to the man. "Excuse me, sir?"

Like José, the cowboy-hat man had no reservations about introducing himself. He stuck out a giant hand for Anna to shake.

"Hello there, young lady. I'm Senator Robert Snickerbottom. I bet you've heard the name."

She nodded. She remembered him not only from his campaign commercials but also from the three hours she spent chasing him around the museum, trying to get an interview last night. And here he was!

"It's an honor to meet you, Senator Snickerbottom," Anna said, edging in front of Henry. "I'm Anna Revere-Hobbs with the *Carter Creek Gazette*, and I was hoping you might have time for an interview."

He chuckled, and Anna smelled chocolate. Evidently, the Tootsie Rolls weren't just for decoration. "Oh, no, little missy," Snickerbottom said. "I need to get a move on. Campaign keeps me busy. Earl! Where are Chuck and Joe? And when's our plane boarding?"

Earl stepped forward, wearing an oversize cowboy hat that kept sliding down over his eyes. "They're getting food." He pointed toward two burly men over at the Cinna-Bunny stand nearby. "As for the flight . . . not any time soon." Earl pushed up his cowboy hat, and then Anna could see his face. He looked a lot like Snickerbottom, only shorter and scrawnier. Like Snickerbottom might look if he shrank eight inches and went a few weeks eating nothing but salad.

"We'd better reschedule some of my appointments in Vermont." Snickerbottom turned back to the kids. "Here's a treat for you." He pulled three Tootsie Rolls from his hat and handed them out. "Y'all have a safe trip." He walked off with Earl at his heels, down the hall to Cinna-Bunny, the cinnamon bun stand with the little rabbit in the apron on its sign.

"Do you know who that *was*?" Anna squealed.

Henry shrugged. "I dunno. When are we going to leave?" Up on the departures screen, the last delayed flight flashed over to canceled. Henry looked ready to punch it.

José looked up from his book. "Tomorrow night at the earliest."

"What are you, some kind of expert?" Henry scoffed. He looked back down at his video game, now running on batteries, and jabbed at some buttons. "Ha! Shot another one."

"Actually, no, but my father is a TV meteorologist in Vermont." José nodded toward a tall, thin man with red hair, red cheeks, and glasses like José's, rushing toward the CNN monitor near the ticket counter. "We just moved from San Francisco, and he's been waiting all season for a good snowstorm." He looked back over at his father, who was bouncing like a kid on Christmas morning as he watched the storm move across the satellite map.

"He looks like my dad when he gets a new piece of legislation to review." Anna pointed to a man in a charcoal gray suit that matched his short curly hair perfectly. He leaned against the ticket counter, talking on a cell phone, and gave Anna a quick wave.

"Anyway," José went on. "This is a huge storm. Dad says we'll be stuck until tomorrow, at least."

"Aw, man!" Henry kicked one of the seats.

"How poor are they that have not patience," José said.

Henry scowled at him. "Did your man Dumbledore say that, too?"

"No." José shook his head. "That one's from Shakespeare."

There was a gasp from near the TV set then, and more people rushed over.

"Storm news?" Anna asked.

"No, looks like something else. Let's go see."

"No!" Henry shouted. They stopped. He looked up at them. "Oh. Not you. It's just that I got killed again."

"How many lives do you get?" Anna asked, walking again.

"Six."

That seemed like more than he deserved, she thought. But she kept it to herself as she looked up at the television.

". . . no leads at this point," the anchorman was saying, "although police say they have reason to believe that the theft may have been an inside job."

"Dude! That happens in my Super-Heist video game all the time." Henry's thumbs twitched as he talked about it. "You get these crimes to solve and half the time it's an inside job. Like this huge bank robbery . . . it turned out one of the tellers did it."

". . . interviewing all possible witnesses." The shot on the TV cut away to a picture of a gigantic flag spread out on a tilted table behind glass. Anna gasped. It was the flag they'd just seen at the Smithsonian!

It was really, really old — she had notes somewhere on exactly how old — and there were rips and holes and everything, and the stars were sort of yellowy instead of white. But somehow, it looked even more beautiful than the brand-new flag that hung outside her father's senate office back home. Not as crisp but more . . . dignified. How could someone steal it?

Anna imagined her mother watching this news at home, fingering the silver jaguar at her neck as she always did when she read about an art theft or something. She'd keep her phone with her every second. Sometimes, nothing happened at all. But sometimes, it would ring, and there would be a flurry of clothes and suitcases and calls to figure out who would pick Anna up from school while her mother was away. It had been happening as long as Anna could remember.

Whenever Anna asked about it, all her mother would say was that the jaguar necklace, passed down from Grandma Revere, meant she was part of a group called the Silver Jaguar Society, whose members were descendants of the world's most creative minds, and who had accepted a promise to protect the work of their ancestors however they could.

Anna always wanted to know more. *Who else was in this society? Were there meetings? What did they do on those trips?*

But the questions piled up like snowdrifts, unanswered. Her mother promised Anna would learn more when she was older. For now, she said, Anna's job for the society was to be good and do her homework and help Dad clean up after dinner. If anyone asked, her mom was on a business trip.

So Anna would do her homework and help with dishes, but she also kept a special notebook for those times. Since her mom never shared details of her secret trips, Anna made them up. She filled pages with her own imagined Silver Jaguar Society missions, chasing down bad guys through the streets of exotic cities like Paris and Rome or wherever she guessed her mom might be. Sometimes, Anna wished her mom would just quit — even though it was an honor, nobody *had* to be in the society, her mom said — but mostly, Anna wished she were old enough to be packing secret suitcases, too.

Anna looked out the airport window, where the world swirled in white. Her mom certainly couldn't travel in this weather. She turned her attention back to the TV.

"... and officials at the Smithsonian are asking anyone with information to come forward immediately."

A woman with long black hair appeared on-screen looking all teary.

"Mom!" José whipped around to his father, who held up a finger for him to wait.

"We are hoping that the person or persons responsible for this crime will come to understand that they possess an irreplaceable piece of America's history." A label came up on the screen while the woman spoke. MARIA SANCHEZ MCGILLIGAN, HISTORICAL TEXTILES EXPERT. "It could be destroyed very easily if it's not kept under certain atmospheric conditions. Time is important. Please ..." She looked directly into the camera. "Return the Star-Spangled Banner to the American people."

FOUR

"The Star-Spangled Banner's been stolen," Anna whispered. She couldn't imagine how. It was enormous. Bigger than her whole living room at home.

"Did you hear that, Harold? Did you?" A short woman with bouncy gray curls and a WORLD'S GREATEST GRANDMA sweatshirt elbowed her husband. "First a giant snowstorm, and now this! This trip to see your old army buddies has been more exciting than I thought it would be."

"Dude," Henry turned to José. "That was your mom on TV? I wonder if she's the one who stole it. That would be so cool!"

"My mother did *not* steal the flag. She's a specialist who restores historical textiles, and she just finished *fixing* the flag so it could go back on display. And furthermore, my mother is part of a —"

"José!" His father's voice was sharp. José jumped, then looked up at his dad and nodded a tiny bit.

"What I was going to say," José said, "is that she has great respect for history. She was going to give a lecture on the flag this week and then finally head home." He turned back to his dad. "Do you think she'll have to stay longer now?"

José's father put an arm around his son. "I'm sure they'll track it down quickly. But yes, the flag may need more repairs once they find it. Mom's probably fit to be tied." The song "Raindrops Keep Fallin' on My Head" played from his pocket, and José's dad pulled out a cell phone. "This is her. Sit tight for a minute." And he stepped toward the ticket counter, next to Anna's dad.

José sat down with his book, and Henry went back to his video game. Anna stared up at the TV, where newspeople were recapping the top stories of the morning: the big blizzard and the flag theft. José's mother appeared on the screen again. She shook her head, and her silver earrings caught the light of the cameras.

"José! What were you going to say about your mom? Being part of something?"

José looked up quickly. "Nothing. She's part of . . . the . . . uh . . . group of people who love history."

Anna's hand flew to her ear. "No, she's not. José, those earrings! She's part of the Silver Jaguar Society, isn't she?"

José put his book down and narrowed his eyes.

"It's okay." Anna tried to keep her voice quiet. "Those earrings? Were they a gift from your grand-mother to your mom?"

José nodded just a bit. "How do *you* know?" he whispered.

"It's okay. We're in it, too. I mean, my mom is." Anna's thoughts were racing so fast her voice couldn't keep up. She was tripping over her words trying. "She has a silver jaguar necklace that looks like your mom's earrings. It's their symbol. This is *amazing*! So do you know about the society? I don't know much, but it's this secret group of people who are all related to famous artists and —"

"Shhh!" José moved closer to her. "It's not going to be secret much longer if you keep shouting about it in a crowded airport."

"Sorry," Anna whispered. "I just can't believe this. Do you know who you're related to? We're descen-dants of Paul Revere."

"Paul Revere, the midnight-ride guy?"

Anna nodded. "He was a silversmith, too. A really good one, I guess. You must be related to somebody who made stuff, too. Right?" She pulled out her notebook.

"Put that away," José said quietly.

"Sorry." Anna slipped the notebook back into her bag. "You're right. My mom would kill me if I wrote this stuff down. But you are related to somebody, right?"

José nodded. "Frida Kahlo."

"Frito who?" Henry asked. He put his game down and moved closer.

"Frida Kahlo. She's a famous artist," Anna said.

"And also . . ." José leaned closer. "My mom says our ancestors in Central America, going way, way back, were some of the founders."

Henry raised an eyebrow at them. "So . . . let me get this right. You guys think that anybody with some . . . magic silver jaguar thing is part of this secret society of yours?"

"Well . . . yeah," Anna said. Coming from Henry, it sounded like something out of a video game.

"That's funny," Henry went on. "My aunt's got one. On a bracelet."

"She does?" Anna grabbed his sleeve and shook a little. "Ohmygosh, Henry! Your family's part of the Silver Jaguar Society, too? This is incredible. Who are you related to?"

"Nobody, s'far as I know." Henry shook her off and picked up his video game.

Anna blocked the screen with her hand. "Henry, seriously! If your aunt has a bracelet like that, she must be part of it. Does she go on a lot of trips?"

"Well, yeah." Henry put his game down again. "And she sure likes art and stuff. She's always all

'Look, Henry!' when we see some dumb old painting or something. But I don't think she's part of any secret mission or anything." He paused, looking down at his game. "That *would* be cool, though."

"Yeah, but, Henry —" Anna stopped short when she saw Snickerbottom heading their way again. Maybe she could interview him now! This story was getting better by the minute.

Anna hurried over to him. "Senator, what do you think about the flag?"

"This theft is a crime against our great nation!" He stood up straight and looked out toward the crowd around the TV monitor, even though it was Anna who had asked the question. "And I'm here to assure the American people that our flag will be recovered." The crowd shifted its attention from the TV to Snickerbottom. "The very best investigators in the nation are on this case. The FBI. The CIA. The SCC."

"SCC?" Anna asked.

"The Snickerbottom Campaign Committee. In a situation like this, every American needs to do his part. I've reassigned some of my key staff members to help with the investigation. We *will* find the flag. And we *will* track down the enemies of America who stole it."

"Enemies of America?" Anna tipped her head. "The newspeople said they don't know who stole it."

"Oh, they always say that. We know better." Robert Snickerbottom gave a loud sniff as if he could smell the enemies of America right there in the airport. "When I'm president, we'll have a stronger, safer nation. Safe for the American people and safe for our flag."

"I see." Anna held up her notebook. "Just a few more questions about your campaign now, Senator. According to the polls —"

"I told you I don't have time for school newspapers, little lady. Too much to do." He walked off with his men following him.

"When he's *president*?" Henry stared down the hallway.

"You don't know who Robert Snickerbottom is?" Anna sighed. At least the airport had wireless Internet access. She tapped at her keyboard, called up a video of Snickerbottom's latest campaign ad, and tipped the screen so Henry could see. "Watch."

The commercial started with a fuzzy black-and-white photograph of a lady who looked like somebody's grandmother. Over the image, a man with a deep voice proclaimed, "Betty Frumble's fine for Vermont. But she doesn't belong in Washington." The image changed to a newspaper headline that read THE COMPROMISE QUEEN with a photo of the woman smiling and holding some kind of cake pan, surrounded by a crowd of people in front of the Vermont State House. The man's voice continued. "America can't afford compromise. We need a leader . . . a man of courage and strength. A true American hero." The image dissolved into a newspaper photo of a way younger Robert Snickerbottom, soaking wet, holding a little boy under one arm and a puppy in the other. Another young man, shorter and skinnier but with the same wavy hair, stood next to him, looking up with awe. HERO SAVES BOY, FAMILY PET FROM ABANDONED WELL, the headline read. And the man's voice finished. "Vote for Robert Snickerbottom, an American hero, for president."

"He's running for president?" Henry asked as the screen faded to black.

Anna nodded. Her laptop battery was running low, so she powered down and slid it into her backpack. "Against Betty Frumble. Wait — don't you live in Vermont? She's our governor, you know."

"Oh." Henry's SuperGamePrism-5000 buzzed again. He flicked the switch to OFF. "So you think that guy'll win? That'd be wicked. I could say I met the president."

Anna shook her head. "Probably not. My dad wants him to win because they're in the same party. They both want immigration reform and stuff like that. But Dad says Snickerbottom's falling behind in the polls."

"Behind that grandma lady from the TV ad?" Henry looked stunned.

"Yep. She's really popular in Vermont. When she was elected governor, she stopped all the political bickering in Montpelier with her 'secret weapon.'" She used her fingers to make quote marks in the air.

"Secret weapon?" Henry's face lit up.

"Berry Maple Oat Nut Crumble," Anna said. "It's her family recipe. She says food brings people together, so she shows up with the Berry Maple Oat Nut Crumble and says anybody willing to listen to the other side gets a big bowl of it with vanilla ice cream."

"And that works?"

"Well, that and a bunch of other stuff. She's an incredible speaker; she's brilliant. But the TV news likes to show the old-lady-with-baked-goods pictures, so whatever. It seems to be working; she's beating Snickerbottom in the polls by quite a bit." Anna fought a smile. She was proud of her dad being a United States senator, and she knew he wanted Snickerbottom to win, but secretly, she loved the idea of a smart lady who did things differently being in charge. She'd love to interview Betty Frumble.

"Anna." Her father walked up briskly. "I need to make more phone calls, so I'm going to head to the business lounge where it's quieter."

"Did you talk to Mom?"

He nodded. "She's beside herself over the flag, but obviously, she can't get here with the weather." Her dad didn't sound sad; he was never thrilled about her mom's secret society trips. "Do you want to come with me or stay here?"

"I'll stay here," Anna said. "I want to get some writing done. This is Henry, by the way."

"Nice to meet you. Where are your folks?"

"My dad's on a cruise with his new wife." Henry said the word *wife* the way most people said *toe jam* or *boogers*. "I've been staying with my aunt, but I'm going home today. Or whenever the snow stops. That flight attendant's in charge of me." Henry nodded toward a tiny dark-haired woman who stood at the ticket counter, swamped with people trying to rebook flights.

"I see, well . . ." Anna's father looked at his watch, then reached for his wallet and handed Anna his credit card. "Take this and get some food for you and your friend whenever you're hungry. Just don't go far." He headed down the hallway.

Anna sank into a chair and realized she'd forgotten about José, whose face was hidden behind his book again. "Oh my gosh, sorry I didn't introduce you. My dad's in a hurry a lot."

"That's okay," José mumbled. He didn't look up

from his book. "He probably wouldn't have been particularly pleased to meet me anyway."

"Why?"

José closed his book and looked up at her. "I'm half Mexican." It came out quiet, like everything he said, but it still sounded like a challenge.

"What do you mean?"

"Immigration reform? Your dad and Snickerbottom are always talking about it on TV."

"So?" Anna said.

"My grandparents came over as migrant workers." José tipped his chin up. "My mother was born here, so she's an American citizen, but some people are still . . . well, *you'd* know."

"Oh, no, it's not like that. My dad worries about jobs, but he likes Mexicans a lot," Anna said quickly. "I mean, he likes people like you. It's, like, the bad ones that he doesn't like. I mean, not that he doesn't like them, too. He probably likes them fine. He just doesn't think some of *those* people should be . . . here."

"Oh." José stared at her and lifted his book. "Sort of like how the Malfoy family only wants pureblood wizards at Hogwarts." He dropped his head and went back to reading.

Anna thought about that. She'd seen the Harry Potter movies, and her father was nothing like Lucius

Malfoy. That guy was a jerk. Her dad worked hard to help people and just wanted to make sure there were jobs for Americans. But the whole idea gave her a rotten feeling, like a little mouse gnawing away in her stomach.

She didn't want to be a Malfoy.

FIVE

For the next two hours, Anna watched the snow outside fall in heavier blankets and the line of angry
travelers at the ticket counter grow longer. Henry
played his video games. José thumbed through a volume of *Bartlett's Familiar Quotations* that looked every
bit as loved as his copy of *Harry Potter*.

"Hey," Anna finally said, nudging José's elbow.
"Do you want to go get some food?" She held her
breath, wondering if he was still upset.

José held up a finger, turned a page, and looked
up. "Sure." Anna let out her breath.

José found his father, who was back at the CNN
screen where new storm reports were coming in. "I'm
going to get a snack, Dad, okay?" He dropped his
backpack at his father's feet with a thud. "Can you
watch this for me?"

"Sure." Mr. McGilligan waved over his shoulder, gazing up at the blue and pink radar images.

Anna turned to Henry. "Are you coming? You should probably tell your flight attendant."

"You kidding? She'll never miss me." Henry flicked a hand toward the counter, where the flight attendant was typing frantically and talking to the first in a long line of irritated passengers.

Anna hoisted her backpack over her shoulder and led them into the main hallway of Terminal B. She had to wait a few seconds for an opening in the river of people pulling luggage and rushing past with briefcases. Everybody was all stuck and clogging the halls like a spring ice jam in the Winooski River back home.

"Hey, there's Pickersgill Diner. Let's get burgers." Henry stepped up to a long, long line that snaked out from a darkened, wood-paneled restaurant.

"Looks like everybody had the same idea," José said. "Get some food and settle in for a long day and night at the airport."

"Man, this stinks," Henry said, kicking the HOST-ESS WILL SEAT YOU sign.

"Yeah, but don't you think it's kind of cool to spend the whole night here?" Anna said. "It'll make a great news story." Anna ran her hand along the edge of the hostess sign, imagining what she'd write. She could talk about the snow, and the flag news, and the crowds. Plus, if she could manage to keep running into Snickerbottom, somewhere in that long night, he would have to give her an interview, wouldn't he?

And who knows who else might be stuck here? All kinds of interesting, important people visited Washington, DC. There could be other dignitaries from the history museum reopening or —

"Oh my gosh!" Anna said it so loudly the woman in front of them turned and stared.

"Sorry," Anna said, but she could barely keep her voice down as she pulled José and Henry into a huddle. "You guys, I just had this thought. What if whoever stole the flag is stuck here, too? *With* the flag!"

José pursed his lips and looked down at the diamond shaped tiles on the floor. "Not likely. You've seen the flag. It's enormous. Trying to sneak it through an airport wouldn't be too bright."

"But you never know, right?" Anna looked around and lowered her voice. "What if the thief is waiting for burgers in this same line. Think about it! We need to investigate." She stood up straight. "It's our responsibility as Silver Jaguar Society members."

"Will you . . . shhh!" José frowned. "First of all, they're not going to be here. And second, even if they were, it's not our job to investigate. We're not society members. My mom says you have to be eighteen."

Anna sighed. "The words *you have to be eighteen* should be banned from the English language. We could *totally* investigate. And we *should*. We're *here*, after all, right here at the airport, and no one else from the society is, are they?" Anna forced her voice quiet again. "I mean, I know it's probably not here, but if it is . . ." If it was, and if they found it . . . that would be the best story ever. And her mom would see that she was plenty old enough and smart enough to know more about the society. "It would be *so* amazing."

"How many?" The hostess, a young woman with spiky pink hair and a small silver nose ring, tapped her clipboard.

"Three, please." Anna craned her neck to get a glimpse of the television behind the bar. Maybe there would be more flag news.

"This way." The hostess led them to a table that almost got hit by the swinging door to the kitchen every time it opened. Anna leaned across the table toward José and Henry.

"So what do you think?"

Henry picked up a menu. "Awesome."

"Awesome, you'll investigate with me?"

"No, awesome, they have root beer floats."

"It's possible," said José, "that someone here could know something, but . . ."

"But what?"

"Do you have macaroni and cheese?" José asked the waitress who had appeared.

"Yep."

"I'll have that."

"I'll have a root beer float, cheeseburger, and fries," Henry said. "With ketchup."

She turned to Anna. "And you?"

"Oh!" Anna flipped menu pages. Why when she was in the middle of a great idea did everybody need to stop to eat all the time? "I'll have a tuna melt with fries."

She handed her menu to the waitress and leaned back in toward José. "You said *but*. But what?"

"For starters, that theft was hours ago. Whoever took the flag is probably far away by now. And also, like I said before, we're not eighteen. It's not our job."

"Not our job? But this is ... it's ... it's like Snickerbottom said. When something like this happens, *every* American has to do his or her part. No matter how old we are. We're here, at the airport, so we should do what we can here and interview people or look for clues or ... Don't you feel like it's all of our responsibility?"

"My responsibility is to knock out these bank robbers." Henry picked up his SuperGamePrism-5000 again. "Otherwise, I can't get to Level Ten."

José looked at Henry, poking at his GamePrism, and shook his head at Anna. "Sorry, I can't believe I'm saying this, but I think I agree with him." He took out his book.

Anna threw her hands in the air. "You are such . . . boys! What is *wrong* with you? You spend your whole lives looking for excitement in video games and movies and books, and then when something big finally happens, you're too busy reading and poking at some SuperGameThingy to do the real, live, exciting thing right there in front of you!"

"Tuna melt?" The waitress held it over the table, floating from person to person.

"That's me," Anna said.

While Henry and José ate their lunch, Anna took advantage of their full mouths to do all the talking.

"Think about it. Everybody who was at that museum reception is either in town or headed home today, and that means that whole big bunches of them are here at the airport. Stuck here. With us. And maybe with the flag! Don't you see?"

José poked the tine of his fork through a single macaroni and lifted it to his mouth. "It's possible," he said.

"It's more than *possible*." Anna picked up the shaker of hot pepper from the table and tipped it back and forth, watching the red and gold flakes tumble on top of one another. "It's *probable*. And if we interview some of those people, I bet we'll get some clues, and if we get enough, they'll start to make sense, like a jigsaw puzzle when you get enough pieces in, and then all of a sudden you can see it's a ship or a carnival scene or whatever and everything's clear, you know?"

Henry stared at her. Then he went back to his game.

José looked up at the television over the bar. The anchorman was on again.

"Turn it up, Morgan!" A muscular man behind the bar hollered, and the hostess raised the volume.

". . . an extremely fragile piece of American history. Authorities continue to investigate all leads, and they say no one with access to the flag chamber has been ruled out as a suspect."

Anna wondered if that included José's mom. She glanced over at him, but his eyes dropped to the last of his macaroni.

"Since the snow has halted traffic out of the city for now, investigators believe that the thief or thieves are still nearby."

"See?" Anna said. "See, I think that's why . . . Are you even listening to me?"

José was staring at the bar. Anna turned to follow his gaze and saw the big guy who had shouted before frantically untying his apron and shuffling through papers next to the cash register.

"Morgan!" he called, so loud that even Henry

looked up from his game. "You need to take over here. I have to go." He handed her an order pad and came out from behind the bar so fast he tripped on the edge, stumbling right into the table where Anna, Henry, and José sat. He reached out to catch himself, and on his upper arm, peeking out from the sleeve of his blue T-shirt, was a tattoo of a curled-up black snake that looked like it was about to strike. Before Anna could get a better look at it, the man had pushed off the table and disappeared out the door.

"That snake-arm guy sure was in a hurry," Henry said. "You done?" He eyed Anna's sandwich. She hadn't even taken a bite.

"No." She stared at the swinging door and wondered where Snake-Arm had gone so quickly. "I mean yes, I'm done. I'll take my tuna melt to go. We need to get started."

Anna paid and boxed up her sandwich, but before she'd taken three steps outside the restaurant, an enormous gray poodle came barreling down the hallway and almost knocked her off her feet. She caught her balance but dropped the box, and her sandwich slid out onto the floor.

"Hammurabi!" called a voice from down the hall.

The poodle skidded to a stop and tipped its head at the voice. It bounded a few steps back toward Anna.

Then in one giant bite, it snarfed up half her tuna melt and took off down the hallway.

"Oh, you must please accept my apologies!" A boy rushed up to them, wringing his hands. He looked a little like José, but smaller and with darker eyes. He wore khaki pants and a long-sleeved polo shirt with SOUNDS FOR A SMALL PLANET embroidered on the chest. He looked off down the hall, where the poodle had paused next to Gate B-15 to chew. "He has been caged up all day long, and we just got the permission to get him out. He is a bit . . ."

"Energetic?" offered José.

"Full of beans?" said Anna, laughing. She wasn't upset over her sandwich; she was too busy thinking to be hungry anymore.

"No, I think he is full of your lunch," the boy said. "Hammurabi!" he called more sharply, and the dog trotted over, licking mayonnaise from his snout.

Anna smiled. "It's a figure of speech. 'Full of beans' means Hammurabi likes to get in trouble."

"Oh!" The boy's face lit up. "That is a new one." He pulled a small sketch pad from his back pocket, took out a charcoal pencil, and began to draw as if he'd forgotten they were there.

"Here is our Hammurabi, full of beans," he said finally, holding up the pad.

Full of beans

"That's awesome!" Henry put down his video game and nodded toward the sketch pad. "You got other drawings in there?"

The boy smiled shyly and flipped through the pages.

Let the cat out of the bag.

Anna smiled at the last one. "That's what my mother says when she sends me to clean my room and I sit in my closet writing instead. It means she's losing her temper . . . getting angry."

"I know," the boy said. "These I have already learned. This is for me the most challenging part of American English. I keep a list of these . . . figures of speech, as you call them." He flipped the sketch pad closed. "I like to draw what they say but do not mean."

"Where are you from?" Anna asked.

"Pakistan. My mother was born there, and my father is from Turkey. Both of my parents are with Sounds for a Small Planet, the orchestra."

Anna nodded. "I saw your dog dancing at the museum reception. He's funny. It's neat that you get to travel with your folks. How old are you?"

"Eight. Too young to be part of the orchestra myself, but my parents play tuba, and the orchestra was needing tubas. Hammurabi and I were . . . ah . . . part of the deal, as you say." He held out his hand. "I'm Sinan. It is a pleasure to meet you."

"I'm Anna, and this is José and Henry. We met at the gate with the delay and all."

"Yes, it is quite a storm." Outside, the wind was picking up. Snow blew horizontally past the big windows. Sinan tucked his sketch pad back into his pocket and gave the poodle a pat on the head.

"What's your dog's name again?" Henry asked. "Hamburger?"

"Hammurabi," Sinan answered. "He is named for an ancient king who united countries and built many things. Temples, canals . . ." He gave his sneaker a shake so Hammurabi would stop drooling on it. "Unfortunately, our Hammurabi would rather chew things apart."

"He's still pretty cool," Henry said, petting the dog.

"Thank you. I should get him back to my parents now. The orchestra members are hoping to play for a bit in the main concourse if they can get the instruments out of the baggage area. Just to pass the time. Perhaps you would like to come listen?"

"Sure," José said.

"I'd love to do that," Anna said. "Let me go tell my dad. That'll be a great way to kill some time."

They headed toward the main concourse with Anna and Hammurabi in the lead, Henry finishing the other half of Anna's sandwich, and Sinan scribbling furiously in his sketch pad the whole way.

Killing time

SIX

The orchestra members were flipping open instru-
ment cases and setting up stands when the kids
reached the open area at the center of the airport
stores and restaurants.

"Ohmygosh, look!" Anna pointed to the coffee
shop, where Robert Snickerbottom leaned on the
counter eating a cinnamon bun.

"Senator Snickerbottom!" Anna rushed up with
Hammurabi so close behind that he skidded on the
tiles when she stopped.

"Whoa there! Get back, ya overgrown froufrou
pup!" Snickerbottom held his cinnamon bun higher
and glowered down at the dog. "I know a would-be
Cinna-Bunny thief when I see one."

"Sit, Hammurabi," Anna said, pointing to the
floor.

Hammurabi sat, but he kept his eyes on the bun high over Snickerbottom's head. "Sorry, Senator Snickerbottom. But now that you're not busy" — she pulled out her mini video recorder — "would you answer a few questions for my school newspaper?"

He chuckled and wiped some frosting from his lip. "You don't give up, do you? But in fact, I *am* busy. I'm meeting with a reporter from the *Washington Post* soon. You should interview one of your little friends here."

"Just a few questions?" Anna pressed the red button to start recording. Maybe if she ignored his "no," he'd answer a question or two. "Like, do you think the Star-Spangled Banner will be recovered?"

Snickerbottom stood up extra straight and used a voice that was a little bigger and deeper. "The flag theft is a crime against America. And I'm doing everything in my power to bring this treasure back to Washington, DC."

"So you think it's gone? Like, out of town?"

Snickerbottom looked surprised. "What gave you that idea?"

"Well, you said you were going to bring it *back* to Washington, which made me think that you think it's not in Washington now. So where do you think it is?"

"Well, I don't know, young lady." He cleared his throat. "I need to get going."

"Just one more question about the campaign," she blurted. She'd been practicing this one; it was the kind of question she watched her mom ask politicians on TV all the time, and she loved it when they were put on the spot. "The latest polls suggest that Vermont governor Betty Frumble would beat you in the primary if the election were held today. Are you still optimistic?"

Snickerbottom waved a big hand in front of him, as if he could knock those silly polls right out of the air. "Of course I'm optimistic. Those polls don't mean anything. They have a margin of error the size of Texas!"

"Even so," Anna said, "she was leading you by double-digit margins in forty-nine states."

"Well, there ya go! We got fifty states, last I checked!" Snickerbottom laughed a booming laugh. Hammurabi's ears twitched. "And as soon as this snowstorm clears out, I'm off on a super-duper, twelve-state campaign swing, starting with Governor Frumble's fine state of Vermont, where I'm sure I'll gain plenty of support." He tipped his big hat, and a Tootsie Roll fell out. He picked it up and handed it to Anna. "Here you go." Then he smoothed his hair before he put the hat back on his head. "And here's a *thought* for you to chew on, too, little missy." Snickerbottom leaned closer. "It ain't over till the fat cat sings." And he walked away.

Sinan flipped open his sketch pad.

"Okay . . . thanks!" Anna called after Snicker-bottom. She turned off her mini video recorder and set it down. She didn't have enough for a whole article; she'd try to catch up with him later.

Anna leaned over to look at Sinan's drawing.

It ain't over till
the fat cat sings.

"That's not really how the saying goes," Anna said. "He got it wrong. It's supposed to be 'till the fat *lady* sings.'"

"Oh." Sinan flipped over his pencil and began erasing the cat, starting with its ears.

"It's a good drawing, though," Henry said, leaning over to see. "I like the way you made the fur look real."

Anna smiled a little. It was weird to see Henry being nice to somebody.

Henry looked at her and frowned. "What? Do I have food in my teeth?"

"No. You just . . . Do you have a little brother or something?"

"Nope. How come?"

"Because . . ." Anna paused. Part of her hated to give Henry a compliment, but it was true, so . . . "Because you seem like you'd be a good big brother."

"Oh." Henry shrugged. "Well, I babysit for my neighbor Will a lot. He's eight, too." Henry looked at Sinan. "Will's pretty cool. I don't know who's going to hang out with him when we move to Boston."

"You're moving?"

"Yeah. When school's over." Henry blinked hard and pointed down the hallway. "So much for Snickerbottom's big interview, huh?"

Anna looked where Henry was pointing and felt all bristly inside. There was no other interview; Snickerbottom was ignoring her, back at the coffee counter with his men. They were whispering and pointing toward the back of the orchestra, where the Japanese drummers were warming up.

"Come meet my parents." Sinan tugged at Anna's jacket sleeve and pulled her in the other direction, toward a couple setting up folding chairs. Sinan spoke to them in a language Anna didn't recognize and then turned. "Ammi, Abba! Meet my friends Anna, José, and Henry from" — he paused — "from the B terminal."

The woman set down a chair and smiled warmly. "It is a pleasure to meet you all." Anna caught a whiff of flowery perfume when Sinan's mother leaned in and held out her hand. Her handshake was strong, like the rest of her. She looked as if she could handle a tuba or pretty much anything else.

Sinan whispered something to his father, who was slightly taller and way skinnier than his mother. The man smiled and held out his hand, too. "I understand we have a thief in our midst."

Anna's eyes got big. "Who do *you* think stole it?"

Sinan's father tipped his head and laughed. "Well, I don't think that's much of a mystery. It's pretty obvious who the guilty party is, isn't it?" He slapped a hand on his leg, and Hammurabi trotted up, his tongue hanging from his mouth, little flakes of tuna still stuck in his chin fur.

"Oh, the *sandwich* thief." Anna tried to hide her disappointment. "That's okay. I wasn't hungry anyway. I'm excited to hear you play. Where do you go next?"

"Vermont. It's our last stop." Sinan's mother smiled a little, but her eyes looked sad. "We had hoped to stay longer in the U.S., but some of the members' visas expire at the end of the month."

"Can't you renew them?" Anna asked. "Maybe my dad could help. He's a senator."

Sinan's mother shook her head. "Our manager spoke with Senator Snickerbottom about it, but it hasn't worked out." She set up the last folding chair, and a trumpet player filled it, warming up with crisp, smooth notes that floated up to the skylights.

Sinan's mother looked around. "I usually help set up the speakers." She put her hands on her hips and waved to a gangly blond man on the other side of the strings. "Guillome! The speakers?"

He shook his head. "Couldn't get them from baggage. Actually, the senator you were talking with before warned us not to request them, said it'd be a whole mess of paperwork, and they may not make it onto the plane if we try to get them out of the baggage area now. You're lucky to have your tuba." Another tuba player blasted a low note from the back row.

"All right, then. We're in a small enough space anyway." Sinan's mother squeezed between two clarinet players, past the trumpets and trombones, and lifted her tuba as the rest of the orchestra settled in. Once they were tuned, they started playing, a song full of energy and swooshes and blustering, like the storm raging outside.

Anna walked to the window to watch the snow. It was falling in bigger, fatter flakes than ever as the taiko drummers pounded out the heartbeat of the song. Anna wondered if they'd make it to Vermont in time for that concert. Nobody was going anywhere for a while.

The fat lady hadn't started singing yet.

There was plenty of time to find the flag.

SEVEN

"You know where I think we should start?" Anna pulled her notebook from her backpack and settled in a chair. After the concert, they'd wandered around the stores a while, but the clerks were getting cranky, so they'd gone back to the gate. "We need a list of suspects. People who might have a reason to take the flag. Then we can see if anyone at the airport looks shady. Like if they act nervous . . . or look around suspiciously . . . or . . ."

"If they're carrying around a giant duffel bag with stars and stripes spilling out all over?" José lowered his book and leaned back against the glass window. Behind him, the tarmac sat quiet and white. It should have been crisscrossing with planes and fuel trucks and luggage carts. But it looked like somebody had spread a big white blanket over it and put the whole thing to sleep. "You did see the flag, right?" José raised an eyebrow at Anna. "You know how big it is?"

"It's not *that* big."

"It's *huge*."

"Sure, but you could roll it up and put it in something." Anna looked around the terminal. Everyone's carry-on luggage was way too small to fit a thirty-four-by-thirty-four-foot flag, though. Finally, her eyes rested on a fat, red cylinder of a garbage can. "It would fit in *there*." She scanned the hallways. "Or it would fit . . . maybe . . ." There really was nowhere else it would fit.

"Well?" José tipped his head toward the trash can. Anna sighed, put down her notebook, walked over, pushed in the flap thingy, and peered inside. It was half empty and too dark to see anything in there except a partly eaten cheeseburger and some scrunched-up napkins halfway down. She smelled onions.

No flag.

Anna plopped back down next to the boys and huffed. "I wasn't saying it *was* there, just that it could have been."

"But it's not." José turned a page in his book.

Anna fought the urge to grab the book from him and fling it out a window into the snow. "You know, you said your mom cares about the flag so much, and you're not even helping. Your family made a *promise* to protect things like this flag. Don't you think your mom would want you to do your part?"

José looked up. "She'd want me to stay out of trouble. Besides, there is *nothing* we can do. Not really." He held up a finger. "Sometimes the key to wisdom is recognizing your limits."

"Who said that?" Anna asked. "Shakespeare?"

"No. My mom." He went back to his book.

"Can't you guys at least help me brainstorm?" Anna flipped her notebook open to a clean page.

"See that guy hiding in the alley? You gotta take him out first. Otherwise, he'll sneak up on you while you're chasing the other robbers. Try again." Henry handed his SuperGamePrism-5000 to Sinan, reached for the bag of chips they'd picked up after the concert, and turned to Anna. "Want some?"

"No, thanks. I don't want grease spots all over my notebook." Anna wrote *Possible Suspects* at the top of a clean white page. The police thought that the flag theft might be an inside job, that someone from the Smithsonian might have been involved. First on the list, she wrote: *Security guard?*

Who else?

Anna looked around. Had anyone been acting strangely here at the airport?

Henry and José acted strangely, but she was pretty sure that's just because they were Henry and José.

There was Snake-Arm from Pickersgill Diner. He

had seemed all hurried after that news report about the flag. Could he be hiding something? It was possible he'd remembered an appointment or had to use the bathroom really bad or something, but maybe, just maybe, he was rushing for a more exciting reason. Anna added *Snake-Arm Diner Man* to the list of suspects.

On TV, the police always talked about motives. Who had the motive to commit a crime? Who would risk everything to try and get away with it?

Halfway down the page, Anna wrote *Possible Motives*. She twirled her pen in her fingers, thinking. Who had a motive to steal the Star-Spangled Banner? Could somebody be planning to sell it? It's not like you could list it on eBay and expect that nobody would notice.

"No! Don't go in there!" Henry yelled so loud that Sinan almost dropped the SuperGamePrism-5000. "That's an ambush. The robbers are waiting in there, and you'll lose all the points you got so far if they trap you."

Anna watched Sinan poke at the buttons. The bank robbers in the game were easy to figure out. They wanted money. But why would somebody want a huge flag? Anna saw a documentary once about this guy who stole a famous painting from a museum — way too famous to sell in public or he'd get caught — but he had this other guy all lined up to buy it already, a private collector who loved the painting — really, really loved it and wanted it in his mansion so he could see it every day. What if the person who took the flag stole it because he or she loved it so much?

Anna was thinking how to write that on the motives list when she heard a man in the next row of seats raising his voice as he spoke into his cell phone.

"No, it is not all right! And it is *not* understandable! Not by any stretch of the — no. Just — Fine, I'm listening."

Anna sat up straighter so she could see over the seats. Between the World's Greatest Grandma and a man who had fallen asleep listening to his iPod sat José's father, his phone pressed tightly to his ear, his brow furrowed, and his face blotchy red. "That's ridiculous!" he said. "No. How could they even —" He paused and squeezed his eyes closed. "I know. I will. I love you, too."

By the time he snapped the phone shut and opened his eyes, Anna, Henry, José, and Sinan were staring over the seats at him.

He took a deep breath. "That was Mom," he said to José. "The police have taken her into custody as a suspect."

EIGHT

"Dude, can you imagine if she did it? Your mom would be some kind of genius!" Henry and the others half walked, half ran to keep up with José's march down the B-terminal hallway. "I mean, it's awesome. That flag must have had alarms and everything, so for her to —"

José whirled around with his finger pointing and almost poked Henry in the chest. "It is *not* awesome. My mother . . ." His voice trembled, but he held up his arm, still pointing at Henry as if daring him to speak. "My mother *loves* that flag. Until last night, I hadn't seen her in three weeks. She lived away from us on and off for six months to work on the restoration. Six *months*!" Henry took a small step back, but José stepped forward to meet him. "She'd *never* take the flag from the chamber. Never. She loves that flag . . . as much as she loves me," he finished quietly.

Henry stepped back again, and this time José let him go. "I didn't mean it like that," Henry said. "I just meant . . . you know, whoever did it — not your mom — but whoever — must have done some cool stuff to get it out." He looked down at the GamePrism in his hands. "Like secret spy stuff. Only in real life."

"Well, you ought to think before you say things like that. How would you like to go three weeks without seeing your mom?"

Henry blinked. "My mom died three years ago."

"Oh." José scuffed his sneaker on the floor tiles. For once, he couldn't seem to come up with a quote.

"I'm sorry, Henry." Anna put her hands in her pockets, then took them out again.

Hammurabi trotted up and dropped Mr. Squeaky at Henry's feet.

Henry gave the toy a kick. "Yeah, well . . . my dad and I have been doing okay. And he's got Bethany now, so you know . . ." Henry shrugged and started walking slowly down the hallway, scuffing his untied sneakers. He turned on his GamePrism and poked at it as he walked.

José, Anna, and Sinan followed Henry past the coffee shop and Cinna-Bunny. Hammurabi ran ahead with Mr. Squeaky in his mouth, dropping the toy every few yards to see if anyone would pick it up and throw it for him. No one did.

Finally, Henry looked up from his game. "Where are we going anyway?"

José shrugged. "I was going to walk around and . . . I don't know. Anything seems better than sitting at the gate."

"I have an idea," Anna said. "We should check on that Snake-Arm guy from the restaurant. He's on my suspect list. And you know . . . Henry's right. Whoever did this must have studied the security system and wanted the flag — no, *needed* it. Needed it enough to risk everything."

Anna stopped in front of Pickersgill Diner, where the dinner line snaked into the hallway, and turned to Henry. "The dog can't go in, so I think you should wait here with Sinan and Hammurabi. José and I will go back to investigate."

The diner was even busier now, with more waitresses carrying bigger, fuller trays of hamburgers.

"Excuse me," Anna said, squeezing past a lady with a stroller near the front of the line. "We're not eating. We . . . need to see someone really quick." She pulled José into the corner by the hostess stand so they could look for Snake-Arm. "He's probably not back yet from wherever he went, but maybe someone will have information."

The kitchen door swung open, and the pink-haired hostess stepped up to them. She held a pile of menus. "How many?"

"We don't need a table," José said. "We're just wondering about someone."

Anna stood on her toes and tried to see into the kitchen, but the door swung shut. "That man who was here before? With the tattoo?"

"Claude Pickersgill. He owns the place. But he left. And you need to leave, too, if you're not ordering. We're busy." The hostess shooed Anna and José back toward the door with her menus.

"Do you know where he went?" Anna asked.

"Said he had to go home early."

"Go home early?" Anna turned her head to the window, where the snow was falling so thick and fast, the planes on the runway were just ghosts covered in white. "I thought the roads were closed! Is he coming back?" Anna called over her shoulder after they'd been ushered all the way back to the hallway.

"Who knows?" The hostess held up menus to the next couple in line. "Table for two?"

"There's definitely something up with that guy," Anna said as she and José left the diner. They found Henry and Sinan sitting in side-by-side shoeshine chairs, leaning together over Henry's GamePrism. The shoeshine guy was nowhere to be found, but

Hammurabi was sniffing at Henry's sneaker as if he might lick it clean.

Henry looked up. "Oh, hey! Did you find the flag? That guy had it hidden in the restaurant's silverware drawer, didn't he?"

Sinan snickered, and even Hammurabi seemed to have a sort of smirk on his face. Anna folded her arms. "You can laugh all you want, but I think that Snake-Arm guy is hiding something. There's no way he just left to go home in the middle of this." Anna gestured toward the window.

"No, that doesn't really add up," José agreed. "But we can't go running out there to track him down. I'm afraid we bit off more than we can chew here."

Sinan's face lit up, and he pulled his sketch pad from his pocket.

While he drew, Henry chased his GamePrism bank robbers.

José patted Hammurabi's head thoughtfully, while Hammurabi looked longingly at the doggy bags being carried out of Pickersgill Diner.

Anna stared out the window at the fat snow-flakes. There had to be something they could do to help while they were stuck here. A little investigating wasn't biting off more than they could chew, was it?

"What do you think?" Sinan held up his sketch.

We bit off more than we can chew.

"Very nice," Anna said. "But I still think —"
"WRROOOF!"
Hammurabi jumped up and barked at a group of men hurrying out of the candy store behind them.

It was Senator Snickerbottom and his crew. "Good boy, Hammurabi!" Anna said. "Maybe I can finish my interview." She headed for the men, but then she stopped and turned. "Look!" she whispered. "It's him!"

They could see half of Snake-Arm's face sticking out from behind a big rack of gummy worms at the candy store entrance. He kept his body hidden but peered down the hallway as Snickerbottom and his men walked away.

Then Snake-Arm looked around, came out from behind the rack, and ran into the electronics store next door.

"He's following Snickerbottom!" Henry said, finally looking up from his game.

Sure enough, Snake-Arm reappeared, half hidden behind a stack of remote control airplanes, and peered down the hall. Ducking in and out, behind book displays and candy counters, Snake-Arm tailed the senator and his men past four more stores.

"Well, forget the bank robbers, then." Henry stood up from the shoeshine chair and tucked his game into his pocket. "We've got a real-life suspect to chase now."

NINE

"So why would Snake-Arm be after Senator Snickerbottom?"

Pacing back and forth in front of the big window of Gate B-16, Anna asked the question over and over. She kept having to step around Henry's GamePrism cord and José's feet, stretched in front of him as he leaned back in his chair watching the snow fall.

They'd crept along, following Snake-Arm following Snickerbottom past three more stores, then up to the door of a bar, where a bouncer guy stopped them and pointed to the sign that read MUST BE 21 TO ENTER.

"So what's the connection?" Anna was so wrapped up in the thought, she nearly tripped over Sinan, who was napping with Hammurabi as his pillow. No matter how unlikely it seemed, Anna could only come up with one answer.

"Snake-Arm has got to be involved in the crime," she said. "I bet . . . I bet he stole the flag and knows that Snickerbottom's campaign team is helping with the investigation, so now he's trying to make sure they don't discover what happened."

"That's dumb," said Henry, putting his GamePrism earbuds into his ears.

"It's not." Anna plopped into the seat next to him and pulled one earbud back out. "Think about it. Why else would he be following him?"

"Maybe Snickerbottom ate at the restaurant and forgot his doggy bag or something."

Anna threw her hands into the air. "Like Snake-Arm would sneak up on him to return his leftover spaghetti?"

Henry unplugged the headphones from his video game, and a blast of gunfire came out of the speakers. His face lit up. "Hey!" he shouted, waking both Sinan and Hammurabi. "Hey! I bet I know what's going on!"

"What is it?" Anna leaned in to look, but all she could see was the yellow and white static of an explosion on the screen.

"Assassination," Henry said, waving the game. "Snake-Arm is involved in a plot to assassinate Senator Snickerbottom!"

"Can you actually assassinate someone who isn't president yet?" Anna asked.

"Any murder with political motivations is an assassination," Henry said with a firm nod. Anna stared. She would have expected José to pull that definition from his brain, but not Henry. "They talk about it in the secret agents meeting in my game, Shadow Rogue Assassin," he explained.

Anna leaned in closer. "What else happens in that game?"

"Here, hold on." Henry popped out his Super-Heist game cartridge and rummaged in his backpack until he found another one. He slipped it into the GamePrism and slid from his chair onto the floor so they could see better. "In Shadow Rogue Assassin, there's this evil guy named Maldisio, and he wants the crown prince dead, but he doesn't want to do it himself, so he hires secret agents to do it for him. Check this out."

They huddled on their knees, leaning over the game screen. Even Hammurabi poked his head into the circle.

"These guys around the table here . . . they're the secret agents, and you choose which one you want to be, see? And then you get your orders from Maldisio. You can choose whether you want to stand guard or drive the escape vehicle or what. So here . . ." Henry pressed some buttons. "We'll be the lookout this time, so what we need to do is make sure that . . ." — he paused, eyes zeroed in on the screen — "that these guys . . ." — his thumbs poked at the GamePrism, and the avatar on-screen kicked and punched until the men who had appeared in the corner were all flat on the ground — "don't get in the way of the assassination." He pressed a few more buttons. "There."

"So . . . why does Maldisio want the crown prince dead?" Anna asked. Maybe it would give her an idea for why Snake-Arm would want to steal the flag.

"It's all about power," Henry said. "Always. If you do everything right, then at the end of the game, Maldisio gets to rule the land."

"Politics ruins the character," José said, nodding. "That's from Otto von Bismarck," he added before Henry could even ask.

"Otto-Man who?"

"Never mind." José shook his head. "Let's think about your game as it relates to our situation. After you help this Maldisio guy get to be prince, Henry, what's in it for you? What do you get for helping?"

"You get to hang out with Maldisio and go to his parties."

Anna sank back on her heels and stared up at the straight lines of window bars breaking the snow outside into perfect white rectangles. The puzzle pieces in her brain weren't fitting like that, no matter how hard she wished they would. "So . . . that could mean that Snake-Arm . . ."

Henry gasped. "Is going to kill Robert Snicker-bottom so *he* can be president instead!"

Anna frowned.

José tipped his head.

It was Sinan who finally spoke up. "Are you not in the habit of electing your president by voting?"

"Oh," said Henry. "Yeah. It was a cool idea, though." He pulled the Shadow Rogue Assassin game from its slot and rummaged through his backpack. "Wanna play Super Larry Tennis?" he asked Sinan.

José pulled out *Harry Potter*. He read for a few minutes until the "Raindrops" song played from a few seats away, where his father had been reading his *WeatherWise* magazine. José leaped up so fast his book flew from his lap. He rushed to his dad's side, leaning in toward the phone.

Finally, Mr. McGilligan hung up and shook his head. "Nothing new. They're still keeping her."

José sank back into his chair and opened his book, but he stayed on the same page for a long, long time.

Anna watched the tennis ball bounce back and forth across the electronic screen from Henry's side to Sinan's side. It reminded her of the ideas pinging around in her head. If she could just get one to slow down long enough to think about it, she'd be all set. It felt like the answer was there, right there, but moving too fast to see clearly. Things had seemed to make so much more sense back when they'd seen Snake-Arm following Senator Snickerbottom.

Anna sprung up from the floor. "I'll be right back. I'm going to the restaurant for a minute." She looked for her dad to tell him, but he was huddled in a meeting with two of his staffers. She waved and pointed down the hallway, and he waved back. Part of her was glad her mom wasn't around to keep track of her, but part of her wished her father would at least ask where she was going.

Anna wandered back to the restaurant, where diners were mopping up ketchup with their last fries. She tried to freeze the scene, like pausing a movie on TV, so her eyes could take in everything.

The dark grain of the tables.

Waitresses hustling to finish serving dessert.

Crumbs under a high chair, from where somebody's little kid probably smushed a whole package of those saltine crackers that show up with the soup.

What was it that she should be noticing? Investigative reporters on TV always saw just the right thing, the thing that made all the pieces come together, made all the lines run straight and true, right to the answer. The door to the kitchen swung the tiniest bit but didn't open. Should she try to peek inside? Could Snake-Arm be back by now?

Anna flipped her notebook to an empty page, but

her pencil felt stuck in the air over it, frozen in the muck of not knowing. She sighed, put her notebook down on the hostess stand, and looked up at the television blaring the news out over the crowded bar area.

There was an update on the storm; an excited weatherman announced that the snowfall had set a new record. He tossed it back to the news anchor, shuffling papers on her desk.

"And just in, we have new information on the Star-Spangled Banner theft."

Anna stepped closer to the TV.

"Police now say it's possible that a gang of international art thieves may be involved. They're looking for this man." The picture cut away to a mug shot of a slender man with tufts of gray hair sticking up over his ears, small wire-framed glasses, and a thin gray mustache. "His name is Vincent Goosen, and he's the reputed leader of the Serpentine Princes, an infamous group of illicit art collectors who are well known to police."

The picture changed to show a side-view mug shot, and Anna sucked in her breath.

Curling around Vincent Goosen's neck was a tattoo of a fat, green-and-black-striped snake.

It wasn't exactly like Snake-Arm's. But it was close enough.

Anna grabbed her notebook and took off running.

TEN

The concourse was thick with travelers, looking sleepier, hungrier, and grumpier by the minute.

"Sorry!" Anna tripped over a purple suitcase being pulled along by a little girl, whose pink sneakers lit up every time she took a step.

"Excuse me." She squeezed through the middle of the line at Cinna-Bunny, dodged one of those airport carts with the whoop-whoop-whooping alarm, nearly crashed into a woman who was waiting to use the restroom, and careened around the corner toward Gate B-16.

Then she stopped so fast that her sneakers squeaked on the shiny floor.

Dozens of people were gathered around a circle of glaring lights and television cameras. The crowd buzzed with an energy that had seeped out of the rest of the sleepy airport hours ago. In the middle of that circle, leaning in toward a cluster of microphones, was Robert Snickerbottom. He looked right into the cameras as he spoke, nodding emphatically, and at one point gesturing out toward the crowd with so much gusto that the reporter standing to his left, a young woman in tippy high-heeled boots, had to duck to avoid the sweep of his arm.

Anna strained to hear what he was saying, but she could only catch a few words.

". . . dedicated the full resources of my campaign . . ."

". . . disturbing developments . . ."

It had to be about the flag. Anna rose on her tiptoes, searching for José or Henry or Sinan. And where was her father? She jumped as high as she could, but her only view was of the wide shoulders of the man in front of her.

"Excuse me." Anna wiggled through the crowd that had filled in behind her. She needed to get back where she could see what was going on. Over at the next gate, the seats were empty except for the skinny man in the cowboy hat who hung around with Snickerbottom. He was hunched over, talking on the phone. She'd ask him what was happening when he finished.

In the meantime, Anna climbed up onto one of the chairs to try and get a better view of the hubbub, but she still couldn't see past the crowd. She wished the man on the phone would hurry up, but he turned away from her and held the phone closer to his mouth.

"Doesn't matter, Zeke. They'll do it when we get to Vermont. That's what he said."

Anna inched closer to him, then stepped up onto the top of the seats to take in more of the scene. Across the hall, she counted four TV cameras and about twice that many reporters scribbling in notepads. Snickerbottom must have called a press conference right here in the airport.

Anna jumped down from the seats, stumbling right into the man in the cowboy hat.

"Hold on!" he growled into his phone, and glared at Anna until she picked herself up and ran back to the crowd. She needed to get up to the front of all those people.

Anna darted through gaps in the crowd, dodging elbows and backpacks until she saw a familiar head of messy black hair in front of her. It was José, with Henry and Sinan in front of him. Sinan's eyes were huge. Henry's mouth hung open.

"Hey!" Anna tapped on José's shoulder.

José turned but put a finger to his lips. "Shhh!"

"What's going on?" she whispered. "Did something happen with the flag?"

He nodded but held up his hand for her to wait.

Anna was close enough to hear now. Close enough to understand why the boys were in shock.

"That's right." Snickerbottom nodded. "We've discovered that the flag is here. Right here at the airport."

"I was right all along!" Anna whispered.

José shushed her again.

"How do the police know?" the tippy-boot reporter asked. "Does that mean you have suspects?"

"Indeed we do."

Anna gasped. "Do you think he knows about Snake-Arm?" She looked around, her heart pounding. Could Snake-Arm be here, too? She didn't see him, but that didn't mean anything. The crowd was too thick to see much at all.

Snickerbottom took a deep breath, and his eyes scanned the crowd. "My team has discovered that a number of . . . suspicious persons from outside the United States" — he paused and shook his head a little — "had access to our national treasure at a private function at the Smithsonian last night. Right before the flag disappeared."

José turned to Anna. "Snake-Arm?"

"Maybe. I never saw him at the museum, though. And is he from outside the United States? He didn't have an accent, did he?" Anna tried to replay his voice in her head.

"What I don't get," José said, "is how someone could have taken the flag the night of that reception."

"I know," Anna said. "Security was so tight. How could Snake-Arm steal it out from under everyone's noses?"

José shrugged. "How could anybody?" And he turned back to the news conference.

Tippy Boots stepped forward then. "So who are these people? And how could they have ended up at such an exclusive event?"

"Well . . ." Snickerbottom waited for the last camera to focus on him before he answered quietly. "They were invited."

The reporters, for once, were silent. The crowd stared.

"Though the investigation is continuing, I can tell you that my team has evidence to suggest that special guests of the museum were involved in the theft. *Musical* guests."

No. Anna shook her head silently. He didn't have the right information at all.

"Sounds for a Small Planet?" Tippy Boots asked, her pen poised above her notepad.

"I'm afraid so. And as you know, members of that group are among us at the airport. They're currently being questioned by the police."

No! How could he say that without any proof? Anna looked at Sinan, who hadn't moved or even blinked. But his brown eyes were shiny with tears. She couldn't stand it. "But, Senator Snickerbottom," she shouted over the crowd, "what about the Serpentine Princes? And why would the musicians want to steal the flag?"

Snickerbottom frowned into the crowd. "There are people in this world who do not share our love for America, young lady. People who, given the opportunity, would seek to destroy this fine nation we've built. Our values. Our beliefs." He turned away from Anna and looked back at the cameras. "And our flag. But we're going to get the Star-Spangled Banner back where it belongs. If you'll excuse me now, I have work to do." He turned and started weaving his way through the crowd.

Anna needed to ask more questions. She'd been in such a rush to find out what was going on, she didn't even think to get it on tape. She never even took out her mini video camera.

She would have run after Snickerbottom and his men if she hadn't seen Sinan's face. He kept shaking his head.

"There is no one," he said quietly. "No one who would do such a thing. No one in the group hates America. We are here for the music. Always the music and the people. Why would this man say such a thing?"

José pulled a rumpled Kleenex from his pocket and handed it to Sinan. "Sometimes, people just want someone to blame."

"It is not right. We are being made into . . . what is the saying that you have for those who are blamed unfairly? Goats that get over the fence?"

Anna tipped her head. "Never heard that one."

Sinan pulled out his sketch pad and flipped through the pages. "Here."

Scapegoat

José nodded slowly. "Yeah. That sounds about right."

"But it's *not* right! It's so totally wrong. And we need to do something." Anna watched Sinan add a few more details to his sketch. And then she remembered another drawing — not on paper, but on skin. On the arm of the man from Pickersgill Diner.

If he was part of Vincent Goosen's art theft gang . . .

If he was the one who stole the flag . . .

And *if* they could prove it, then the police would have to leave the orchestra people alone.

"I need to tell you guys what I found out." Anna put an arm around Sinan. "Let's go find your mom and dad. We can talk on the way."

ELEVEN

"So let me get this right . . ." José rubbed his eyes under his glasses as they walked. "You're saying that this tattoo is evidence that the guy from the diner is involved? I don't know, Anna."

"Dude, she's totally right," Henry said. "I told you that Snake-Arm guy was acting like an assassin!"

"I never said *that*," Anna said as they walked back into the area with the shops. "But I do think we need to investigate him. Because if he's connected to that Vincent Goosen guy and the Serpentine Prince gang, then —"

Hammurabi's barking interrupted her. It wasn't the friendly sort of barking he did when he wanted attention. It was sharper and deeper. And scared.

The area where the orchestra had played just hours

ago was swarming with police officers and airport security guards. Anna couldn't see Hammurabi, but she spotted Sinan's parents standing with the trombone players, talking with two policemen.

"What is this?" Sinan whispered.

Hammurabi barked again.

"Where is my dog?" Sinan's voice squeaked as he climbed up on a chair searching the crowd until his eyes settled on his mom and dad. "Why are Ammi and Abba with your officers? What is happening?"

José took Sinan's hand and pulled him from the chair. "It's okay. They're just talking with the police. In America, even if somebody thinks you might be involved in a crime, you're innocent until proven guilty. They didn't do anything wrong; they'll be fine." His voice wobbled on the last word, and Anna could tell he was thinking about his own mom, talking with police, too, in another part of DC.

Just as Sinan's eyes relaxed, there was another eruption of barking. Over by the coffee counter, two burly airport security officers were forcing Hammurabi into a cage.

Sinan tugged away from José and took off.

Henry ran after him. "Come on!" he called over his shoulder. "He's going to get himself in trouble."

By the time they made it through the crowd, Sinan was clutching the front of the cage. Hammurabi was all crunched up in there — it wasn't nearly big enough for him — whimpering and licking Sinan's fingers through the bars.

"What are you doing?" Anna walked right up to the airport security guard who stood by the cage. He was only a little taller than Anna, with short brown hair and a mustache and a belly that hung over his thick black belt. He either didn't hear Anna or ignored her.

"Excuse me." She tapped his elbow. "That's my friend's dog."

"Mphh." He brushed off his elbow, as if she'd gotten him dirty by tapping him, and refolded his arms. "That dog is going back into the baggage area."

"But the storm has delayed everything for so long!" Anna said. "He can't stay down there by himself."

"Hammurabi gets lonely," Sinan said quietly.

Another security guard came and lifted Hammurabi's cage. He nodded to the first guard. "I'll run this downstairs, and you start over there." He nodded off to the side, where it looked as if all of the group's instruments had been stacked — no, it looked as if they'd almost been *thrown* into a big lumpy mountain of music. "They'll check all that stuff down below. The rest of this group's baggage — a few bigger pieces, I guess — is buried too deep in the suitcases to bring it out now, but they'll go through that when the plane gets to Vermont. If there's enough evidence for arrests, the authorities there will be ready."

Hammurabi's nails scratched wildly at the bottom of the cage as the man bounced him down the hall. They disappeared behind a door that said AUTHORIZED PERSONNEL ONLY.

Sinan's eyes pooled with tears.

Anna bit her lip.

José patted Sinan's shoulder.

"You know," Henry said, "I got this game called Jailbreak where you're a bank robber and you gotta break your accomplice out of his cell so you can find the hidden money and go to Argentina. We could sneak into baggage claim and bust Hammurabi outta there and then get on a plane to . . . I don't know . . . Mexico or someplace."

"Henry! This is serious. Innocent people are in trouble." Anna took a deep breath. When innocent people got in trouble on TV crime dramas, there was only one way they ever got out of it. The real bad guys had to be uncovered. They needed to find out for sure if Snake-Arm was part of that international art-theft gang.

"Look." She pulled them into a tight circle, out of the way of the rolling luggage and the coffee line. "It's late, and there's no way our plane is getting out tonight anyway, so here's what I think we should do. We take Sinan to his parents and head back to B-16 so *our* parents" — she looked at Henry — "and your flight attendant lady don't freak out. We try to sleep. And in the morning, we head straight to Pickersgill Diner.

Maybe Snake-Arm will be back for the breakfast rush, and we can see what he's up to. If we stay on his tail long enough, he might lead us to the flag. It's worth trying at least, isn't it?"

"I don't know," José said. "Maybe we should let all this go. I know my mom didn't have anything to do with the flag's disappearance." He looked at Sinan. "And I know your parents didn't, either. If we let the police and everybody figure that out on their own, won't it all blow over without us getting involved?"

"Dude!" Henry looked at José incredulously. "You're already involved. Hasn't your mom spent, like, her whole life trying to protect stuff like this flag? And didn't she spend the last . . . I dunno . . . six months or something fixing it? And now some bunch of creepy snake-men stole it, and she's getting blamed? Doesn't that make you mad?"

"Well . . ." José pushed up his glasses. "Well, yes, but . . ."

"Come on!" Henry paused for a moment; then he made his voice deep. "The test of any man lies in action."

José's mouth dropped open. "You read Pindar?"

"Huh?"

"Pindar, the Ancient Greek poet. You just quoted him!"

Henry shook his head. "No, I didn't. I've never heard of that guy. I was quoting Maldisio. He says that thing about action right before he takes the crown in the game."

"No. That's from Pindar," José insisted. "'I will not steep my speech in lies; the test of any man lies in action.'"

"Yeah, well, maybe your Pinhead guy stole it from Maldisio. Anyway, his point was you can't just talk about stuff all the time. Eventually, you have to *do* something."

José nodded slowly. "Okay," he said. "I'm in."

"If being *in* means you wish to be of help," Sinan said, "then I am in, too."

Anna put a hand on his shoulder. "That's good, and we'll come get you in the morning to help. Right now, your parents are looking for you."

Sinan's mother had spotted him and was making her way through the crowd. "There you are!" She pulled Sinan into her and kissed the top of his head. "It has been a long day, hasn't it, *jaanu*?"

Sinan squirmed and made the same face Anna made when her mother called her *honey bear*. She guessed *jaanu* probably meant something like that.

"Let's get you a snack and a pillow." Sinan's mother took his hand and nodded to José, Henry, and Anna. "Thank you for being a friend to our boy today."

They had taken only three steps when Sinan tripped over something and there was a loud squeak.

"Mr. Squeaky!" It was the rubber clown toy, so well loved that its nose had faded from red to pink with white rubber flecks. Sinan's eyes filled with tears as he picked it up. "Hammurabi will never be able to sleep without Mr. Squeaky." He looked around, but the security guards who had taken the dog were long gone. "Excuse me," he asked an officer who was leaning up against the keyboard. "Do you know where I can find my dog? He needs this."

"You people are staying right here," the officer growled.

Sinan started to argue. "You don't understand. He will be —" But his mother pulled him away.

"Oh, my Sinan . . . Hammurabi is named for a brave king. He will be all right. And he will have his Mr. Squeaky back tomorrow." Sinan's mother took his hand — the one that wasn't clutching the rubber clown — and started to lead him away.

"Wait!" Sinan tugged away from his mother. He squeezed the clown slowly, and it let out a long, high, wheezy noise. Sinan sighed. "I have to go to the bathroom first." He pointed toward the restrooms next to the frozen yogurt stand.

"Be quick." His mother kissed his head.

"I will see you tomorrow." Sinan waved to Anna, Henry, and José, then gave the clown one last squeak and walked away.

TWELVE

The eleven o'clock news was on when they got back to Gate B-16. José's father was in front of the television, listening to the end of a flag update.

"Dad," José said, "have you heard —"

"Shhh!" His father's eyes were red, his smile gone.

"And finally," the news announcer continued, "there's still no sign of Vincent Goosen, leader of the infamous art-theft gang known as the Serpentine Princes. Police are asking anyone with information about his whereabouts to call their tip line immediately, but do not approach this man. Goosen and the other gang members are known to be armed and extremely dangerous. We'll keep you updated."

A commercial came on, and José's dad turned to them.

"Sorry," he said. "I'm just . . . exhausted. And worried about Mom. Did you get dinner?"

José nodded. "I'm all set. Any news?"

Mr. McGilligan took off his glasses and rubbed his eyes. "They're — the police are still . . . interested in her as a suspect. They're holding her for now."

"In *jail*?" José's mouth hung open.

"At the police station. They say she's the last person who had access to the flag — apparently, she did a final check on it late last night, after the party — and they keep asking her if she saw anyone else, anyone suspicious."

"Did she?"

Mr. McGilligan shook his head. "Nope. She said the chamber was quiet — blissfully quiet after the big shindig."

"Mr. McGilligan." Anna couldn't hold back. "We actually have some information that might help. That Vincent guy from TV? There's another man here at the airport with a snake tattoo, and he's acting all suspicious, so we think he might be part of the gang!"

Mr. McGilligan gave a tired smile. "There must be thousands of snake tattoos in this world. Trust me . . . the police would know if a member of the Serpentine Princes had purchased an airplane ticket. I'm sure they've already been through the airline records and know exactly who's here."

"So what are they going to do?" José's voice was getting higher. "Are they going to keep Mom until they find it? What if they *never* find it?"

"They're going to find it."

"Can we at least call her cell phone and say good night?" José swiped at a tear rolling down his cheek. Anna looked away.

"Sure," José's father said, and he dialed. But then there was only quiet.

"She's not answering," he said finally, and when Anna looked back, Mr. McGilligan had put his arm around José. "Her battery probably died. Don't worry — it's all going to be fine. Mom wants to stay in town anyway, in case the flag needs more work when they find it. And I just met Anna's father over at the airline counter; he says they have new suspects, so maybe that will be our answer." He lifted his head and nodded toward the corner, where Anna finally saw her father, squinting down at his cell phone. It was plugged into the outlet she and Henry had fought over that morning. It seemed like days ago now.

"Who are those other suspects?" Anna asked, but Mr. McGilligan shrugged.

Anna sighed. She would have bet her notebook that they were the same suspects Senator Snickerbottom told the reporters about without even having proof. She needed to share what she'd learned about Snake-Arm. "I'm going to talk to my dad," Anna said.

"Dad!" She tapped the shoulder of his suit coat. "I need to talk to you. I just got back from —"

"One minute!" He held up the hand that wasn't holding his phone and paused. "Yes, I'm still here. Sure . . . she'll be there with a crew whenever we arrive. Okay, bye."

"Who was that?" Anna said, still staring at the pocket where he'd put his phone.

"Senator Snickerbottom. News tip for Mom."

"News tip?" Anna's fingers twitched. Where was her notebook? "About what?"

"Well . . ." Her father looked past her to José and Henry, who were getting settled a few chairs down, and lowered his voice. "You can't share this with your pals."

Anna nodded.

"Senator Snickerbottom is quite confident they're going to find the flag when we get to Vermont."

Vermont? That didn't fit with her Snake-Arm theory. "They think the flag's in Vermont?"

"Well, it's not there now. It's here."

"Then why don't they find it here?"

"If you'd ever seen an airport baggage area, you'd understand." Anna's father held his arms out wide. "They believe the flag has been checked as baggage, but they're not entirely sure about the . . . ah . . . packaging, and with all the luggage piled up, it would be like looking for a needle in a haystack. They're going to inspect all the baggage after it's unloaded in Vermont instead."

"How do they know all this? And why do they think it's going to Vermont?"

"That's the . . . destination of the primary suspects."

"Dad, if this is about the orchestra members, then —"

The notes of "Hail to the Chief" rang out from his pocket, and he pulled out his phone. "Hold on, this is Mom. . . . Hey, what's up?"

He turned away from Anna, but she could hear him sharing what Senator Snickerbottom said about Vermont and suspects. Snickerbottom was totally blaming the orchestra. Anna scooted around her father so he couldn't miss seeing her. She held out her hand and whispered, "Can I talk when you're done, please?"

Her father held up a finger. "Okay . . . yeah . . . Of course I made sure she had dinner." He raised his eyebrows at Anna, and she nodded. "Okay, then. See you soon. Love you. Here's Anna."

"Mom?" The phone felt warm against her cheek. Anna could almost imagine it was her mom's hand resting there.

The voice that came through was warm, too. Warm, but worried. "What are you up to, kiddo? Keeping Dad out of trouble?"

"Yeah, and guess what? We've been investigating the flag theft because —"

"We? Who is we?"

"Me and Henry and José, these guys who were at the party at the museum last night and they're from Vermont, and you're not going to believe this, but . . ." — Anna lowered her voice, even though no one was really near them — "their families are part of the Silver Jaguar Society, too!"

"Anna, listen to me. This —"

"Don't worry, we're just checking things out, but we already know that Senator Snickerbottom's wrong about the suspect thing. He thinks it's the orchestra, but we think there's somebody here from the Serpentine Princes, so —"

"What?!" Anna almost dropped the phone, her mother's voice was so sharp. "There? There at the airport?"

"Yeah," she said, but her mother's fearful tone of voice made her pause.

"Anna," her mother said. "You have no idea how much danger you may be in if this is true. I want you to —"

"Why? It's not like some Serpentine Prince guy would care about a bunch of —"

"Anna Revere-Hobbs. I am not going to sit here five hundred miles away and share society secrets on a nonsecure cell phone. But I will tell you that this is over your head. Way over."

"Aw, Mom, we're not doing anything dumb, just investigating a little. We're practically Silver Jaguar Society members — I mean, I know we're not old enough, but there aren't any grown-up members here, so I figured —"

"Stop. First of all, yes, there are."

"There are?" Anna felt her heart jump. "Who are they? Mom, we totally need to talk to them."

"And second," her mother continued as if she hadn't even spoken, "you are not practically members. You are *children*."

"But, Mom —"

"And when you hang up this phone, you are to sit down at that gate and — Where's Dad?"

Anna looked around. He'd gone down the hall to talk with some guy in a suit. "He's right here."

"Then you are to sit down next to him and write in your journal or read a magazine and stay out of this flag business. If the Serpentine Princes really are — Wait, why do you think they're at the airport?"

"We saw this guy who has a tattoo like Vincent Goosen's. You know who that is, right?"

"How do *you* know Vince?"

"I don't know him, I just —" Anna's head was so full of questions she felt it might explode. Why did her mother sound so scared? And *Vince*? Her mom was on a first-name basis with this —

Anna heard her mother let out a shaky breath. "Anna, there is something you need to know about Vincent Goosen. But first, *how* do you know about him at all?"

"I don't *know* him. He's been on the news is all. How do *you* know him?"

A gust of wind whipped the snow outside into a whirlwind at the same time static crackled over the phone.

"Mom?"

"Did you lose her?" Anna's dad was back. But her mom was gone from the line. "We can call her later on," he said. "I need to check my e-mail now." He took the phone, plopped down in a seat, and started poking at it with the same energy Henry used to press his GamePrism buttons.

He'd be on that thing all night, Anna could already tell. She didn't sit down next to him as her mom had ordered. Instead, she gave him a wave and wandered over to José and Henry, who had been joined by a flustered flight attendant talking into a two-way radio.

"Yes, I have him here." Her eyes narrowed at Henry. "He's been . . . he says he has been in the gate area the whole time."

Henry shrugged and nodded. "Except for when I went out to get a burger. Guy's gotta eat, right?"

She frowned and pressed the radio button again. "All right, we'll keep checking on him. I'm heading back your way now." She clipped the radio onto her belt. "You're to stay here. Understand?"

Henry nodded. "Perfectly."

She shot one last strict look at Henry and hurried off down the hall.

"You guys," Anna said after the flight attendant left, "my mom says there are Silver Jaguar Society members here."

"There are?" José raised his eyebrows. "How many? And who are they?"

"She wouldn't say."

"Well, that's helpful." Henry looked around at the crowds huddled in their stiff airport seats. "We'll just check all these thousands of people for weird cat jewelry. Should be no problem at all." He pulled out his GamePrism. "Anybody wanna play Jailbreak? It'll be good practice."

"For what?" José asked.

Henry grinned. "*Our* secret jailbreak mission."

"Oh, no. No. We are not breaking a poodle out of baggage claim. We have to be sensible." Anna plopped down on a chair of her own and felt as if all her energy had finally drained out of her. "In the morning, we'll go to the diner and see if Snake-Arm is there."

"Sounds okay to me," José yawned and slid to the floor, using his jacket as a blanket and *Harry Potter* as his pillow.

Anna tipped her head back, and somehow, even with her thoughts swirling with stars and stripes, snakes and security guards, fell asleep.

THIRTEEN

"Anna! Anna!"

Anna didn't know if it had been ten minutes or an hour when she woke. The airport was darker, and at first, she thought the voice was part of a dream. But it didn't go away.

"Anna! I am in need of your help."

She blinked and saw Sinan's mother. Her eyes darted from chair to empty chair, full of worry. "Have you seen Sinan?"

"No. He was going to meet you after he used the bathroom."

"I thought he might be with you." Sinan's mother blinked fast. "He never came back from the bathroom."

"But where would he go?" Anna whispered. Her eyes had adjusted to the lights now. Henry was slumped over a chair, dozing, and José was still sound asleep on the floor. Even her father had drifted off in his seat, his mouth hanging open, hands folded over his cell phone on his chest. Anna could see the message light blinking between his fingers.

Sinan's mother shook her head. "We do not know," she whispered, looking nervously around the gate area. "I'm not supposed to be here. They've restricted us to a small area down the hall, but we are so worried. We thought perhaps he was hungry and went off to find something to eat — he loves the pizza — but it has been more than an hour. And I do not believe he had his backpack with his money."

"He didn't," Anna said. "All he had was —"

"There she is!" The security guards who had caged Hammurabi were stepping briskly over backpacks and purses, headed right toward them.

Sinan's mother shrank back against the window. "I am sorry. I know we were to stay in the area you set out for us, but my son —"

"Let's go." One of the guards reached for his handcuffs.

"Please." Sinan's mother raised her hands. "There is no need for that. I will come with you."

"Darn right you will. You've got some questions to answer."

The other guard grabbed her elbow and led her

back down the darkening hallway before Anna could even find her voice.

That poor lady! She was just looking for her son, and they were treating her like a criminal. And Anna hadn't even had a chance to finish telling her.

Sinan didn't have his bag with him. He didn't have anything.

Except Mr. Squeaky.

Anna closed her eyes.

She pictured the chewed-up toy in Sinan's hands.

She heard its wheezy squeak.

And she knew where Sinan had gone.

"Wake up!" Anna poked José. She tugged on Henry's sleeve and tried to ignore the trickle of drool coming out of his mouth. "Come on, you guys, get up!"

"Whaa?" Henry rubbed his forehead with the heel of his palm, wiped the drool on his sleeve, and blinked. "What?"

"It's Sinan." Her words tumbled out, one on top of another. "His mother was here, and you know when he went to the bathroom before and he had Mr. Squeaky? He never went back to his parents, and I think I know where he is, but before I could even tell his mom, they took her away, and I don't think they'll let us see her if we try to go over there now."

Henry squinted at her. "*What?*"

"I think Sinan went to look for Hammurabi. We need to find him."

"So . . . what exactly are you proposing?" José asked.

Anna took a deep breath. "We have to break into wherever they keep the luggage."

There was a long pause.

A very long pause.

"Ordinarily, I'd say that what you're proposing would be impossible as a result of airport security." José scratched his head slowly.

"But . . . ?" Anna's eyes were huge. "You said ordinarily. There has to be a *but*."

"Everybody has a butt." Henry snickered.

Anna glared at him.

"Sorry, but you kind of set that one up."

She turned back to José. "But . . . ?"

"But if ever there were a time when it might be possible for three minors to slip into the baggage area unnoticed . . ." He glanced out the window, where a million huge, feathery snowflakes swirled in the runway lights as if giants were having a feather-pillow fight on the tarmac.

Then he turned back to the terminal, where the only other person awake was the World's Greatest Grandma, knitting what looked like a big green sock. Even she was starting to doze off.

"If ever there were a time when it might — just might — be possible," José said, "I'd say that time is right now."

FOURTEEN

"Are you sure this is the only way to get in?" Anna hurried along beside Henry and José. They'd left hastily scribbled notes about walking over to Terminal C to find a snack, just in case her father and Mr. McGilligan woke up before they got back. "It seems so risky."

"Let's see . . . three kids sneaking into the baggage-handling department of an airport without an adult going with them or even knowing where they are. Oh! And there's a big guy with a tattoo around here somewhere who may be trying to kill the next president." Henry scratched his chin. "Can't imagine why you think it's risky."

"Well, we *have* to find Sinan. I just . . . thought there might be a different way in with . . . stairs or something."

"Don't worry," José said as they passed the food court. Even the Cinna-Bunny stand was closed. "In theory, the chute will be angled so the luggage items will have a stable landing no matter how far down the baggage-handling level is. That means we should have a pretty stable landing, too."

They walked down a long hallway back to the security checkpoint, and José pulled open the glass door. There was no metal detector to walk through to get out of the terminal — only in.

The check-in area, so busy and bustling when they'd arrived this morning, was eerily empty. Only one counter was staffed, by a JetBlue lady eating a cupcake and reading a book called *Ten Days to a Flatter Belly*.

"Back here." Henry ducked behind an empty American Airlines counter. Anna and José followed, crouching down behind a computer monitor that stared back at them with a list of canceled flights.

"That's where we need to go." Henry pointed to an idle conveyor belt next to them. Any other time, it probably would have been chugging along with luggage, but now it looked as if the snowstorm had frozen it in place. The belt led away from the counter and disappeared into an opening in the wall. Rubber strips hung down, blocking their view of whatever was on the other side.

"So that leads to the . . . baggage place?" Anna's

heart thumped like one of those orchestra drums. "How do we know it's safe?"

"It's not safe." Henry's voice was matter-of-fact. "It's meant for suitcases, not people."

"Well, that's comforting. You know, I —"

"Shhh!" José grabbed her elbow and yanked her back down behind the counter. "It's him!"

Snake-Arm was heading in their direction. He had changed out of his apron from the diner and was wearing the same heavy, fluorescent orange vest the baggage handlers wore outside.

"He works in baggage, too?" Anna whispered. She heard her own voice quiver and remembered her mom's anxious tone when the Serpentine Princes came up in their phone conversation before they got cut off. What had she been about to tell Anna about Vincent Goosen?

"Stay down," Henry whispered. "Here he comes."

Snake-Arm hurried past their counter and leaned up against the United Airlines desk as if he were talking with someone behind it. But no one was there.

"That's weird," Anna said. "It's almost like —"

"Shhh!" José and Henry said together, just as Snake-Arm stretched a long arm over the counter. He must have pressed a button or something, because the conveyor belt started to move. Snake-Arm glanced around the check-in area, but the JetBlue woman never looked up from her book, and Anna, José, and

Henry were tucked behind the American Airlines counter, barely breathing.

Snake-Arm sauntered over to the moving conveyor belt and sat down on it. He tucked his long legs in, hugged his bulky knees into his even bulkier chest, rode through the opening in the wall, and disappeared. The black rubber strips swung gently and settled back in place behind him as the belt came to a stop.

José stared at the swinging flaps.

"You think he's a real baggage guy, or did he, like, steal that outfit?" Henry's eyes got big. "That'd be like the game Golden Oath. There's a treasure hidden in this thousand-year-old castle full of nuns. So you gotta dress up like a nun and sneak in to knock out the guards."

"Are the guards nuns, too?" José asked.

Henry nodded. "Ninja nuns."

Anna frowned. "But there's no treasure here." As soon as she said it, she realized she might be wrong. If the flag was here, there was indeed a treasure at the airport. "You guys . . ." Her eyes got bigger and bigger. "If Snake-Arm works in baggage, he had the perfect opportunity to hide the flag in a really big suitcase or something, and now he's going to check on it. Or . . . move it. Or hide it better. Or . . . or something! We need to stop him!"

She turned to José and gestured toward the conveyor belt. "You can go ahead."

José shook his head. "Women and children first."

Anna put her hands on her hips. "Who's *that* quote from?"

José shrugged. "Anonymous."

"Figures. Some scared anonymous *man*. Come on, José. What happened to the Ancient Greek action poet?"

"Yeah," Henry said. "Do it for Pinhead."

"*Pindar*," José said. He took a deep breath. "Fine." He crawled gingerly onto the belt, as if he expected it to leap out from under him.

Anna climbed on behind him and settled in, cross-legged. "All right." She nodded at Henry. "Let's get this thing moving."

"Ready?" Henry peered behind the check-in counter, where Snake-Arm had found whatever button or switch he'd needed to get the belt moving. "Must be this one." Henry poised a finger in the air. "Hold on, 'cause here we go!" He pressed the button and leaped onto the belt just as it rumbled to life. "This is awesome!"

"Oh!" Anna's stomach turned a flip as she rode behind José, headed for that black hole in the wall. On their way to wherever it ended up.

The rubber flaps brushed against her face, and on the other side, there was only darkness. Before Anna's eyes had a chance to adjust, she heard José's cry.

"*Whoooaa!!!*"

FIFTEEN

"José?" Anna leaned forward, reaching for him in the blackness, but there was nothing. Right away, she found out why.

The conveyor belt dropped away from under her bottom, and she fell. "*Whoooaa!*"

Anna landed on something soft, lucky for her.

It was unlucky for José.

"Get your knee out of my stomach!" he hissed.

"Sorry, I —" But Anna's knee was the least of José's worries when Henry came down the chute feet first and landed on both of them.

"Wow," he said as Anna and José tried to catch their breath. "That didn't hurt at all."

"Shhh! We don't want him to hear us." Anna crawled out from under Henry, scrambling over the heap of duffel bags that had helped to break their fall, and looked around. They were definitely in the right place.

The cavernous room had to be ten times the size of Anna's school gymnasium at home. It was cool, with high ceilings and dim fluorescent light, and crammed full of baggage in every size and color. Near the chute Anna, Henry, and José had just flown down were several more like it, maybe to carry baggage from other airlines.

Deeper in the room, bigger pieces of baggage — crates and cases and cartons — were piled along both side walls. The not-so-gigantic pieces — suitcases and backpacks, smaller cartons and kids' car seats — lined a conveyor belt that snaked through the center of the room twisting over on itself and looping around. It climbed hills and plunged down again, a giant roller coaster for suitcases. In the shadowy light way across the room, the belt split into several different tracks that disappeared into holes in the far wall.

The conveyor belt wasn't moving, though, and there wasn't a single baggage worker to be found.

"Doesn't anybody work here?" Henry whispered.

"Maybe they're all on break since no flights are leaving," Anna said. She looked around. "So now what? These bags must be headed all over the country, all over the world, even. We need to find the ones for our flight to Vermont. That's where Hammurabi would be, wouldn't it? And I bet that's where Sinan will have ended up. I wonder —"

"Shhh!" Henry shoved her head down and pulled a big red duffel bag over the top of her. She started to push it off but heard noise from the far side of the room. Like someone throwing things.

Anna wiggled the duffel bag to the side enough so she could see. Someone was indeed throwing suitcases out of the shadows over there. When the person stepped into the light, Anna gasped.

"It's *him*!" she whispered.

Snake-Arm sent a set of golf clubs clattering onto the belt, then paused. Anna froze, afraid he'd heard her, but he never looked back in their direction; he just cursed and lumbered over to the conveyor belt. He ran his hand along the smooth metal rails that kept the luggage on the belt. When he got to a place where the track started to rise toward the ceiling, he hoisted himself up and climbed along the belt on his hands and knees, toward the high ceiling and around a curve, until they couldn't see him anymore.

Anna waited to make sure he was gone, then pushed the duffel bag off her face with a grunt. "I don't know what someone has packed in this bag, but it stinks to high heaven."

Henry poked at the bag. "Hockey gear, maybe. The tag says it's headed to Buffalo."

Anna looked, and sure enough, the white loopy sticker the airline had attached to the bag's handle was marked BUF. "We need to find the ones marked BTV — that's what my boarding pass called the Burlington airport." She crawled over the heap of suitcases. "These are all BUF. Wait — there's BOS. That must be Boston."

Henry made a noise that was halfway between a grunt and a growl.

"What's wrong with Boston?" Anna said.

"One, it's not BTV," Henry answered, "and two, I'm being *forced* to move there. With my dad and his new wife."

"Oh." Anna wasn't sure what do say, so she started calling out letters on tags again. "ROC. LAX. Another BUF."

"TPA. ORD. ATL." Henry tossed bag after bag off the heap and sent them clunking onto the cement floor. Anna and José had to jump off to the side to avoid a maroon suitcase on wheels that came whooshing down from the baggage chute.

"Where are the BTV bags? It's like they disappeared." Henry's forehead shone with sweat as he checked the last bag that had been in the pile. Another BUF.

"Well, when we got here, there were still flights scheduled to leave," Anna said, "so our luggage might have gone out by the planes." Her eyes followed the swirling maze of conveyor belts. She counted four places where the belts disappeared into the opposite wall, behind rubber flaps like upstairs. Four exits to somewhere. "We should check the bags on the belt, too. One of those tunnels must lead to the Burlington baggage."

A deep metallic *thunk* made them all jump. There was a *rumble-creak-hum* of motors grumbling awake, and conveyor belts all around the room started up again.

"Don't move," Anna whispered. "It might be Snake-Arm!"

They froze. Anna held her breath until she thought she'd explode. But there was no sign of him. No sign of anyone.

"Maybe they started it from up there." José nodded toward the top of the baggage chute. "Looks like more luggage."

The baggage that had been frozen in time chugged along past them now, in a colorful suitcase parade.

"Well, this is easier than climbing all over them," Henry said. "Spread out, and we can watch for Burlington ones."

They stationed themselves at three turns on the conveyor belt. Anna would rather have stayed together, but she saw Henry's point. They'd be less likely to miss something this way.

She watched the bags pass.

Big green suitcase. BUF.

Medium red with a silver ribbon tied to the handle. BUF.

Little princess suitcase. TPA.

Big black suitcase with its sticker folded over itself. It passed by before Anna could turn it to see the destination. Probably another BUF.

But what if it wasn't?

She hoisted herself up onto the belt next to a maroon BOS suitcase with wheels, then climbed over a couple of ORD duffel bags.

As soon as she reached the black suitcase, she had to duck and flatten herself against it to avoid clunking her head on a crisscrossing baggage belt that made a sort of bridge over the one she was riding on. She sat up and straightened the sticker.

"Oh my gosh! BTV! BTV! You guys! Over here!" She called and looked over her shoulder to where she thought Henry and José should be, but she'd taken so many twists and turns through the huge room on the snaking conveyor belt that all she saw were more curves and loops and suitcases.

Were there any landmarks in this gigantic room? She turned to face forward again and found herself ascending the section of belt that led way up by the ceiling. Way up where Snake-Arm had gone before.

She looked over her shoulder again, but the boys weren't there. She looked back down at the big black suitcase.

BTV.

This bag was the only thing that could lead them to Sinan. Alone or not, she had to stay with it.

SIXTEEN

Anna flattened herself on top of the black suitcase and took a deep breath. She felt the cold zipper of the little side pocket against her cheek and hung on tight as the belt climbed higher.

Now, way up by the steel-beamed ceiling, Anna could peer over the edge. Conveyor belts hummed and squeaked through the room below, twisting and looping, climbing and plunging over and around one another.

Anna tried to trace the path her BTV suitcase would take. Her eyes followed the belt up ahead, around a hairpin curve, then back alongside the same belt for a while before it took a steep climb and looped off toward the other side of the room where they'd first come in. Big plastic carts were stacked on one of the belts over there, and she couldn't see past them.

Where were the boys? She was looking over her shoulder and nearly fell off the belt when the suitcase made that hairpin turn. When she regained her balance, she thought she heard the echo of a voice on the far side of the room. Maybe Henry and José were coming. She closed her eyes, trying to tune out the drone of the conveyor belt motors and find the voice again, but it was gone.

Anna felt herself sliding backward as the suitcase started up a big slope. She held on and was all the way to the top before she realized that this hill dropped off into another steep plunge. She would have screamed if she'd had time.

But she didn't.

Still clutching the handle of the suitcase, she landed flat on her stomach at the bottom of the ramp, then tumbled another three feet onto a pile of bags that had slid off the belt after the plunge. The BTV suitcase landed on top of her. "Oomph!"

"What was that?" A man's voice — it wasn't Henry or José — drifted over the top of a huge plastic cart filled with suitcases. Anna held her breath. Something in the duffel bag underneath her poked into her ribs, but she didn't dare move.

"What was what?" Another voice. Lower than the first. Was it Snake-Arm? She tried to remember his voice from the restaurant, but she couldn't be sure.

"I thought I heard somebody."

Anna couldn't make out what they said next. She closed her eyes, trying to sort out words from the humming of the motors. ". . . middle of the night. I told you, the handlers are all off duty. Just a suitcase falling off the belt or something. We'll probably hear more coming through now that the system's turned back on."

The voice had a familiar tone to it, but Anna still couldn't hear clearly enough to say for sure it was Snake-Arm. There was a faint clinking sound, too, like someone juggling change in a pocket. Then more clunking. More thumping of tossed bags.

Another duffel bag barreled down the ramp — "Oof!" — and pinned Anna down.

"See? That's what I heard before!"

"I'm telling you, it's the bags. Now get moving. We still have all these to check. I can't believe you didn't have the brains to mark the thing somehow."

"But it had to fit right back in with all their other stuff. What was I supposed to do? Write *FLAG* on the case in chalk?"

"Shut your piehole and keep going."

Anna's heart pounded so hard she thought it would burst. She'd been right all along; the flag was *here*, and those men had it! Or at least, they expected to find it soon.

She strained to hear the voices. Did one of them belong to Snake-Arm? It sounded familiar. But who was the other man? And how many Serpentine Prince members were at the airport? What if it was Vincent Goosen himself? Anna swallowed hard. From under the duffel bags, she could hear something like big boxes being pushed around, scraping on the concrete floor.

"Nope. Not this one."

She shifted under the suitcase, and something poked into her hip. Her mini video camera in her pocket! If she could get to a place where she could see the men without being seen herself, she could take video of them — maybe even with the flag — and she'd have evidence to prove José's mother and Sinan's family and all the orchestra people were innocent.

Anna squeezed her eyes closed; she could do this. She could solve the mystery and then José's mom and Sinan's parents would be okay. She'd have the story of all stories for the newspaper, and Snickerbottom would give her an interview, and then they'd *have* to let her be in the Silver Jaguar Society no matter how old she was. She just had to get up the nerve.

Little by little, Anna wiggled out from under the bags.

She held her breath.

Had they heard her moving? She doubted it. The noises from the other side of the luggage carts were getting louder, if anything. More clinking change. More thumping. It sounded as if they'd dropped something big.

"Blast it! That was my toe!"

Anna tucked her knees into her chest and rolled to the side, sliding off the pile of bags until she was kneeling next to it on the floor. She pulled the camera out of her pocket and turned it on. She crawled as close as she dared but still couldn't see a thing. The voices were louder and clearer, though.

"Quit fidgeting and help me. And what *is* that you keep clinking in your pocket?"

"Sorry. It's just these."

Anna heard more clinking but couldn't see what *these* were.

"*What* in the —?! You *brought* them here from the museum?"

"I wanted to get outta there. I wasn't thinking. I'll just — I'll put 'em back with the flag when we find it."

"You'll *put* them back in your pocket. Now."

"Fine." *Clink.* "How come?"

"Because they're covered in your fingerprints, you dimwit! Hold on to 'em and toss 'em in some garbage can in Vermont when it's all done."

Anna's breath caught in her throat. With every word she overheard it became more obvious that Senator Snickerbottom was right! The flag *was* headed to Vermont. But right now it was *here*. And she was trapped in this room with the men who stole it.

"Did you check this one yet?" The voices had to be right on the other side of those carts. Anna bit her lip.

Where could she go to see them without being spotted? Her eyes followed the conveyor belt, snaking around the room. At one point, not far from where they'd first come in, the belt climbed a gradual, long slope. Then there was an even longer stretch of straight belt that was elevated. It would be the best place to see anything in the room, but there was no cover. No railing on the belt way up there. No place to hide.

"Got that one already. Come on, we need to hurry up. They'll be back soon."

As quietly as she could, Anna heaved the big BTV suitcase back up onto the metal edge of the conveyor belt. She'd have to make herself a place to hide. She piled two duffel bags onto the belt, climbed up herself, and wiggled in between them. She slipped her camera from her pocket and pressed the button to start recording as the belt began to climb the slope.

"You got something?" An excited voice, even louder this time, came from below.

This would be her only chance to record evidence.

Anna still couldn't see the men. Somehow, they'd changed position or she'd miscalculated, but they were directly below her. She couldn't come out from her hiding place — they'd spot her for sure — so keeping her head down between the bags, she clutched the camera and stretched her arm as far as it could reach, until her hand stuck out over the edge of the belt. Anna shook off a chill that was half cold, half fear that she was about to be seen, that whoever was down there, clunking things around, would spot the camera with its Rudolph-red RECORD light in her hand, dangling over the belt.

"Well, here we are! Jackpot!"

"About time, little brother. Get what we need and let's go."

Anna's hand shook so much she was afraid she'd drop the camera.

"You got scissors or something?"

"The thing's two hundred years old. Just tear a piece off."

A new chill settled on Anna as the belt rumbled along under her knees. They were going to *tear* the flag? That beautiful, dignified old flag? Anna wasn't sure if she actually heard it or if she imagined the soft rip, but it felt as if something had torn in her heart. She lifted her head the tiniest bit to see where she was on the conveyor belt. The higher-up stretch was a long one, but it had to be ending soon.

"Hey! What was that?" The lower voice said, and Anna yanked her arm back into her chest. Her camera caught the edge of the belt and she lost her grip. It clattered to the cement floor, and Anna braced herself for the men's reaction.

Instead, she heard deep, loud barking.

"What the — What's a dog doing down here?"

Oh, *no!* Anna gasped. *Not now. Not now.*

"Hammurabi! Come, boy!"

She should have known Sinan would be right behind him, but the sound of his little voice made her heart sink.

There was nothing she could do but stay hidden between the bags and ride away from them, but she heard everything.

"Got him!"

"Well, there. You seem to be in the wrong place, now, don't you?"

Hammurabi's bark bounced off the hard walls, more and more frantic, until something made him yelp and go quiet.

"Please, sir . . ."

"A busy place like this, all kinds of bad things could happen. It'd be mighty easy for a kid to get lost. Or hurt real bad. He might even go missing."

It was the last thing Anna heard before she felt rubber strips tugging at her hair. The conveyor belt pulled her into one of the dark tunnels she'd seen from the far side of the room, and the voices faded away behind her.

SEVENTEEN

At the end of the tunnel, the conveyor belt came together with a much bigger one, like an on-ramp joining an interstate highway. It stretched down a long, chilly hallway, and every few yards, there was a mechanical arm. As scanners read luggage tags, the arms moved like flippers on a pinball machine. They opened to keep some suitcases moving on the main ramp and closed to direct others to different belts. Some bags got shuttled off to the side and rode smaller conveyor belts up to high baggage racks that lined the walls, almost to the ceiling. The racks were teetering with bags, maybe because so many planes had been delayed. Other suitcases got kicked off the ramp altogether and dumped into big rectangular carts on the ground.

Off to Anna's left, standing next to one of those carts, were José and Henry.

"Dude, we thought you got lost in there. We've been waiting for, like, *ever*."

Anna tripped over herself trying to get her limbs unfolded and climb out from between the bags.

"Sinan's in there!" She jumped to the ground, letting the black BTV suitcase go on without her. It didn't matter where it went now; she knew exactly where Sinan was.

In trouble.

"Sinan's back in that room. And there are two of them. We have to go for help!"

"Slow down." José held up a hand. "What are you talking about? *Who* are you talking about?"

"I don't *know* who, but I heard voices — two men — and —"

"Was one of them Snake-Arm?" Henry asked.

"I — maybe. Probably. I'm not sure, but *listen*, will you? They were arguing, and one kept clinking something in his pocket, and they were clunking boxes and containers around and talking about the *flag*. It's *there*. They have it in *there*!"

"They have the flag? THE flag?" Henry held his arms wide.

Anna nodded.

"Dude, that's awesome!"

"It's awful." José whispered. "You said Sinan is in there now? *With* those men?"

"He ran in after Hammurabi while those men were . . ." She took a deep breath. "I think they were ripping a piece off from the flag."

"*Ripping* a piece from it?" José's mouth fell open. "Are you sure? What exactly did you see?"

"I didn't *see* much, but I heard them talking, and I heard the ripping."

"What else?"

"That's about it. I was trying to videotape, but —"

"You have *video*?" José's eyes lit up. Then he stared at her empty hands.

"But I dropped the camera."

Henry shook his head. "Aw, *man* . . . You'd totally lose points for that."

"This is not pretend, Henry!" Anna whirled around to face him. "You think everything is just a dumb game, and I don't know where you two were when I was in there with those guys, but let me tell you something. They are *real* live bad guys — not some characters you can control with your thumbs. They're real. They're scary. And they caught Sinan."

"They *caught* him?" Henry's jaw dropped.

"*Yes!* They grabbed him, and one of the men started talking about how a kid could . . . could disappear in there, and oh!" Anna's voice trembled. "My mom said how dangerous the Serpentine Princes are, and the way they were talking, I think they might really hurt him. Sinan would have seen *everything* where he was . . . their faces . . . the flag." She swallowed hard. "He's in huge trouble."

Henry's face turned to stone, his mouth tight, his eyes focused on the tunnel that led back to the larger baggage room. "We need to get him out of there. We need to —"

"What we need is help," José said. "But we just broke the law sneaking into an off-limits area of the airport, so unless we can prove what Anna heard is true, we're not going to get help. We're going to get yelled at."

"What we need . . ." Anna looked over her shoulder, toward the tunnel.

José finished her thought. ". . . is that video camera." He blinked a few times, fast, and tugged at his eyebrow. "Do you know where you dropped it?"

"Kind of." She could still hear the men's voices — *all kinds of bad things could happen.* "But it fell a long way. It might not even work anymore. And don't you think it's too dangerous?"

"What's wrong with you?" Henry's voice was sharp. "*You're* the one who wanted to be Little Miss Secret Society. *You're* the one who said this isn't a video game. Sinan is *alone* in there with those guys. He's eight years old. Eight. We have to go." He jumped up onto the conveyor belt with one foot on each of the metal edges, the only parts that weren't moving in the wrong direction. "Whoever's coming with me, keep your feet to the metal edges. You're going to have to get down on all fours to get through the tunnel." Teetering, he took a couple of tentative steps, then squatted and put his hands down on the edges in front of him, moving hand-hand-foot-foot all the way up to the rubber strips before he looked over his shoulder. "Who's with me?"

José bit his lip and mumbled something.

"What was that?"

"A coward turns away, but a brave man's choice is danger." José said it but didn't sound as if he really believed it.

"Yeah." Henry nodded. "I like whoever said that."

"Euripides."

"Well, if you believe that, then follow me." Henry turned and headed into the tunnel.

José took a deep breath and climbed onto the belt. He looked wobbly, but he followed Henry, hand-hand-foot-foot, back toward the big room.

Anna's knees threatened to buckle under her. In her mind, she heard the man's deep voice again — *a busy place like this, all kinds of bad things could happen. It'd be mighty easy for a kid to get lost. Or hurt real bad. He might even go missing* — but she knew Henry was right.

Still shaking, she hoisted herself back up onto the belt, stepped onto the outside edges, caught her balance, and followed the boys through the tunnel.

EIGHTEEN

The cave of conveyor belts looked even more enormous this time. Where *was* she before? Was it that corner to her right, or by the pile of crates on the other side? Every snaky curve of the belt looked the same.

"Down here!" José hissed, and tugged at her sweatshirt from the floor underneath the belt.

She jumped down — farther than she thought — and caught her breath when she heard the echoing thump of her sneakers on the concrete. She huddled next to José and Henry, listening for a "Hey, what was that?" or a "Get that kid!" But there was only the hum of the belts, emptier and lonelier than they'd been before.

Henry grabbed her arm and pulled her into the shadows under the conveyor belt. "Okay, where were they?"

Anna peered out at the ribbons of black and silver that wound over and around themselves, and shrugged. "It all looks the same." But then she spotted the place where the belt looped around, high over the ground. "Wait! Over there! I think that's where I was when I videotaped them. That high part. I was looking down, and there were tons of boxes and cases and bags along that wall."

"Let's go." Henry climbed back onto the belt. Anna and José scrambled up behind him, and the belt carried them up the ramp.

Anna held her breath when they reached the top and made the turn that would take her back over the spot where the men had grabbed Sinan.

But the men were gone.

So was Sinan.

And so was Hammurabi.

Anna turned to the boys. "They were right down there, next to those —"

"Shhh!" Henry pointed to a stack of boxes underneath them.

Anna caught a flash of neon orange among the crates. She heard a loud grunt, then the scrape of wood against the floor. She lifted her head a bit and saw a big, blue-jeaned bottom wedged between two of the larger containers. When the bottom backed itself out from between the boxes, its owner stood up and put his hands on his hips.

His face was turned away from them, but his tattoo wasn't.

Snake-Arm!

Anna felt a tap on her sneaker and dared to look over her shoulder. José had lifted his head a few inches, and underneath his chin, he was pointing a finger ahead of them, toward a shadowy cave of crates about fifteen feet from where Snake-Arm was standing.

Against the wall was a tall black case; it didn't look special until Anna saw the lid lift, just an inch or two, as they rode past.

She stared at the case over her shoulder as they drifted away from it.

It happened again. The top must have been unlatched; it kept coming up a tiny bit. This time, it stayed open for a few seconds before closing again.

Almost as if someone were inside, peeking out.

Anna was about to twist around for a better look when she heard a thump. Henry had jumped down from the conveyor belt and was gesturing for them to come, too.

Was he crazy? Snake-Arm had wedged himself back in among the boxes, but he was still where he could hear them — and *see* them if he turned around. There weren't even any bags to hide behind here!

Anna shook her head at Henry but heard another thump. José was down, too — motioning for her to follow. She jumped and scrambled over to the boys. "Now what?" she whispered. "He's right there!"

Snake-Arm was pushing one of the black cases, wiggling it along inches at a time. Beads of sweat shone on his forehead.

He bent over to catch his breath, and when he did, the other case, over in the corner, lifted open again. The lid rose higher this time, until they could see Sinan's mop of black hair, then his dark eyes peering out. He must have gotten away. But how long could he hide?

Snake-Arm was facing the other way. Henry waved frantically until they saw Sinan's eyes light up and knew he'd seen them. Then Henry held up one finger. Sinan nodded and disappeared back into the case, the lid lowering slowly over his head.

Henry grabbed Anna's and José's sleeves and tugged them farther away from Snake-Arm and Sinan, into the shadows of one of the belts.

"You guys create a distraction," Henry whispered. "I'll go get him."

Anna's mouth hung open. "Isn't calling attention to ourselves the dumbest thing we could do right now?"

"Don't be seen — just heard. So Snake-Arm will leave to check out the noise, and I'll have time to get Sinan out of there."

"That's assuming Snake-Arm is alone," José whispered, turning to Anna. "Didn't you say there were two of them?"

"I heard two voices before."

"Well . . ." José paused. "I don't see or hear a second man now." He took a shaky breath. "Let us step out into the night and pursue that flighty temptress, adventure."

Anna stared at him.

"Uh . . . that was Dumbledore, in case you were —"

"You guys . . ." Henry pointed to the case in the corner. The box lid lifted again. Sinan.

Anna nodded. "We have to do something."

"Okay. So you guys go . . ." Henry's eyes darted around the room.

"There." José pointed to the far corner, where one section of the baggage belt was stacked especially high.

Henry nodded. "Perfect."

They heard a grunt. Snake-Arm had opened one of the bigger trunks and was leaning into it, his bottom sticking out the top.

"Go now," Henry whispered, "while he's busy."

NINETEEN

Anna followed José over belts, around cartons and boxes, under a looping ramp, and up onto the lumpy heap of luggage they'd spotted from across the room.

"Here." José crouched behind two stacked suitcases and pulled a guitar case from the pile. Quietly — *click, click* — he flipped up the two metal latches that held it shut. "This'll sound good on the concrete."

Anna scanned the pile of bags. What else would be loud enough to steal Snake-Arm's attention away from Sinan?

"Help me pull these out." She tugged on the handle of a golf bag that had to be packed full of clubs; it weighed a ton.

Zipper tooth by zipper tooth, so it wouldn't make noise, Anna undid the top of the bag. Her hands trembled and fumbled, but finally, she lifted the cover, and a bouquet of shiny golf clubs gleamed inside. One of the clubs was so huge, it apparently needed its own name — BIG BERTHA was etched on the handle.

"That's perfect," José whispered. "We need to make as much noise as we can, as fast as we can, and then get out of here."

"Where are we going again?" Anna searched the room for the tunnel that led back to the long hallway.

"There." José pointed to the tunnel way across the room.

"We're supposed to run all that way? There's no cover, nothing to hide us."

"Well . . ." — José swallowed hard — "at least we'll be headed away from Snake-Arm."

"What if he comes after us?"

"Then we will have done our job, and Henry and Sinan can get away. Besides . . . we . . . we'll have a good lead." As if that settled the matter, José picked up the guitar case and braced himself against a big green suitcase at the edge of the belt. "Ready?"

Anna heaved the golf bag over her shoulder and got one hand under the bottom of it. "Ready. You want to count or something?" Her arms trembled.

"One . . ."

Anna gripped the handle of the bag more tightly.

"Two . . ."

She peeked over the edge of the belt.

"THREE!" José sprung out of his crouch and flung the open guitar case off the belt, farther than Anna could have imagined someone so skinny could throw. It clunked off the metal edge of another belt, fell from its velvet interior and bounced with a reverberating *THUNGGG* off the cement floor. Anna froze, waiting for the gruff voice, the thudding boot steps.

"Do it — *fast* — and let's go!" José lowered himself over the edge of the ramp, and Anna snapped out of her spell. She heaved the golf bag up over her shoulder and tipped it so the clubs spilled out like pickup sticks, clattering, clanging, and twanging onto the floor.

"Come on!" José was already down, looking around wildly. Within seconds, heavy footsteps came thunking across the cement floor. Anna dropped the golf bag — there was no time to climb down carefully — and jumped.

A sharp pain shot through her ankle when she landed, but she limped after José, tripping over scattered golf clubs, ducking between suitcases, in and out of the looping conveyor belts.

The thumping steps behind her grew louder and louder. She didn't dare slow down to look over her shoulder, even for a second. She knew it was the clunking of those big green work boots even before she heard Snake-Arm's voice.

"Hey you kids! Stop right there! STOP!" The voice boomed over the hum of the conveyor belt motors and fueled Anna to move even faster.

"*Go!!*" She caught up to José and shoved him on, toward the belt that led through the tunnel in the far wall. The pounding boots were getting louder; he had to be getting close. There was a crash and a clatter. A deep voice cursed not far behind them, but Anna kept moving.

"Quick, climb up!" Her breaths came in short, quick gasps, and every muscle in her body tensed as she waited for José to climb onto the belt so she could follow. "Hurry!"

She risked a glimpse over her shoulder, ducking to see under the maze of conveyor belts. Snake-Arm was two belts away from them and had apparently tripped over whatever it was they heard clattering. Under the belts, Anna could see hands, knees, and green work boots, all scrambling to get back up. "Hurry! He's coming!"

She gave José a shove up onto the belt and started to pull herself up, but a big paisley suitcase came merging in from another path and pushed her right off the edge of the ramp.

The footsteps came closer.

"Anna, come on!" José was crouched backward on the belt, facing her but riding away toward the tunnel. His eyes widened. "Hurry!"

Anna flung herself onto the belt, shoved aside a car seat coming toward her — why was more luggage showing up all of a sudden? — and scrambled over the bulging paisley suitcase. José knelt next to her and unzipped it.

"What are you doing?"

"Looking for something we can use to defend ourselves!"

"Well, it's not like you're going to find a baseball bat or something in there. Let's go!"

"Hold on." José tossed out two dress shirts, a few loose brown socks, and a pair of red, white, and blue striped boxer shorts that Anna might have stopped to laugh at if they hadn't been in so much trouble.

"He's *coming*! And he's three times our size, José! Just *go*!"

"No! We need to stop him or we'll never get away."

Anna looked back. Snake-Arm was struggling to pull himself onto the belt after them. "Stop him? With what, José? A fancy pair of underpants? Stop him with *what*?"

"This." José pushed the suitcase toward Anna. Lining the bottom of the bag was a virtual beauty salon. Big, glugging, economy-size bottles of Gotta-Be-Hot shampoo and conditioner. Three cans of Glamour-Hold hair spray. Styling mousse. Two combs, three brushes, a blow-dryer, and a big tub of Powder Perfect face powder.

"*What?* Are we supposed to beautify him to death?" Anna heard a grunt and looked behind her; the big lug had hoisted himself halfway onto the ramp and was kicking his legs behind him, wiggling up the rest of the way. "We need to *go!*" Anna pushed José toward the tunnel, but he pushed back.

"Quick!" He popped the lids off the two cans of hair spray and shoved them into Anna's hands. "Take these!" He tucked the powder under his arm and frantically started unscrewing the top of the biggest shampoo bottle as he climbed back over the suitcase. "Come on!"

Snake-Arm was up on the ramp, crawling on hands and knees toward them.

"Stop right there," he said. "I know you think I'm just some baggage handler, but —"

"We know who you are!" Anna's voice was the only brave part of her. The hair spray cans trembled in her hands.

"I doubt that very much," Snake-Arm growled, teetering to his feet. He looked even more enormous up here; Anna felt as if she were facing down a mountain. "But you need to come back here with me, or you're going to be in trouble with people a lot tougher than I am."

He was just feet away from José now, and Anna was next in line. How they could possibly be in any more trouble, she couldn't imagine.

"Okay," José said, his voice shaking. "We're coming . . . BACK!" On that word, he yanked the face powder from under his arm. The lid went flying, and José flung the whole tub of powder at Snake-Arm. A huge cloud of white exploded in his face, and he doubled over, coughing.

José squeezed the bottle of shampoo for all he was worth, emptying every drop onto the belt between them and Snake-Arm. He took a step back and pushed Anna forward. "Get him!"

She imagined the twin hair spray cans were guns or lightsabers — something more powerful than hair spray, anyway — held both arms in front of her, and pulled the triggers.

PHFFFFFTTTT!!!!!!

"Aawwwwgh!!"

"Go!" Anna felt José tugging on her elbow. She dropped the cans clattering onto the concrete floor and took off, leaping over the paisley suitcase and ducking with José through the flapping black rubber strips into the next room, where they both climbed down from the conveyor belt and darted into the shadows underneath.

"Shhh!" José whispered, panting. "Stay hidden."

Anna nodded, grateful for a minute to rest. She couldn't catch her breath, and her ankle throbbed. "Do you think he's coming?" she whispered.

Her answer came from the other side of the flapping rubber strips.

Thumping boot steps.

A loud curse, and then —

Ka-thunk-thud-THUD! As if someone had dropped an extra-large duffel bag full of ski boots onto the belt from way up high.

Or as if an extra-large man had slipped in shampoo and tumbled off a conveyor belt to the floor.

Finally, there was a low, grumbling moan.

"Sounds like he's been beautified," José said quietly. "Let's get back to Gate B-16 and make sure Henry and Sinan made it out."

TWENTY

"Where on earth have you been?"

José's father came hurrying down the hall with an airport security guard only seconds after Anna and José had found their way through some kind of luggage storage room, down a poorly lit hallway, and back into the check-in area. They'd just ducked around to the customer side of the American Airlines counter when Mr. McGilligan spotted them. He hurried up to them, lugging his briefcase over one shoulder and José's bulging black backpack over the other.

"Sorry." José shuffled up to his father. "We were seeing if there was anything better to eat out here."

"Anything better to eat? You two had no way to get back through security without your boarding passes. Do you realize that? The snow's letting up. Flights will be leaving again soon. What were you thinking?" Mr. McGilligan's cheeks were red and his mouth turned down, but he pulled José into a hug. "You had me scared. Your mother's going to kill me when she hears about this."

José's face lit up. "Have you heard from her?"

His father's shoulders sagged. "No. She's still not answering her phone. But I'm sure she would have called if anything had changed." But his voice broke as he said so.

"*What?*" José asked. "What is it? It's not like the police are going to hurt her or anything, right?"

His father shook his head. "It's not the police I worry about. It's . . . other people who might be involved in this. If they find out that Mom's part of . . ." He shook his head. "I'm sure she's safe with the police, even if they do still consider her a suspect."

Anna knew right away which "other people" Mr. McGilligan meant. "The Serpentine Princes? How would they even know about the Silver Jaguar Society?"

Mr. McGilligan stared at her. "How do *you* know about the Silver Jaguar Society?" His eyes shifted to José.

"José didn't say anything," Anna said quickly. "My mom is in it, and I'm the one who brought it up, when I saw your wife's earrings when she was on TV." She paused for a moment, until the confused look on Mr.

McGilligan's face settled into understanding. "But how would the Serpentine Princes know?"

Mr. McGilligan sighed. "The same way you know — personal experience."

José gasped. "One of them is related to a member?"

"Not quite," Mr. McGilligan looked around and lowered his voice. "One of them *was* a member."

Anna forgot to whisper. "What?!"

"Shhh!" Mr. McGilligan held a finger to his lips. "I suppose you've heard of Vincent Goosen? The leader of the Serpentine Princes?"

Anna remembered her mom on the phone. *There is something you need to know about Vincent Goosen.*

"Vincent Goosen," Mr. McGilligan whispered, "used to be on our side."

José blinked twice. "But I thought to be in the Silver Jaguar Society, you had to be —"

"A descendant of a famous artist or inventor. You do. And he was . . . is . . . related to a famous Dutch artist."

"Which one?" Anna asked.

"Rembrandt."

"Rembrandt!" Anna forgot to be quiet again.

"Shhh!"

"But . . . how did he end up . . . ?"

Mr. McGilligan looked at his watch. "Talk to your mom when you get home. For right now, realize that these people are extremely dangerous. That's the only reason I'm telling you all this. When I couldn't find you before . . ." He trailed off, and his expression kept flipping back and forth between stern and relieved. "No more wandering off." Mr. McGilligan put an arm around José's shoulders, and they all headed down the hallway. "And here," he said, shrugging off José's backpack and handing it over. "You need to take care of your own stuff. This thing weighs a ton."

When they got back to the security screening area, Mr. McGilligan explained that Anna's boarding pass was back at the gate. That didn't go over well until he mentioned that it was with her father, *Senator* Hobbs, and then security let them through.

The whole way back, Anna searched the sleepy crowds for signs of Henry or Sinan. Her eyes scanned the seats in every waiting area — all empty or full of snoring grown-ups.

Henry and Sinan weren't back at the gate either, but Anna found her dad, who had woken up and resumed making phone calls. He gave her a quick wave, but he was frowning, looking out the big window at the snow. It had tapered off from that feather-pillow explosion of a blizzard to a few quiet flakes drifting down around the plows clearing the runways.

"I'm going to check on our flight status," Mr. McGilligan said, heading for the counter. "Stay here."

As soon as he was gone, Anna turned to José. "Where *are* Henry and Sinan? What if Snake-Arm has them both?"

José's brows knitted together over his dark eyes. "It's too soon to jump to any of those conclusions," he said, but his voice wavered. "Let's give it a little time. I bet they'll find their way back here, and if for some reason, they don't, then —"

"Hobbs! Senator Hobbs! I need to talk with you!" A booming voice echoed off the walls.

"It's Snickerbottom!" Anna said. With one hand clutching his cowboy hat so it wouldn't fly off, he ran down the hallway as fast as a big man could run in high-heeled cowboy boots. His men scurried along behind him. "He's coming to see my dad, José. We can tell *him* about Snake-Arm and the flag! And he can take his security guys into the baggage area to make sure Henry and Sinan are okay."

Anna tugged her notebook from her backpack and ran off down the hallway. José lagged behind her, weighed down by his backpack.

"What do you have in there, bricks?"

"Not quite," he said, catching up. He unzipped the bag so she could peek inside. It was stuffed not only with the Harry Potter book he'd been reading but also the other six titles in the series, plus his notebook and quotations book.

"Did you have to bring them *all*?"

José looked at her as if she'd suggested he leave one of his ears at home. "I like to keep my books with me. Just in case I need them."

Anna rolled her eyes. "José, I hate to break it to you, but your books aren't magically going to help us. Come *on*."

"You said that about the shampoo and hair spray, and that worked out." His hand tightened around the backpack strap at his shoulder. "Besides, I can go plenty fast with this."

Anna sighed. "Fine. Let's go."

Snickerbottom seemed to draw a crowd wherever he went, and by the time he and his entourage reached Anna's father, a few dozen people were pressing in on the group, snapping photos and shaking hands. Anna was out of patience; she started running and lost José in the crowd.

The World's Greatest Grandma was there, pulling her husband behind her. "Come on, Harold! There he is!" She waved wildly at Snickerbottom. "I'd vote for you twice if they'd let me, Senator!"

"Well, I'll be an armadillo's Uncle Albert!" Senator Snickerbottom caught his breath and straightened his hat. "You folks sure do know how to make a fellow feel appreciated." He paused to shake some hands and give out some Tootsie Rolls from his hat.

"Now if you'll excuse me for a few moments, I need to talk with Senator Hobbs. As much as we're all aching to get to the Green Mountain State, we have business to deal with before that plane takes off."

The people milled away, but Anna ducked under one of the seats nearby. If she tried to talk with Snickerbottom now, he'd send her off with everybody else, but if she stayed close, maybe she could catch him when he finished with her dad.

"Quite a fan club you have there." Anna's father smiled. "Now, what can I do for you?"

Snickerbottom looked over his shoulder at a woman pushing a stroller past the gate. When she was gone, he leaned in closer to Anna's father. "Tell your lovely wife to bring an *extra* news crew to meet the plane. This is way off the record, but the police have found hard, cold evidence connecting those artsy, all-over-the-world orchestra types to the missing flag."

Anna's father's eyes widened. "What kind of evidence?"

Senator Snickerbottom leaned in closer. His men stood nearby, their eyes darting from side to side. The skinny one with the cowboy hat dug his hands into his pockets and jingled his coins. Anna caught a flash of silver as one fell out and bounced on the carpeted floor. The man just kept on jingling.

Snickerbottom lowered his voice, but Anna could still hear. "Let's just say it was evidence of the red, white, and blue variety. They got an anonymous tip and found a torn bit of flag snagged on the hinge of a tuba case."

Anna sucked in her breath. Sinan's parents both played tuba! And she knew exactly where that bit of flag had come from and who put it there. Snake-Arm and the Serpentine Princes were trying to frame the orchestra!

Sinan's parents were already in trouble. What would happen to them now? And what would happen to Sinan?

Just as Anna ducked down to crawl out from under the chair — she had to tell them, and no one would care she'd been eavesdropping when she had such important information — she spotted José peeking out from behind a recycling bin on the other side of her father and Senator Snickerbottom. José caught her eye and shook his head.

Anna frowned. Apparently, he couldn't hear what was going on from way over there. She *had* to say something. Anna leaned out from under the seat to crawl into the open, but something made her glance up again. This time, while her father and Snickerbottom looked out the window at the dwindling snowstorm, José shook his head again, so urgently she felt as if she could actually see the thoughts spilling from his brain.

No. No. No! NO!!

Anna tucked herself back under the chair and waited.

"Are you sure?" she heard her father say. He said something else, too, but Snickerbottom's guard with the clinking pocket change was making it hard to hear.

"Sure as shoofly pie, Hobbs! They have a piece of the flag. What more do you want?"

"Well, shouldn't we call the Smithsonian then? And the police?" Anna's father looked over Snickerbottom's shoulder at his security guards. "I'm sure you have a fine security team, but . . ."

"Listen, Hobbs. I came here to let you know your wife would have a story. Not to ask for advice. I've talked with airport police and — grab-nabbit! I don't need to explain this to you. I'm going to be the next president of the United States!" Snickerbottom wheeled around. "Stop that jingling, Earl, and let's go! We have work to do."

Snickerbottom blustered back toward the concourse with his men behind him.

Anna scooted out from under the chair and ran after them.

"Senator! Senator Snickerbottom! I need to talk to you. It's important!"

He turned briefly to wave at her, but kept walking and reached for his hat.

"Senator!"

A Tootsie Roll landed at her feet, just as an airport security guard took her by the elbow. "All right, young lady. The senator has business to take care of, and you need to get on back to your family."

"But —"

He grabbed her shoulders and turned her back toward the gate. "Go on."

She ran back to her father.

"Dad, I have to talk to you. It's important!"

"Oh, there you are. Use the bathroom, okay? Looks like flights are about to start leaving, so we'll probably be getting ready to —" His hand flew to his cell phone in his pocket. "Hold on! I need to take this."

"But, Dad, the —"

He held up a finger, turned away, and started walking down the hallway.

Anna turned to lean against the window. The cold glass pressed against her forehead as she watched the snowplows backing up, pushing forward again. She wished they would slow down. Or get flat tires or something. She needed time. She had to tell her dad — or *somebody* who mattered — the truth about the flag before they left for Vermont. Because then Snake-Arm would be long gone, and Sinan's mother or father would be on an airplane with threads of stolen flag in their tuba case, and then nobody would believe her.

She whirled around to go after her father — she'd grab the phone from him and *make* him listen — and almost crashed into José.

"We have a problem," he said quietly. "A big one."

"Well, *duh*!" Anna said. "Did you hear what Snickerbottom was saying back there? Snake-Arm framed Sinan's parents! They put that ripped piece of flag in one of their tuba cases, and if they get on that plane and then pick up their luggage in Burlington, then —"

"Anna, stop." José's voice was still quiet. "It wasn't only Snake-Arm." His face was pale.

"What?" She scrunched up her eyes. "There was that other guy, too — they talked about ripping the flag. I heard it rip, José. It was definitely Snake-Arm!"

"You heard one of those men clinking something in his pocket, right?" José slowly pulled a hand out of his own pocket. In it was some kind of shiny metal gizmo.

"What's that?"

José looked down at the hardware resting in the palm of his hand. "It's a clamp. It fell out of his pocket." He nodded down the hallway.

"Snickerbottom's security guy?" Anna remembered him clinking his change. "I still don't see —" But suddenly, she did see. Or rather, she heard. The clinking sound. The same one she'd heard from her perch in the baggage room.

No.

It couldn't have been them.

But the voices . . . voices that sounded familiar but too quiet to place. Anna shivered.

"Oh!" She looked down the hall and saw men in suits standing in line way down at the Cinna-Bunny stand. How could Snickerbottom's security guard possibly be involved in something like this? She forced her voice down to something that sounded calm. "José. Do you really think . . . ?"

José was already nodding. "I know."

Anna shook her head slowly. "But . . . we can't be sure that was the clinking I heard in the baggage room, right? Just because he had a clamp-thingy in his pocket."

"It's not just any clamp-thingy. I've seen these before, Anna. When my mom ordered them for the flag restoration project." José held the clamp up to the window. "This is one of one hundred fifty clamps, custom made to fit around the edges of a table at the Smithsonian Museum of American History, to secure the edges of the Star-Spangled Banner."

"It was them," Anna whispered. And there they were, leaning against the cinnamon bun stand way down the hall. Snickerbottom's big hat tipped back as he laughed. Was he laughing because he was about to send innocent musicians to prison? Anna shook her head. "But why would Snickerbottom do that?

Why would he be involved with the Serpentine Princes?"

José shrugged. "Money?"

"He doesn't need money. He has tons raised for his campaign already." She should know. Her father had dragged her to enough fund-raising dinners. "Besides, it's not like they can go out and sell the flag, right?"

José shook his head. "My mom deals with a lot of museums, and they worry about theft of smaller, lesser-known objects more than the big ones. Famous ones are too hard to unload."

"And too . . . big." Anna couldn't imagine anyone traveling the world with that gigantic flag in a big bag or something, trying to sell it. "So why would they want the flag?"

José shook his head and shrugged a little. "It's a treasure. But I don't know what anyone could possibly do with it. Unless they just . . . want it for themselves. Or maybe they have a buyer already lined up."

"We have to tell someone, José! They might still have Sinan somewhere — and Henry, too! We have to —"

"We have to be smart," José interrupted. "Henry and Sinan are probably fine. Maybe they're back with the orchestra or —"

"Wait!" Anna couldn't get all the pieces together in her head fast enough. "Go back. This means

Snickerbottom and Snake-Arm are . . . working together?"

"It looks that way. But we can't prove any of it. We need evidence."

Anna's stomach twisted. He was right. Nobody was going to believe a couple of kids — kids who'd already wandered off and gotten in trouble — over the man who was probably going to be the next president.

Then a new, awful thought occurred to Anna. "José, you need to get rid of that clamp before you get in trouble, too! Your mom's already —"

"I'm keeping this right here for now." José slid the clamp into his pocket. "But it's not enough. We need more."

"Ladies and gentlemen . . ." A loud voice came over the airport speakers. "We're pleased to report that flights will be resuming at nine A.M. Please check at your gate for updated departure times."

"José." Anna's voice shook. The pieces were coming together now. "The videotape."

"You lost it."

"I did. But we know where it is." She took a deep breath. She couldn't believe what she was about to suggest, but without the camera, they could talk all they wanted and no one would believe them. "And we need to go back."

TWENTY-ONE

"Attention, passengers . . ."

When the loudspeaker came on, Anna stopped so fast that José almost tripped over her.

"What's the matter?"

She held up a hand and tipped her head to listen.

". . . Flight 2544 with service to Fort Lauderdale, departing from Gate C-12 . . ."

"Never mind." Anna resumed her power walk down the hallway. "But we need to keep an ear on those announcements. We *have* to make it back to get on the plane."

They dodged suitcases and strollers and pressed on through the crowd. It seemed as if every traveler in the airport was swarming toward the B and C gates to check their departure times. Anna and José were virtually the only ones going in the opposite direction — back toward the security checkpoint. Back to the check-in area where they'd plummeted down the chute in the middle of the night.

"Will you hurry up?" Anna snapped at José. "Couldn't you have left that dumb backpack at the gate?"

"My dad says he's tired of watching it for me."

"It's books, José. Not a national treasure. Not some secret weapon. Just books."

He switched it to the other shoulder and kept walking.

"Attention, passengers," the loudspeaker voice droned. "Soon, we will begin pre-boarding Flight 2712, with service to Burlington, Vermont. Passengers with small children and those requiring extra assistance will be welcome to board at that time."

Anna's heart sank. "We're not going to make it."

"I'll hurry." José dodged a custodial worker rolling a garbage can out of the ladies' room and kept going.

Anna jogged to catch up with him. "José, stop. There's no way we can —"

"Yes, there *is*. There *has* to be." He walked faster.

Anna grabbed his arm. "It's too far. We *won't* make it back!"

He whirled around. "Look, maybe you've forgotten this, but my mom is still — I don't even know where — and this is our last chance to fix everything. We *need* that camera! We need a faster way to —" José stopped and looked wildly around the terminal. "There!" He pointed to one of the counters, where passengers swarmed around a single, swamped airline worker. One of those airport carts — the kind that made the whoop-whoop-whooping noises — sat abandoned by the gate.

"Come on!" José grabbed Anna's hand and yanked her toward the counter. They ducked down next to the cart.

"José, we can't do this!" Sneaking into baggage was risky enough; she couldn't even imagine the trouble they'd be in if they actually stole this thing.

"We'll never make it, otherwise." He dropped his backpack into the basket thing on the back of the cart and leaned in to look at the buttons next to the steering wheel. "Okay, this makes sense. Get in."

"José, you're acting like Henry. This is like some video game or movie stunt; it'll never work in real life. We'll get caught and then we'll never get back down there!"

"Attention, passengers. We are now ready to begin pre-boarding Flight 2712, with service to Burlington, Vermont. Passengers needing special assistance should board at this time. General boarding will begin soon."

"Come on!" José's eyes were huge. He grabbed Anna's shoulder, pushing her toward the cart. "Get *in*!"

Anna's whole body felt like Jell-O. She couldn't do it. It was a stupid idea. It was a . . . a *Henry* idea, and it wasn't going to work.

"No." She wrenched away from José and whirled around.

And there was Snake-Arm striding down the long hallway.

When he spotted her, he broke into a run.

Anna leaped into the cart, gripped José's arm, and yanked him into the seat next to her. "Come on! He's coming! Snake-Arm is coming. GO!"

José slammed the heel of his hand down onto the green button.

Nothing happened.

Snake-Arm was two gates away, dodging through the crowd.

"It doesn't seem to be working." José's voice trembled. "Maybe the battery's dead?"

Anna pushed his hand aside and pressed the button herself. It didn't even make a sound. She pounded on it.

Nothing.

She looked up. Snake-Arm had been swallowed up in the crowd. She couldn't see him anywhere.

"Try the other button!"

José pressed the red button.

Again, nothing.

"There's this key thing, too." José frowned thoughtfully.

Where was Henry when you needed him? He probably had a SuperGamePrism Steal-the-Airport-Cart game and would have had them zooming down the hall by now.

"Well, try turning the key! Try anything!" Anna searched the crowd again. There! Just a gate away now, Snake-Arm was pushing past a woman in a wheelchair, his eyes locked on Anna.

"So I have this turned now . . ." José said. "I think if we —"

"Do it!" Anna reached past him and slammed her hand onto the green button again. This time, the cart motor rumbled. "Now GO!"

José pushed the level to HIGH and the cart lurched. *WHOOP-WHOOP-WHOOOOOP!!*

"Shhh! Turn that off! We'll get caught!"

José looked down, and they nearly ran over a businessman who was texting on his phone. He leaped out of the way as Anna grabbed the wheel, and the cart careened around a corner.

Anna steered while José poked at the buttons under the wheel. "There doesn't seem to be an off button for the whooping thing."

"Then just watch where you're going!" They were headed for the busiest part of the concourse — the food court — and if nothing else, the whooping was warning people out of the way.

Anna looked back over her shoulder. Snake-Arm was still running. Or at least trying to run. If it weren't for the thick crowds, he would have caught them already. Even so, the gap between them was closing.

"Can't we go faster?"

"I don't think so," José said, looking down again. "I have it on high, unless there's a different control for —"

"Look out!!"

The cart clipped the edge of a soft-pretzel stand. The little man who'd been serving pretzels dove out of the way just in time to avoid being trapped when the cart teetered and tipped over. Soda cans clattered and rolled in every direction, and hot pretzels rained onto the airport floor.

"He's okay! Keep going!" Anna shouted.

Up ahead, two hallways converged, and the crowds grew even thicker. One hallway led back to the check-in area. Back to the baggage room.

"Attention passengers, we'll now begin general boarding Flight 2712 with service to Burlington, Vermont. Passengers seated in zones five and six are welcome to board at this time."

José glanced at Anna. "What zone are you in?"

"I don't *know*! Watch OUT!"

José yanked the steering wheel hard to the right and just missed a lady with a stroller.

"It's getting too crowded!" He swerved again to avoid a little girl who was skipping backward across the hall with her purple suitcase. "We can't drive through all this."

Anna looked back. Snake-Arm was gaining ground. "We'll have to leave it and try to disappear into the crowd," she said. "We're smaller. We'll be able to move faster than he will."

When they reached the intersection of the two hallways, Anna elbowed José. "Ready?"

He nodded. "Now!"

He slammed on the emergency brake, and the cart jerked to a stop. The steering wheel dug into Anna's ribs, but she leaped out anyway. "This way!" She grabbed José's hand — he pulled back long enough to yank his backpack from the cart — and they disappeared into the river of people flowing down the hall.

TWENTY-TWO

Anna and José darted between passengers, leaped over pull-along suitcases, and squeezed their way through the smallest gaps in the crowd. Excitement — or maybe fear — had apparently given José a burst of energy, even with his thousand-pound backpack thumping against him as he ran.

"Here's the door we need!" Anna pointed, and a strong hand clamped around her arm.

"Whoa there!" A barrel-chested man in an airport security uniform stepped in front of them. "You sure you want to be heading *this* way? If you have a flight to catch, you're not gonna have much time to get back through security."

The loudspeaker came on again. "Flight 2712 to Burlington, Vermont. Now boarding passengers in zone four."

"We know. We're just . . . getting something really quick. Our flight's not leaving for a while, and we have our boarding passes and everything." Anna held hers up, and the guard opened the door so they could pass through.

She kept turning to look back as they hurried down the hallway, but Snake-Arm was gone.

"I still don't understand," Anna said when her heart finally stopped turning handsprings in her chest. "Why? Why would Snickerbottom be involved with a . . ."

She trailed off.

And stared. The check-in area that had been so deserted before was now clogged with people.

Businessmen carrying briefcases.

Kids licking sticky lollipops.

Lines and lines of people, barely moving.

And every desk was staffed with at least two airline employees poking at their computers.

"This isn't going to work," Anna said. "We can't sneak in now. Look at all the —"

"Quick!" José grabbed her arm and yanked her under the rope into the check-in line, dodging passengers whose patience was already stretched thin.

"Hey!"

"Where are your parents?"

"Line's back there!"

José ignored them, pulled Anna behind him, and finally dove onto the floor next to two little boys sprawled out amid four enormous green suitcases. They were playing hockey with pennies and Popsicle sticks, while their parents talked on cell phones nearby.

"What are you doing?" Anna hissed.

"You guys wanna play hockey?" the littler boy asked.

"Not right now, thanks," José said. He turned to Anna and said in a low voice, "Don't turn around now, but they're here."

"Snake-Arm?" Anna gasped.

"No. Snickerbottom and his guys."

Anna peeked over her shoulder. Sure enough, men in suits and cowboy hats were weaving through the crowd, headed their way.

"We need to get out of here!" she said. Then, "No wait! We need to blend in." She turned to the boy who'd invited them to play hockey. "Do you have any more Popsicle sticks?"

He nodded. "They're kinda sticky. Is that okay?"

"Fine." Anna took one and glanced over her shoulder. She couldn't see Snickerbottom anymore. Where had he gone?

José took a stick, too, made a distracted swipe at the penny, and looked down the line of passengers.

"There they are. They're coming right up the line, talking to people."

"Score!" The bigger of the two boys called.

"No fair! This new guy on my team wasn't paying attention. Do over!"

"Keep your head down," José whispered to Anna. "They're right here."

Anna stared at her purple-stained Popsicle stick — it must have been a grape one — and pushed the penny along the polished floor, her ears perked.

"Excuse me, have you seen a young man, about so tall . . ." She recognized the voice immediately this time. It was behind her. Too close. "His parents are members of the orchestra group that's about to leave town, and he's apparently run off, the little dickens. We're trying to help find him."

Anna lifted her head just enough to see their cowboy boots walking past, up to the American Airlines counter.

". . . possible he never left the baggage room. Maybe we missed him," one of the men muttered.

Then Anna heard Snickerbottom say, "We won't miss him this time."

"Are you playing, or what?" The bigger boy shook his Popsicle stick at Anna.

She looked down and got her penny back into play, but her mind wasn't on the game. Snickerbottom hadn't caught up with Henry and Sinan . . . *yet*. But he wasn't giving up.

"Anna, look!" José dropped his Popsicle stick and scrambled to his feet, pointing. Snickerbottom was having a conversation with the woman at the counter, an excited, hand-waving sort of conversation. The woman motioned to the other agent behind the counter, who came over and listened as Snickerbottom talked and waved his hands around some more. He sure was making a scene. The computer was perched on the edge of the counter, and he kept nudging it with his elbow.

"I can't hear what he's saying," Anna said. "It could be anything, so —"

There was a smash and a flash of sparks at the counter as a computer crashed to the floor. Snickerbottom was looking ten kinds of sorry and helping to pick up the pieces, but from the way he'd kept bumping into the thing, Anna guessed he had trashed it on purpose.

"Look!" José pointed to the next counter, where the smallest of Snickerbottom's three guards, the cowboy-hatted, pocket-clinking man, was drifting slowly toward the luggage conveyor belt. He looked around once, twice, crawled onto the belt, and made himself as flat as he could, as if he wanted to sink right down into it. He shot a look over his shoulder as the belt slid silently along, pulling him behind the flapping rubber strips.

"You still playing?" The littler boy tugged the bottom of Anna's pant leg. "It's your turn now!"

Her turn.

Their turn.

Anna stared at the baggage belt, the chaos up at the counter as airline workers brought out brooms and tried to calm irate passengers who were now going to wait even longer in line, and she whispered to José, "Follow me."

It had been such a long day that kids were running all over, and nobody paid attention to Anna and José weaving through the crowd. Not even when they crept behind the American Airlines check-in area and up to the baggage belt.

"I don't care who he is. He's going to pay for that computer!" a man in an American Airlines uniform was saying. "Now where's the other broom?"

José eased his backpack off his shoulder, hugged it to his chest, and raised his eyebrows at Anna.

She nodded.

They crouched low and crawled onto the luggage belt, just before it disappeared under the rubber strips.

This time, Anna went first — down the long, dark plunge — and scrambled out of the way before José came plummeting down after.

"What in the devil!" A man in a DayGlo orange vest stood over them. He adjusted his name tag — GEORGE MALBUT, US AIRWAYS BAGGAGE. "Hey, Tom! We aren't back from break more'n a minute and look — two kids down the baggage chute!"

"We're sorry." Anna tried to stand, but her feet were tangled in the suitcase pile. "We . . . needed to get something out of our suitcase." José sat next to her, still clutching his backpack, and staring in shock. She hoped he was thinking of an idea.

George Malbut nudged the other baggage handler. "Go tell Tucker. He'll call somebody to escort 'em up to security."

The man hurried across the room toward another worker with stripes on the shoulders of his vest. Anna was in no hurry to meet Tucker. She started scrambling down from the heap of bags.

"Hey, where you goin'?"

"Getting down before I get hit by flying luggage." As if to prove her point, a Thomas the Tank Engine suitcase came sailing through the chute, just missing her.

José hoisted his backpack onto his shoulder and climbed down beside her. "So, do you gentlemen go through all this baggage?" he asked. "It must be a fascinating job."

"Oh, you betcha!" George Malbut's eyes lit up. "You wouldn't believe some of the things we see."

Anna stared. Here they were, probably about to be arrested, and José was interviewing the baggage handler? When George turned to find an example of oversize luggage, José jerked his head in the direction of the big crates where they'd been before. Anna could just make out a glint of silver on the ground. Her camera!

"This one time, my buddy Sammy lifts a suitcase and hears a rattlin' coming from inside."

Slowly, Anna backed away.

"He starts to unzip the thing, and I say, 'You sure you wanna do that?'"

Anna ducked into a shadow under the baggage belt and looked back.

"Then Sammy screams — 'Eeeyaaaghhh!' He throws the suitcase clear across the room, and there on the floor's a snake — three, maybe four feet long."

"Really?" José stepped to the side to block the view of Anna. She ducked out from under the belt.

"Sammy's hopping all over like he's got fire ants in his drawers, and I thought he musta got bit."

The concrete floor was cool and grainy under Anna's hands as she crawled toward the camera. Twenty feet away.

"So I say, 'Sammy, did he getcha?'"

Anna crept forward. Ten feet.

"Then he knocks a golf bag on the floor and clubs

fall out all over, so he grabs one and swings it over his head. . . ."

"Wow. Did he kill the snake?" she heard José ask. She was almost there.

"Nope. Missed. One of our other guys came running in, scooped the snake up with his bare hand, and zipped it up in a duffel bag. I guess he's all into handling snakes for a hobby or somethin'."

Anna was reaching for the camera when she heard a sniffle.

She froze.

There was a sneeze, so close she felt tiny water droplets on the back of her neck.

Slowly, she turned her head.

In the shadows between two wooden crates stood Snickerbottom's security guard.

He lifted one hand and wiped his nose.

In the other hand, he held a knife.

TWENTY-THREE

The man put a finger to his chapped lips, and his meaning was clear.

Quiet.

Or else.

The ceiling lights reflected off the blade of his knife.

Anna took a shuddery breath. She could feel her kneecaps pressing into the concrete, the grit under her palms. The camera was just out of her reach. But maybe if she could creep forward a bit. Could she grab it and run fast enough to get away?

Snickerbottom's security guard sniffled again.

Anna looked back into the shadows.

And it happened all at once.

"ACHOO!!"

"Hey! Who's there?!" boomed a voice from over where they'd come in.

And when Snickerbottom's guard ducked back into the shadows, Anna lunged forward, closed her hand around the video camera, floundered to her feet, and ran.

She circled back, ducked under baggage belts, stumbled over golf clubs that still littered the floor from earlier. She gripped the camera tight in her hand and pumped her arms, willing herself to move faster.

But this wasn't the abandoned baggage cave it had been before. Heads turned. Heads of baggage handlers in bright orange vests. Was one of them Snake-Arm? Anna wasn't about to slow down to find out. She had to get out of here with the camera. That camera was the key to everything.

She lunged under one of the belts and paused. Where was José? Was he still waiting where they'd come in? Where the baggage handler had caught them and told them to stay?

She couldn't go back that way. She couldn't risk losing the camera to some bossy suitcase lugger before she got out and had a chance to show her father — or someone — the truth.

She climbed out from under the belt. She'd have to go out the way they'd escaped before — through the tunnel on the far side of the room.

Anna slipped between a couple of luggage bins just in time to disappear before two orange-vested baggage guys jogged by.

"Tucker thought she went this way," the first man panted.

"She couldna got too far."

When their voices faded, Anna ducked out from her hiding place and ran in what she hoped was the right direction. But who knew? Where *was* she in this twisting, looping maze? Noises crammed together in her ears — engines, bags thumping against one another as they switched from one belt to another, rusty wheels creaking whenever one of the big carts filled up and rolled down a ramp.

Anna needed it all to stop so she could think. She felt like she was going in circles.

Where was the tunnel? It had to be near this belt where the —

Whoooaa!!

Anna's foot hit something slick on the concrete and flew out from under her. She reeled, twisting and flapping her arms to keep her balance, and slammed her wrist on the metal edge of a belt before she went down hard, right on her tailbone.

The camera flew from her hand, and her head slammed back on the concrete floor. Tiny lights danced as the pain radiated through her head.

She could smell shampoo. Sticky sweet. Her stomach churned.

"Tsk. Tsk. Tsk."

Someone was standing over her. Anna couldn't make out the face. Too blurry. She closed her eyes and hoped he would go away.

He didn't.

"You know, with all the dangerous machinery, this is no place for children. Hand over that camera, and we'll get you out of here safe and sound."

Anna opened her eyes and blinked until the weaselly face of Snickerbottom's security guard came into focus. The knife's blade still glinted in his hand.

"S'gone," she mumbled. She hoped it had flown far, far away from him.

"Gone?" The man narrowed his eyes and inched closer to her. Then Anna saw another shape rising behind him. A big Henry-shape. It was holding something high in the air. Getting closer and closer.

Anna lifted her head. It pounded. "Yes, gone."

The man took a step toward Anna, but before his foot even hit the floor, Henry swung the Big Bertha golf club right at the man's head.

Snickerbottom's security guard collapsed like a scarecrow off its pole. Anna had to scramble out of the way so he wouldn't fall on her.

"Come on!" Henry reached to help her up, but she pulled back.

"No! The camera!" She dropped to her hands and knees, but the only thing on the floor was shampoo. Where could the camera have gone?

Anna peered underneath the belt. Her head throbbed, and her eyes were still blurry, but there — a flash of silver — there it was!

Anna snake-wiggled her way under the luggage belt to reach the camera, tucked in a dusty corner. She wiggled back and leaned against Henry. "I'm kind of woozy."

"We need to get the other guys and get out of here." Henry started pulling her deeper into the room.

"Where *are* the other guys?" Anna whispered.

"I thought José was with you."

"*Was.* I lost him."

"We'll find him. Sinan is hiding back there," Henry whispered, climbing over a duffel bag that had fallen off one of the belts. "We were looking for Hammurabi, but then I heard you and José and saw you were in trouble. I made him promise not to come out until I got back."

Henry slowed down when they got to a wall lined with big black cases and wooden crates. "He was back here."

Anna waited, keeping watch over her shoulder, while Henry stepped up to one of the crates. "Sinan, it's me," he whispered. "We gotta go."

Anna's head pounded, especially right behind her eyes. She closed her eyes and reached up to rub them, and a hand clamped around her wrist.

"Have a little accident?"

She gasped, and the sick, sweet smell of stale cocoa filled her nose.

Tootsie Rolls.

It was Robert Snickerbottom himself.

TWENTY-FOUR

"And *you* — back in the crates — stop right there!"

Henry's head popped up from behind a crate, and his eyes widened, round and scared.

Snickerbottom growled, "You come here nice and slow, young man, if you want things to go all right for your friend."

Henry stepped forward. "Okay, okay. I'm not going anywhere." He pulled his GamePrism from his pocket and poked at a few buttons.

Anna's mouth dropped. How could he even think of playing a video game right now?

"That's good," Snickerbottom muttered. "Play your little game and stay put." He turned to Anna. "I know what you saw before, missy, and you are not going to ruin this for me. You have no idea what I went through to steal that flag. The Star-Spangled Banner is staying right where it is, and I am getting on a plane for Vermont. You are going to tell me where you put that camera, and then you're going to keep your mouth shut."

Snickerbottom's stale cocoa breath was hot on Anna's face, and his fingers tightened around her wrist, but somehow, he still hadn't noticed that her other hand was closed around the camera. If she could get it to Henry, maybe he could run and get help. Someone running for president wouldn't really hurt her, would he?

But then she remembered the voice she'd heard from high up on the luggage belt, when the two men had Sinan.

A busy place like this, all kinds of bad things could happen. It'd be mighty easy for a kid to get lost. Or hurt real bad. He might even go missing.

"Hey!" Snickerbottom jerked his head toward Henry, who was easing out from amid the crates and cases, still holding his GamePrism. "Get over here." This Snickerbottom sounded so different from the kindhearted, smooth-talking man on the TV commercials, as if he wasn't the man who had saved the boy from the well at all. "I want you where you can't pull any funny business."

As Henry stepped forward, Anna caught a flash of

motion behind him. The top of a crate lifting open. Two dark eyes peering out. Sinan again. *Oh, no! Stay put*, she thought.

"Listen," Henry said. He held his GamePrism in front of him and moved closer to Snickerbottom very slowly, the way you walked if you had a very full cup of water you didn't want to spill. "You have this all wrong. We don't have any idea what's going on here. We don't care if you stole the flag. We just came to find our friend who wandered away. We need to get back to —"

"You're not getting back anywhere." Snickerbottom let Anna's hand go roughly but grabbed her by the elbow so hard she was sure that she'd have finger-shaped bruises tomorrow. Her arm throbbed, and her head felt as if someone was boring into it with a dull screwdriver. Why had they ever come back here?

Then she felt the cool weight of the camera in her hand and remembered.

It was as if her thought slid right under Snickerbottom's white cowboy hat and into his brain. His eyes snaked down her arm, and a slow smile spread over his face when he spotted the camera. "I'll take that."

"Henry, *catch*!"

In a single twisting motion, Anna wrenched herself away from Snickerbottom and flung the camera in Henry's direction.

Still holding his video game in one hand, Henry snatched the camera out of the air with the other hand and took off. He glanced back at Anna over his shoulder.

"Run!" she screamed, even though Snickerbottom had both her arms pinned behind her back. "Go!"

"Earl!" Snickerbottom's voice echoed off the room's cool walls. "Get that kid!" He turned to Anna. "You." He was so close she could see the brown stains on his teeth. "You want a news story, do you?"

Anna tried wrenching away again, but Snickerbottom's grip on her arms tightened, and she winced.

"If you think you're going to destroy everything I worked for — everything I . . ." Snickerbottom tipped his head to the side. Anna thought she'd heard something, too. A weird *scratch-thump*.

"If you think . . ."

Scratch-thump. There it was again. Coming from the direction of Sinan's crate.

Scratch-thump.

With his fingers still digging into Anna's arms, Snickerbottom took a step back from her, toward the crate, and tipped his ear toward it.

Scratch-thump.

Keep quiet, Sinan. She didn't need him in trouble, too.

Scratch-thump.

Snickerbottom dragged Anna along behind him and stepped up to the crate.

It was quiet.

He waited.

Anna heard thumping, but this time it was her heart, fighting to get out of her chest. Fighting to get out of this awful place with this awful, awful man.

Snickerbottom tipped his head.

Still quiet.

He turned back to Anna.

"If you think —" Snickerbottom stopped again.

Scratch-thump.

"What in the dad-blabbit is that?" He turned to Anna, unwrapping his fingers from her arm. "Don't even think of making a move," he growled, and stepped toward the crate.

He held his ear to the side of it.

Quiet.

He ran his hand up the edge, to the rim, and tipped his head again.

Quiet.

He pulled a smaller case over to the big one and stepped up on it — *thunk* — with one big cowboy boot, then pulled himself the rest of the way up. He flicked the latch on the case — *click, click, click, click* — closed, then open, closed, then open again, and braced his hands to lift it up.

But the lid flew open on its own.

"*BarrRROOWF!*"

Hammurabi bounded from the crate and leaped at Snickerbottom. His giant paws thumped against Snickerbottom's shoulders, and his jaws snapped at the big white cowboy hat as Snickerbottom teetered off the crate and tumbled to the floor.

"Stop! Licking! Me!" Snickerbottom sputtered. "Get off!"

But Hammurabi was hungry.

And one Tootsie Roll was left on the hat.

Anna scrambled over to the crate. Sinan was already doing a sort of chin-up on the edge, trying to pull himself out.

"Hurry!" She grabbed his arms and tugged until he could fling a leg over the edge and clamber the rest of the way out. "Come on! Our flight's going to be leaving any second. We need to get back to the gate!"

They started running.

"What about Hammurabi?" Sinan looked back at his dog straddling the still-struggling Snickerbottom, chomping on a Tootsie Roll, and dripping brown drool onto the senator's crisp white shirt. "Chocolate's not good for him! And we can't leave him!"

"Hammurabi's a big dog. One Tootsie Roll won't hurt him. And he's taking care of himself fine. Let's go!" Anna took Sinan's hand and pulled him toward the tunnel she hoped Henry had gone through with the camera, the tunnel she hoped José had somehow managed to find, too.

"Watch out for the shampoo!" She caught Sinan just as he started to slip, gave him a boost up onto the belt, and climbed up after him. They rode the flat black belt into the tunnel until they could barely hear the sounds of barking and cursing on the other side.

TWENTY-FIVE

"There you are!" Henry sprang up from under the belt as soon as Anna and Sinan came through. He almost gave Anna a heart attack.

"Don't do things like that!" She climbed off the belt while Henry helped Sinan down. They were back in the long, wide hallway with the on-ramps and off-ramps, the baggage stacked on high racks to the ceiling, and carts parked along the walls. "Have you seen José?"

"Nope." Henry pulled the tiny video camera from his back pocket. "As soon as you tossed me this, I took off. I've been waiting here."

The beeping of an electric cart, high-pitched and even, made Anna whirl around. A man in an orange vest was riding toward them from the far end of the long hallway.

"No!" she breathed. "Snake-Arm!"

"He hasn't seen us yet." Henry ducked under the conveyor belt, motioning for Anna and Sinan to follow him. They crawled through to the other side and hid behind one of the big rectangular carts. Henry poked his head out. "Let's see where he's going."

"Henry, we can't just sit here and wait," Anna hissed as he pulled his head back in. "Our plane is going to leave. We have to get out there with the camera. We have to —"

The beeping stopped.

Oh, no, oh, no. Let him keep going, Anna thought. *Let the cart start up again.*

But instead of beeping, there were footsteps. Clunky boot steps on the concrete. Coming in their direction.

Ka-thunk. Ka-thunk. Closer and closer the boots came, until they had to be standing just on the other side of the wheeled car. Henry put a finger to his lips, and Sinan nodded. Then Henry put both hands on the top of the cart and braced his legs. He gave Anna a meaningful look, and she did the same.

"Count of three," Henry mouthed, barely whispering the words. "One."

Ka-thunk.

"Two."

Ka-thunk.

"Three!"

Anna pushed so hard she fell forward, arms splayed out to try and catch herself, and got all tangled up with Henry, who had fallen, too. From the floor, she heard boot steps stumbling backward and then a great "Oof!" She looked up in time to see Snake-Arm trip over the belt behind him and fall.

"Let's go!" Henry pulled Anna to her feet and grabbed Sinan's hand. "We have to get back to our gate and hope José finds us there."

Anna shook her head. "There's no time to get all the way back there. There must be a way we can get right out to the plane — the luggage gets there, doesn't it?"

Snake-Arm moaned from the floor.

Anna looked over, terrified, but he was . . . waving at her? He wasn't making any move to come after them. He mumbled again.

It sounded like . . . letters.

"What'd he say?" Henry asked, peering over the luggage belt.

"BTV. You want BTV." Snake-Arm lifted his head weakly and pointed toward the luggage cart they'd used to flatten him. BTV was printed in red block letters on the side.

Anna stared. Was he actually trying to help them?

"There." He pointed again, and something flashed in the light. Something silver.

"Wait!" Anna rushed up and stared. On his right hand, Snake-Arm wore a thick silver ring in the shape of a jaguar.

"You're a member of the Silver Jaguar Society!" she shouted.

"Shhh!" Snake-Arm looked as if she'd slapped him. "How do you know about that?"

"My mother has a necklace like that, from my grandma. And José's mom, and Henry's . . ." she began, but her thoughts were spinning so fast she could barely think. "But that means all this time . . . You're not with the Serpentine Princes at all. You're . . . you're with us!"

"I'm with the flag."

"Wait!" Henry said. "What's with the snake tattoo, then?"

Snake-Arm winced and pulled up his sleeve. Underneath the snake were the letters *VSAH*. "Virginia Society of Amateur Herpetologists," he said. "Always been fascinated with snakes, so I joined a few years ago. We go out and tag 'em to help monitor populations."

Sinan stepped behind Henry, unsure, but Anna knew the story was true. "You're the one who saved the baggage guy from the rattlesnake!" she cried.

Snake-Arm squinted. "You know Sammy? How do —" He stopped mid-sentence, and his eyes lit up when he saw the camera in Henry's hand. "Hey! You got something on there?"

"Maybe," Henry said.

"If you do," Snake-Arm said, "it may be the only chance to save the flag. Get to your plane. And get that to the police." He nodded toward the camera, then squinted his eyes shut, as if moving his head made it hurt. He raised a hand slowly and pointed toward the luggage cart. "Hide in there. It'll end up where you need to be, and you'll be safe."

"Can't we call for help now? Don't you have a phone or something?" Anna asked.

"I had this." Snake-Arm held up a small two-way radio. "But it got broken when I slipped in the shampoo."

"Err . . . sorry," Anna said.

"S'okay. You didn't know." Snake-Arm shrugged, then winced and held his shoulder. "Go now. And hurry up. They'll be after you."

"What about you?" Anna asked. It didn't feel right to leave a fellow Silver Jaguar Society member in danger.

"I can't get around right now, but I'll be fine." He wiggled his way under one of the lowest conveyor belts. "I'm kinda dizzy, too, so I'm gonna duck under here and rest for now. When you get out, let somebody know I'm here."

Henry wheeled the cart back to where it had been and gave Sinan a boost to get inside; then he climbed in himself. Anna followed him, and they crawled way to the back, pulling a green duffel bag in after them.

"Gross. It smells like gym socks in here," Anna said. "Henry, you do have my camera, right?"

"Yeah," Henry whispered. "But listen, I . . . uh . . . tried to play the video and nothing happened, so I —"

"*What?*" Anna grabbed the camera from him and pressed the power button. Nothing happened. It couldn't be out of batteries; she'd just charged it. She held it to her ear and shook. The broken rattling sound made her heart sink.

"Oh, no!" she whispered. "It *did* break when it fell. We did this all for nothing!"

Next to her, Anna felt Sinan trembling. "I want to go home," he said in a sniffly voice.

"No, it's going to be okay," Henry said. "When I was back there, I —"

"Shhh!"

Clunking cowboy boots — Anna knew the sound so well now, it made her shudder — landed on the floor on this side of the tunnel. Then a second set of feet — quieter than the first. The footsteps got louder, closer to the BTV cart, and Anna held her breath, shaking.

Then the footsteps stopped.

Then the sound of boots, pivoting in place. Anna could picture his buggy eyes searching the room. Had they landed on their cart?

"They could be anywhere." It was Snickerbottom's voice; Anna couldn't mistake it now. "Start checking those carts."

More footsteps.

Closer footsteps.

Anna looked frantically at Henry in the muffled light, but all she could make out were his wide eyes, full of fear. Video games never prepared him for this.

"Check that one."

The footsteps came closer. Was *that one* their cart? Anna couldn't tell, but it was only a matter of time. They couldn't come out of hiding. They couldn't run. Where would they go?

A motor hummed; it sounded like another conveyor belt. Anna hoped Snake-Arm was okay under there. She heard suitcases clunking against one another as more baggage moved into the room, through the maze, up onto shelves, down into carts.

Snickerbottom's security guy spoke again. "Nothing here but hockey bags."

"How about that one?"

This time, the clunking steps were so loud, so close, so easy to hear over the moving belt and rustling baggage. Anna sucked in her breath and waited for their cover, the green duffel bag, to be pulled away.

The footsteps stopped.

"Just bags." The voice came from right above her.

"Well, check under 'em."

Anna felt the green duffel bag start to move, start to brush against her hair. She squeezed her eyes shut, as if that could stop it from happening, stop them from being found.

And then she heard a tremendous *THUMP*.

And an *OOMPH!*

And a half second later, a big clunky *THUD*.

Fast, clunking boot steps. And a "Boss, you okay?"

"Grab-blabbit!" Snickerbottom let loose a few more words that wouldn't have sounded good in a campaign commercial at all. Anna peeked out from under the duffel bag for a second.

Snickerbottom was on his back, his cowboy hat knocked off, scowling and rubbing his head. Next to him was a black backpack, resting quietly on the concrete floor. It didn't look large enough to have knocked over such a big man. Snickerbottom stretched out his leg and kicked it. "Stupid thing!" It barely moved.

"Musta fallen from up there," the other man said, looking up at the high baggage racks. "Bad luck." He reached down a hand, but Snickerbottom brushed it away, crawled over to his hat, put it on, and stood up, wincing.

"I'll give you bad luck. Earl, you have been nothing but an unreliable, worthless piece of . . ." He started to turn, and Anna pulled the green bag back over her head. "We *need* to catch that lug of a boy with the camera!"

"Don't really look like he's here, though."

"So we need to get back to the gate. Get *moving*!"

Anna listened as Snickerbottom struggled to his feet. She waited until the footsteps faded away, then started to move the duffel bag, but Henry pulled her down. "Wait!" he whispered.

There was a new sound, softer than the cowboy boot steps.

Sneaker thumps, coming from above them.

A quiet voice. "Anna? Henry?"

"José!" Anna threw aside the duffel bag and jumped from the cart so fast she tripped over the side and ended up sprawled on the floor herself, staring up at José as he climbed down one of the tall metal ladders that stretched up to the high luggage racks along the walls.

"You were up *there*?" Henry's eyes were wide with admiration as he looked up — way up to a baggage rack that had to be thirty feet above the floor.

"Where do you think the bag came from?" José walked to the backpack, heaved it from the ground, and slung it over his shoulder.

"Dude, you're a genius. You're like Maldisio times ten," Henry said.

"Thanks." José grinned and turned to Anna. "I told you. I like to keep my books with me. Just in case I need them." He looked at Anna's empty hands. "Please tell me you found the camera?"

"I did, but it was broken." Her face fell. "We don't have anything."

"Yeah, but listen," Henry said. "When I was —"

A thumping noise by the conveyor belt tunnel made them all freeze, but it was only a second before they knew it was friendly noise.

"BarrRROOWF!!"

"Hammurabi!" Sinan ran to him and hugged him so hard it looked as if he might never let go, until a door slammed at the far end of the room.

"Okay, then," a man's voice echoed off the walls. "Last check — I think there may be one more cart full of bags if there's time."

"Well, now we're in a pickle," José said.

Sinan's face lit up and he reached for the sketch pad in his pocket.

"Draw it later! Get in here, quick!" Henry reached out and yanked José into the luggage cart. The five of them scrunched together into the back of the cart. Anna felt the corner of one of José's books poking her in the shoulder — not that she'd ever complain about that now — and Hammurabi's hot breath on her neck.

Between all their heads, Anna could see work boots approaching. She put an arm around Hammurabi, willing him to stay quiet as the boots paused next to the cart. *Please don't bend and look inside,* she thought. *Please don't look inside.*

The man in the work boots sighed. "They always miss something." He bent down and heaved the green duffel bag back into the cart. Anna heard a quiet "Oomf!" from José, but the man in the work boots was already talking into his walkie-talkie.

"All set. Just the one last cart." He reached up and swung down a door, sending them into total darkness. Now it smelled like dog *and* smelly socks. "Is there time for us to run it out?" There was a pause. "All right, we'll get it marked for the next flight, then."

Anna's heart dropped. No! It *couldn't* be the next flight. It had to be *this* one! They had to get out to that plane.

"What are we going to do?" she whispered.

"Shhh." She wasn't sure if it was José or Henry talking. "Wait."

There was a thump.

Then footsteps that faded away to nothing.

"Okay." The voice had been Henry. He shoved the duffel bag to the side and forced the door of the cart open. "We'll have to get out there ourselves."

"How?" Anna was ready to start throwing things, she felt so frustrated. Couldn't one thing go their way?

"Excuse me. Sir?" Henry was bending down to look under the conveyor belt. Anna had forgotten Snake-Arm was there. His eyes were closed, but they fluttered open.

"Hey there," Henry said. "I don't know if you heard, but this baggage that we're . . . uh . . . hiding in . . . is being held for another flight. But we need to get to the first flight. How do we get out to the tarmac from here?"

"ULD."

"Huh?"

José walked over from the cart. "I thought Burlington was BTV."

"ULD. Unit Loading Device." Snake-Arm pointed to a small vehicle at the end of the hallway. It looked a little like the cart Anna and José had stolen — no, borrowed — earlier. Snake-Arm handed José a small key, groaned, and closed his eyes again.

José held the key as if it were a poisonous caterpillar. "I'm not sure this is going to work," he said. "That vehicle looks way more complicated than the inside carts, and I don't think —"

"Gimme that." Henry swiped the key from José's hand. "You guys get ready to load back into the cart. We're going for a ride."

"Wait!" Snake-Arm's eyes popped open. Wincing, he lifted himself halfway off the ground and wiggled out of his DayGlo orange vest. With a weak arm, he held it up to Henry. "Here. You're a big enough kid. Put this on, and they'll never notice you don't really work here."

Henry put on the vest, ran to the far end of the hall, hopped into the cart, inserted the key, and turned it. He pressed a few buttons — leave it to Henry to know which ones would do the job — and grinned when the motor rumbled on.

"Just like Sim Airport," he shouted as the vehicle rumbled down the hall. "Now, this hooks onto the other cart, and away we go. Load up!"

Anna, José, and Sinan piled back inside and tugged Hammurabi and the green duffel bag in after them. Anna pulled down the door, plunging them back into the smelly-dog darkness. They heard the rumbling get closer, then a click, and then their cart lurched forward as Henry towed it out of its parking spot and . . . somewhere. Anna hoped he knew where he was going.

The cart lurched, went over a bump, and then started picking up speed.

"Henry?" Anna called. "It's kind of fast!"

But he didn't answer. Anna felt Sinan next to her. She took his hand and held on. Hammurabi licked her cheek, and she got a nose full of dog breath.

At least they were on their way somewhere.

And they were going faster by the second.

TWENTY-SIX

"Think we'll be there soon?" Anna whispered to José, trying to keep her voice calm. He didn't say anything, but she thought she felt him nod against her shoulder.

Hammurabi whined.

"Shhh . . . it's okay," Sinan whispered. "Brave Hammurabi. Brave boy. When we get home, you'll have —"

"Hey!" Anna interrupted. "I think we're finally slowing down!"

Then came a *clunk*, and all four of them lurched toward the back of the cart, smooshing Anna against the wall.

It felt cooler. Cold, even.

Voices drifted through the cracks. Not Henry's voice. Where had he gone?

"Thought we were done loading, Tucker!"

"Nah, hold up, George! Looks like this one's gotta go, too. Start unloading it while I check the plane."

The door of the cart swung open, and a thick hand grabbed the duffel bag. The bag disappeared, and a man bent over to reach into the cart. His hand was halfway in, probably to grab another suitcase handle, but he pulled it back out and put his hands on his hips.

"What in the devil?"

It was George Malbut, US Airways Baggage, from before.

"Wha — what in the — you kids! Again? How in the devil —"

"You never know what you'll find in the baggage, huh? At least it's not a snake this time." José climbed out of the cart. "It's a long story, sir, but our parents are on this plane. We need them. And we need to talk with the police."

George Malbut gaped as Sinan and Anna unfolded their cramped legs and climbed out of the cart. Hammurabi bounded onto the tarmac last, wagging his tail.

"José," Anna hissed, catching up to him. "We don't have anything to show the police, remember? The camera . . . We don't have the evidence."

"Yes, we do." Henry jumped from the seat of the

unit loading device, pulled his SuperGamePrism-5000 from his pocket and held it up. "Right here."

"Henry, I'm serious. How is your video game supposed to help?"

"Look." Henry poked at the buttons and held up the game so Anna and José could see. Snickerbottom appeared on the game screen, and his voice came growling out of the speaker.

"I know what you saw before, missy, and you are not going to ruin this for me. You have no idea what I went through to steal that flag. The Star-Spangled Banner is staying right where it is, and I am getting on a plane for Vermont."

Anna's heart soared like a jet taking off. "That thing has a *video* camera?"

Henry nodded. "I tried to tell you, but stuff kept happening. Back in the baggage room, I was pretty sure Snickerbottom was going to get your camera from you, so I figured I'd make us a backup."

"Henry!" She felt like hugging him. "You . . . you deserve, like, twelve extra lives for that!"

Henry grinned. He took off his orange vest and handed it to George Malbut. "Can you give this back to the guy with the tattoo for me? He's back in that hallway with the bags. He told us to talk to the police. And he's hurt, so you should probably get him a doctor, too."

George held the vest, shaking his head. "I don't

know what you kids have been up to, but you're going to talk with the police all right." George Malbut nodded toward the terminal. Two police cars approached with flashing lights.

Anna looked up at the plane. She scanned the row of faces in the windows, looking for her father, but then realized he'd never get on the plane without her. She did see Snickerbottom, though. Even from way down here, she could tell he was shouting.

"Senator Snickerbottom doesn't look too pleased," she said, pointing.

"Bet he's not." Henry held up his GamePrism and grinned.

"Aw, him?" George the baggage handler said. "He's all in a snit because they told him they found some damage to his luggage while they were loading it. Never shoulda told him about it before he got on the plane."

The police cars turned on their sirens. The red and blue lights flashed bright on the piles of newly cleared snow.

"What kind of damage was it?" José asked over the sirens.

George Malbut snickered. "Apparently, somebody handled the bag a little too rough, and all his shampoo and whatnot came out and spilled all over. Got on everything, I heard. Even his boxer shorts. Musta been a ton of the stuff." He glanced up at the plane where Senator Snickerbottom scowled from his window. "He does like his hairdo, that one."

A car door slammed, and a Washington, DC, police officer came toward them. Anna's father stepped out of the passenger seat, and José's father climbed out of the back. Mr. McGilligan held his hands up to the sky, where the sun was finally beginning to burn through gray snow clouds.

"What in the world . . . ?"

Anna's father folded his arms in front of him. "Where on earth . . . ?"

"Dad, I . . ." Anna didn't know where to begin.

But Henry came through. "We know where the flag is." He held up his SuperGamePrism-5000. "And we can prove who stole it."

TWENTY-SEVEN

With a flight that was already more than twenty-four hours late, you'd think the passengers on the plane would have been impatient about another delay. But they understood.

After all, they'd all watched the same TV news report about the flag that Anna and Henry and José had seen in the terminal, just a few minutes after they'd met. They'd watched the news updates all through the day and night, including the ones that reflected on the significance of that American flag. How it had flown over Fort McHenry, through the fog and the smoke, still flying the morning after the British bombing. How Francis Scott Key said he had seen it from the ship in the harbor where he was being held prisoner. How it inspired him to write a song that inspired a nation. How that nation is known as the land of the free and the home of the brave, still today.

So the passengers were patient while police boarded their plane and removed Robert Snickerbottom in handcuffs, along with the skinny security guard who turned out to be Robert's little brother, Earl. They were patient while baggage handlers, working with police, carefully unloaded all of the luggage until they found a large speaker case that belonged to the orchestra Sounds for a Small Planet, and inside that case, the enormous flag frayed and faded with one more small piece missing, but otherwise unharmed. The case was supposed to hold the last of three big speakers that the group had used at the museum performance, but the case had gone missing before the orchestra packed up for the night, so the speaker was packed in a makeshift carton instead.

Thankfully, the passengers could watch satellite television while the plane waited on the runway, so they ate their small bags of pretzels and sipped their Cokes and listened through their headphones as the news anchors pieced together what had happened.

"Good evening," said a wavy-haired anchorman on the screen. "It has been a stunning day at the airport, where the region's two top news stories — our record-setting blizzard and the theft of the Star-Spangled Banner — came together late this morning in what can only be called an incredible story."

The TV station cut away to video of Snickerbottom and his brother being led from the plane.

"Look, there I am!" The World's Greatest Grandma nudged her husband, who was dozing over his novel. "See me there, Harold? I'm in the third window, see? You can kind of see my hair. . . ."

The anchorman's voice continued over the video. "Police say presidential candidate Senator Robert Snickerbottom orchestrated the theft of the flag and planned to frame several members of the international orchestra Sounds for a Small Planet, which played at the recent reopening of the Smithsonian Museum of American History. Snickerbottom's brother, Earl, who is now cooperating with the investigation, told NewsChannel Nine that his brother planned the whole theft so that he could recover the flag himself, solving the mystery and appearing as a hero to the American people."

The video cut to a sound bite from Earl. "Bobby, he always loves being the hero," Earl told the camera. "He puts that campaign video of him saving that boy and his puppy on TV every chance he gets. Savin' the puppy. Savin' the puppy. S'all we ever heard about at home. Savin' the puppy. Anyhow, he was falling behind that Frumble lady in the polls and got to thinking he needed a bigger way to be a hero. So we went and stole the flag. Didn't go so well, I s'pose."

The anchorman came back on camera. "We're

going to go live now to the Smithsonian, with more on how this could have happened. NewsChannel Nine's Veronica Mays is at the museum. Veronica, what can you tell us?"

"Well, Dave, museum officials are embarrassed that this could happen at all. They're conducting a full review of security procedures, but right now, it looks like the problem comes down to access to restricted areas and security staff. At a news conference just moments ago, Museum Director Erma Emma Jones told us that Snickerbottom and his security team were actually *allowed* in the off-limits flag chamber for a private tour the night of the museum reception."

Erma Emma Jones appeared on the screen, standing at a microphone with her lips pursed together so tightly, it was a wonder she could speak. But she did. "We are dismayed that such a thing could happen. We have been in the habit of allowing some restricted access to the museum's . . . ah . . . privileged guests, though we'll obviously be reviewing that policy now. But yes, we've discovered that Senator Snickerbottom and his security team intentionally sneaked an extra person into what was supposed to be a tour group of four. Though our head curator who led the tour was aware of the fifth guest, he was called out of the flag chamber during the tour to assist with an emergency in the First Ladies exhibit. We believe it's likely that

Snickerbottom also had one of his men create that emergency —"

A reporter's voice called out, "What emergency was that?"

"Well," Ms. Jones said, "a mouse was set loose in the display case holding Michelle Obama's inaugural ball gown. It could have been severely damaged by nibbling, and as I am . . . not fond of mice, I summoned Mr. Brodie to take care of it. At any rate, we have concluded that during this . . . interruption . . . one of Snickerbottom's men hid himself in the chamber until the group was escorted out, and in the confusion, the officer who left with the men believed there were only four of them, as the original list had indicated."

"Aren't there security cameras?" a reporter asked.

"Well, yes. The guard who was on duty monitoring those cameras has gone missing, along with Snickerbottom's campaign manager, Zeke Skipworth. The police believe the guard was paid to remain quiet while Earl Snickerbottom removed the flag from the chamber in a stolen case belonging to the orchestra, left the building with it, and later made sure that it was slipped in with the rest of the orchestra's baggage. Rest assured, we are conducting a full review of security."

"Thank you, Ms. Jones," the reporter said. "And now we have someone who is most happy to see the flag recovered: Maria Sanchez McGilligan, who spent several months restoring this artifact. What do you have to add?"

José's mother appeared on the screen, looking exhausted but relieved. Her silver jaguar earrings glimmered. "I'd just like to say that we're thankful the flag is coming home."

The anchorman came back on-screen then. "Indeed. And now, the most remarkable part of this story. The heist of the Star-Spangled Banner might still be a mystery if it weren't for a few clever young people who uncovered the plot during their long night at the snowed-in airport. Our crew at the airport joins us now with that part of the story."

The screen cut to the tippy-boot reporter in a light raincoat, shivering on the windy runway.

"Look, Harold!" The World's Greatest Grandma nudged her husband, waking him up. "There she is! You can see her out the window there with those kids and the police, and there she is on TV!"

"I'm Melinda Gomez, live at the airport," the woman on the runway said. "I'm here with four special kids who saved the day." The camera widened out to show Anna, José, Henry, and Sinan. Every once in a while, Hammurabi would jump up on one of the kids so viewers could see him, too. "Tell me, kids, how did you first come to believe the flag might be here at the airport?"

Down on the runway, with the TV lights shining in their faces, Henry looked at José. José looked at Anna. Anna looked at Henry. How had they come to figure out the flag was there? It had started off as such a crazy idea, and yet, they'd all been pulled along in its wake. It was almost as if they were *supposed* to find the flag . . . as if this kind of detective work was in their blood. And it was. But they couldn't say so now.

"We just had a hunch," Henry said finally. "And you know, there was nothing else to do all those hours, so we checked it out and it . . . uh . . . it was right."

"Remarkable," said Melinda Gomez, beaming. "And I understand you were in some sticky situations back there. Were you ever afraid?"

"Nah, never," Henry said.

"Yes," said Anna and José at the same time. Anna looked over at Henry. "And he was, too." Out of the corner of her eye, she caught a glimpse of movement and turned to see Snake-Arm being loaded into an ambulance nearby. "Oh! And we actually had some help from —"

But just then, Snake-Arm lifted his head from the stretcher, met her eyes, and raised a finger to his lips.

Anna paused. Of course. The Silver Jaguar Society was still a secret, even if it felt a little bigger, a little more real to her now. "Um . . . we had help from Hammurabi here." She gave the dog a pat on the head.

Melinda Gomez laughed and looked into the camera. "Brave kids and a brave dog, if you ask me." She turned back to the kids. "You four must be pretty close to have worked together so well. How long have you been friends?"

José looked at his watch. "About twenty-six hours. Since yesterday morning."

"When she stole my electrical outlet," Henry added, pointing to Anna.

Melinda Gomez put a hand to her ear. "Okay," she said. "I'm getting word that police have finished questioning Senator Snickerbottom and will be . . . What's that?" She held her finger to her ear again. "And will be escorting him directly to jail. He's accused of grand theft and conspiracy, and more charges may follow."

The camera panned to show two police officers leading Snickerbottom away from the terminal and ducking his head down to fit into the backseat of a police car. One of the officers held his cowboy hat. The Tootsie Rolls were gone; all that remained were smears of chocolate dog drool.

"Well, there you have it," Melinda Gomez said, and then turned to Sinan. "You've been awfully quiet, young man. Anything to add after all this?"

Sinan looked at the microphone for a couple of seconds. "I think that now . . . how do you say it?" He reached into his back pocket for his sketch pad and flipped through the pages until he found what he was looking for and smiled. "I am pleased that all this is over, and the fat cat" — Anna nudged him — "I mean, the fat lady . . . sings."

It ain't over till ~~the fat cat sings.~~ the fat lady sings.

The passengers could be heard applauding loudly as the police car carrying Robert Snickerbottom pulled away from the plane. They applauded when Sinan, Henry, José, Anna, and their parents boarded the plane — and again when the announcement came that Hammurabi would be allowed to ride in first class as a pet offering special services.

They clapped once more — loudest of all — when the plane finally taxied to the runway, fired up its engines, and took off for Vermont.

TWENTY-EIGHT

"Henry?" Anna poked at his shoulder between the seats. He was sitting right in front of her, in the first row so his flight attendant could finally say she was doing her job and keeping an eye on him.

He didn't answer.

She peeked between the seats. He was jabbing his thumbs at his SuperGamePrism.

"Henry!"

The video game beeped. "Aw, man! You made me die." Henry whirled around. "Can't a guy relax a little?"

"Sorry. It's just . . . I never got to talk to you again about your aunt with the bracelet and everything."

"Yeah?"

"Well, now that we know a little more about the

society, don't you want to ask her about it? You must want to know who you're related to, right?"

"I guess." He shrugged and turned back to his game.

Anna frowned. Now that the excitement was over, he was acting like the old Henry, the one who was all grumpy about his electrical outlet. She poked him again. "What's wrong? Aren't you happy to be going home?"

Henry turned. "Home is going to be a little different when I get there, and in a few months, I'm moving anyway."

"Oh." She had forgotten about his dad's wedding and his move to Boston. Coming back to a house with a new stepmom was probably enough family drama without worrying about which ancestor left you in charge of his or her artifacts.

Before this week, Anna had imagined her mother's Silver Jaguar Society trips more as secret meetings in ballrooms than anything truly dangerous. Now, she knew better — but she still wanted to know more.

"Dad?" Anna leaned across the aisle and rustled his newspaper.

"Hmm?"

She decided to go for it. "Seeing as how I'm pretty much a member of the Silver Jaguar Society now, I was wondering —"

"What?" He put down his paper and stared at her.

"Well, you know, since it was Henry and José and I who took care of things for the society in DC. Their families are involved, too. There were no other members, except Snake-Arm the baggage guy, so . . ."

Her father tipped his head. "Snake-Arm the baggage guy?"

"Well, he's not just a baggage guy. He runs Pickersgill Diner, too. But he has the jaguar on his ring. You know . . . Mom's jaguar. And he told us he was working for the flag. He's part of the society. And I figure now that Henry and José and I, you know, solved the whole thing . . . well . . ."

Her father looked up at the little airplane reading lights over their seats and shook his head.

"I figured now we can . . . officially be in the society, too?" Anna finished in a quiet voice.

"That," her father said, "is not happening." He shook his head. "If you have questions, talk to your mother. This is her territory." He went back to his newspaper.

Anna sighed, leaned against the window, and watched the bumpy clouds fly past below until the plane finally sank into them and came out the bottom, and she could see the Green Mountains, and the lake, and home.

"Mom!" Mrs. Revere-Hobbs was waiting along with her news crew, though the story they ended up with was a whole lot different from the one Senator Snickerbottom had promised.

"Give me a minute." Mrs. Revere-Hobbs waved her news cameras off to the side and gave Anna a huge hug. "I am so glad you're home." She kissed Anna on the head and leaned over to hug her husband. "I missed you guys."

"Missed you, too, Molly." He gave her a quick kiss on the cheek and then whispered into her ear — loud enough for Anna to hear but out of the range of the cameras — "She met one of your Silver Jaguar friends. Guy from the diner?"

Mrs. Revere-Hobbs pulled back and looked at Anna with wide eyes. "You met Claude?"

"I guess," Anna said. "We called him Snake-Arm. He was nice once we figured out he was on our side." Anna took a deep breath. "Mom, listen. I know you said I wouldn't be involved in the society until I was older, but it's kind of too late for that now."

Her mother crossed her arms. "Really."

"Because we totally caught the bad guys. So I was thinking . . ." Anna looked up at the ceiling. "You do such important work with the news and the Silver Jaguar Society and —"

"And you have your homework and your school

newspaper, Anna. You're twelve. *Twelve.* Don't be in a hurry to grow up."

"I *am* in a hurry!" Anna didn't mean to raise her voice, but it all came glugging out like that shampoo back in the baggage room. "I can't help it. I want to *do* something . . . something more important than a school newspaper. And I did, Mom. *We* did. Henry and José and me!"

"These are the kids you told me about on the phone? Whose families are also in the society?" Her mother blinked, then looked at her dad. "Can you explain some of this? Where were you all this time?"

"Oh, he was right there watching me," Anna assured her mother. "Except for when we went to get lunch and sneak down to the baggage rooms."

"Thanks," her father said to Anna. "Thanks a lot." He turned to her mom. "Molly . . . it's been a busy couple of days." They stepped off to the side, whispering, and left Anna to watch the crowds pass. Her dad pointed toward José and his father, over by the baggage carousel, then to Henry and his dad, hugging next to the car rental place.

"All right," her mother said when she came back. "That's some story." She took a deep breath. "I'm . . . not sure what else there is to say. You already know our family is part of the Silver Jaguar Society, Anna, that we're bound by our lineage to protect the world's artifacts, and —"

"*You're* part of the society. You said I couldn't be in it yet."

"Not until you're eighteen. That's how it works."

"Yeah, but —"

"Anna, let me finish. I understand that you and your friends were incredibly brave. But you were also incredibly foolish. The kinds of people we deal with play for keeps." She swallowed hard. "They're dangerous."

"Like the Serpentine Princes?" Anna asked.

Her mother nodded. "Even though it turns out they weren't involved this time. They're always out there. And others like them."

Anna pictured her mother in her news-anchor suit and silver necklace, facing down the man with the snake-neck tattoo from the mug shot. All those times, all those trips she'd taken over the years, she was dealing with guys like that? It sounded too much like one of Henry's video games.

Where *were* Henry and José? She wanted to say good-bye.

"Anna?" Her mother brought her attention back with a hand on her shoulder.

"This whole thing is like that *National Treasure* movie or something."

Her mother sighed. "It feels that way some-times. Only it's real. And you're right. You do need to know more. *They* know about *us* — the world's art thieves and illicit treasure hunters know our group exists, and —"

"I *know*, Mom. Because Vincent Goosen used to be part of the society. José's dad told us, but he said I had to ask you if I wanted to know more. So what happened? Why did he leave" — she wanted to say "and join the dark side," but then it would really sound too much like a movie — "and start stealing art instead of protecting it? Didn't he care?"

Mrs. Revere-Hobbs stared at Anna as if she weren't quite sure who she was looking at anymore. Finally, she said, "He did care — and still cares — about art very much. He loves it, perhaps more than anyone I've ever known. And ten years ago, Vince was one of our bravest, most dedicated members."

"What happened?"

Mrs. Revere-Hobbs shook her head. "He volun-teered almost every hour of his life, went on more and more dangerous missions, until it consumed him. And then somehow, protecting the artifacts . . . saving them . . . wasn't enough. He wanted to pos-sess them."

"So he started . . . stealing art instead of protect-ing it?"

"He did. And he's very good at it. And very danger-ous. As I said, he knows who we are." Anna's mom put both hands on her shoulders and held her gaze. "And since you were involved in the recovery of the flag, he'll know about you now, too. They all will."

They? Anna thought about Vincent Goosen. About Snickerbottom being led off in handcuffs, and she imagined a whole bunch more of them. She took a shuddery breath. "So Paul Revere got us into all this, huh?"

"Good old Paul. Never could mind his own busi-ness." Her mother nodded, and the light caught her necklace.

"How come it's a jaguar?" Anna asked suddenly.

"The society started hundreds of years ago in Central America, by those who wanted to protect treasures from the conquistadors. It was originally named for Ixchel, the Mayan goddess of creativity, among other things. Her symbol is a jaguar. Over the years, people forgot about the goddess and just remembered the jaguar part." Anna's mother lifted the pendant from her neck, and Anna stared at its smooth lines. It was just like the jaguar on Snake-Arm's ring.

That reminded her. "So Claude Pickersgill . . . is related to . . . who?"

"Did you get to walk through the flag exhibit at the museum?"

Anna nodded.

"Remember the portrait of the lady next to the punch bowl?"

Anna nodded again. "She was all strict looking."

"That's Mary Pickersgill," her mother said. "The Baltimore seamstress who sewed the flag. Claude is her great-great-great-grandson. He is *extremely* committed to the flag. To the whole society, but to the flag in particular."

Anna's head was spinning. Her father was lugging his suitcase off the baggage carousel. The crowd was starting to thin. She spotted José with his dad and Henry in a corner, huddled in serious conversation with a stocky man who looked like an older, taller Henry. A tall woman stood off to the side with their bags.

"So . . . wait —" Anna thought about Henry's aunt and her necklace. "Do you know all the other members?"

"Not all, but some. We're just . . . called when we're needed. Sometimes, we meet while we're traveling."

Anna thought back to the electrical outlet at Gate B-16. They'd met while traveling, all right. "Mom, José's family is related to the artist Frida Kahlo and to some of the founders from Central America, he said. Henry's aunt is in the society, too. Do you know her? Do you know who they're related to?"

Her mother looked up and smiled a little. "You should probably ask Henry that question."

Henry was headed their way, along with his dad, the woman who must be his stepmom, José and his father, and Anna's dad. They were pulling suitcases, and the baggage carousel spun around behind them, empty except for that one smelly green duffel bag.

José and Henry walked up to Anna, leaving the parents to talk on their own. Anna was so full of wondering she didn't know what to ask first.

Henry broke the silence. "Dude, this has been one weird day." And that made all of them laugh.

Anna looked over toward the luggage carousel, where the moms and dads were shaking hands, introducing themselves as if they were getting kids together for a playdate or something.

"That's lame," Henry said.

"What's lame?" Anna frowned.

"They need a secret handshake or something. The society should have . . . I don't know . . . some cooler way for members to meet."

"You should work on that," José said.

Henry nodded.

Anna hesitated but figured it would be her last chance to ask. "Did you find out who you're related to, Henry?"

"Yeah. Grace Wisher. She sewed the flag, I guess."

"Wasn't that Mary Pickersgill?" Anna said. "She's Snake-Arm's ancestor."

José snapped his fingers. "Yeah, but the guide at the museum said there was an indentured servant who worked with her. Grace Wisher!"

Henry nodded. "From what my dad was telling me, Grace Wisher sounds pretty cool. She and her mom were freed slaves." He smiled a little. "You know, she ought to have her portrait in the museum, too, instead of Mary getting all the credit."

"You should write a letter to the Smithsonian," Anna said. "I'll help if you want."

"Thanks." Henry nodded. "I might do that. It . . . uh . . . turns out my mom was in this society with Aunt Lucinda, too. Dad says Mom felt a real connection to this Wisher lady. She was all . . . proud of her." He bit his lip a little. "So I figure if they ever need me for the Silver Jaguar Society, I'm in."

Anna nodded. "Me, too. And you know what I think?" But before she could say what she thought, two giant paws thumped up on her back and almost knocked her to her knees. "Hammurabi!" she squealed. He licked her cheek as if it were covered in pizza sauce.

"Sorry!" Sinan said, tugging on Hammurabi's collar. "He was caged up so long that he is happy to be . . . ah . . . tasting his freedom, I think you say?" He flipped open his sketch pad.

Tasting freedom

"I wanted to say thank you," Sinan said, holding Hammurabi's collar. "You did a great kindness for my family and our friends." He hugged Anna, then José, then Henry, whose eyes were starting to water.

"Ah, shoot," Henry said, swiping his eyes with his sweatshirt sleeve. "It was nothing. Turns out it's our job anyway."

"Sinan! We must catch our bus!" His parents were waving from near the door, along with the other musicians.

"Thank you," Sinan said again. "You are all . . ."

"The bee's knees?" Anna said.

"How about the bomb?" Henry asked.

"I think we're the cream of the crop," José said, waving to Sinan as he ran off. "That should give him plenty to draw on the bus ride."

Anna watched as Sinan took his mother's hand and left the airport with Hammurabi trotting along beside him.

Anna knew she should say good-bye to Henry and José, but how did you say good-bye after something like this? There was no secret handshake, after all.

"Well," she said, "it sure would be great to see you guys again."

"About that . . ." Anna felt a hand on her shoulder. Her mom and the other parents had come over from the baggage carousel.

"Here's the thing," Henry's dad said, putting an arm around his son. "We parents have been talking, and we think it would be a crime for the three of you not to keep in touch."

"Does that mean we get to be in the society now and come with you on your trips and hunt down the Serpentine Princes and everything?" Anna bounced a little. "We'll be Silver Jaguars together!"

"Not exactly," her mother said, smiling a little. "But you may get to come on a trip now and then, sort of as apprentices. It's not something we do lightly. But . . . historically, there have been a few other situations where kids under eighteen have become involved in cases, for reasons beyond our control, so the society came up with a special designation for that group of underage members."

"Members!" Anna squealed. "We're members!"

"You're *junior* members," her mother said. "You still won't be full members until you're eighteen."

"I don't care what we're called as long as we get to do something." Anna bounced on her toes until her mom gave her "the look."

"You're *not* going to be chasing down art thieves on stolen airport carts."

"You heard about that, huh?"

"It came in a news update at work." Her mother smiled a little. "Anyway, being a junior member of the society is *not* going to put you in danger; in fact, it's the opposite. Now that you've been involved, you'll need to know more about how we work." Her face grew more serious. "And how to be safe now that they know who you are."

"No missions, then?" José asked. Anna couldn't decide if he sounded relieved or disappointed.

"No missions for you. However, *if* things come up and we're called to help, and *if* there's a safe place for you to stay, you might be able to come along now and then."

"Well, that's a start." Anna leaned into her mom for a hug, and pretty soon José's and Henry's dads had their arms wrapped around their kids, too.

"You know," Anna said, "this whole thing still feels like a movie or something."

"You know what it feels like?" José waved his Harry Potter book in the air. "It's like when Harry finds out he's really a wizard and Voldemort's after him, and he has all these new powers to fight him."

"Only I don't think we get new powers," Anna said.

"If we were playing Intergalactic Treasure Hunters, right about now is when the game would ding to tell us we found a new cache of weapons." Henry looked around the empty baggage area as if he were waiting for weapons to appear, but just the one duffel bag kept riding around and around, and it wasn't full of anything particularly powerful, unless you counted smelly socks.

"Sorry to disappoint you," Anna's mother said, "but there are no wands or weapon caches. Even when you turn eighteen, you won't get any special gifts — only extra responsibility."

"That kinda stinks," Henry said.

"That's kinda life," his dad said. "Sometimes, the world throws changes at you, and you have to deal with it, whether you feel ready or not." He had tears in his eyes, and Anna wondered why until she remembered Henry's mom. Mr. Thorn must have felt as if the whole world was dropped on his shoulders when she died and he had to take care of Henry by himself. He wiped his eyes with the back of his sleeve. "When something is your responsibility, you just do it. Like you guys did back in DC."

José was nodding slowly. "It's like Dumbledore

says," he said finally. "The universe does not give us situations that we are not equipped to handle."

"Yep," Henry said. "And when you've got good friends to back you up, you can kick pretty much anybody's butt."

José grinned. "Is that another quote from Maldisio?"

"Nah. I made that one up myself." Henry looked at his dad. "Can we get cheeseburgers on the way home?"

His father nodded. "You bet."

Anna bit her lip. Her parents were waiting, too. "I do hope I see you guys again." She held out her hand to José. He shook it. Then she turned to Henry.

Henry frowned. "I still say we need a cool handshake."

Anna laughed and gave him a light punch on the shoulder. "How's that until you come up with something better?"

"That's a start," Henry said. "Till next time."

José nodded. "Until next time."

Anna followed her parents out the automatic doors, pulling her suitcase behind her. Somehow, it felt heavier than it had on the way here.

Maybe she was tired from her long night at the airport.

Or maybe it was all that extra responsibility, the weight of a promise made by her ancestors that was hers to carry now.

**TURN THE PAGE FOR A SNEAK
PEEK AT ANNA, JOSÉ, AND
HENRY'S NEXT THRILLING
ADVENTURE,
HIDE AND SEEK!**

In the next room, the walls were a gentle cream color, but the carpet and curtains were the blue of deep summer sky, and the walls were lined with softly lit display cases that seemed to glow golden.

José stepped up to a case full of animal sculptures — golden monkeys, frogs, and birds — and some creatures that looked half human, half jaguar. Were-jaguars?

He found a panel on the wall, hoping it would explain. The exhibit, the panel said, was called *Culture and Columbus: Treasures of the New World*, and it was made up of "newly discovered treasures of Central America's indigenous peoples" and "priceless artifacts from the age of Spanish exploration." Most of those artifacts, as far as José could tell, seemed to be big, heavy guns.

The collection was about to go on an international tour, starting in Boston.

"José, come here. You have to see this!" Anna called from across the room. José's mom and dad, who had been chatting with a White House historian near the door, headed for the display as well.

José stepped up to the glass and bent down. "That's the Jaguar Cup?"

The chalice glowed a soft yellow. Beautiful — but its shape surprised José. Instead of a simple jaguar as he'd expected, or even a human representation of the jaguar goddess, Ixchel, this cup had two faces — the gleaming eyes and powerful jaws of a jaguar on one side of the vessel, and on the other, the dagger-toothed shape of a serpent.

José shivered a little. How could the sacred symbol of the Silver Jaguar Society also include the chilling image of its most prominent adversaries? The kids had never come in contact with anyone from the Serpentine Prince gang of international art thieves, but they'd heard enough stories to make the image of jaguar and snake together on one cup something that José couldn't reconcile.

When he looked up, his mother was frowning, too.

"Isn't that just . . . so wrong?" he whispered, leaning up so he couldn't be overheard. "Why would they have a snake on there?"

His mother squinted into the case. "Because," she said quietly, "our ancestors who founded the society believed in balance. They knew that to ignore the darker side of humanity was to invite disaster, so this cup celebrates the jaguar — all that's positive about the human world — at the same time it acknowledges the existence of evil. Knowing evil — drinking from its cup — prepared them to face it with courage."

But she didn't look up from the case, and her frown lines deepened. She leaned over and whispered something to Anna's mom and to Henry's aunt

Lucinda, and all three of the women leaned closer to the case, staring. They looked at one another for a long time, and finally, Anna's mom nodded.

"You know," Anna said, inserting herself into their quiet. "I wish we could take it out and, like, touch it at least."

"Or drink out of it!" Henry said. "That would be so sick."

Anna nodded and whispered to her mom, "So if I'd been one of the original Silver Jaguar Society members, this is the cup I'd have held in my hands — this very cup — to drink from at the ritual of initiation?" Her eyes glinted with excitement, and José could tell that in her mind, Anna was back in the fifteenth century with that cup in her hands.

"No," her mom whispered, slowly shaking her head.

"But . . ." Anna tipped her head, confused. "You said the Jaguar Cup was part of that ceremony when —"

"Shh." Her mother held up a hand.

"The Jaguar Cup *was* part of that ceremony," José's mother whispered into their tight circle while the other visitors thinned out, heading for the State Dining Room and probably the hot dog cart outside on Pennsylvania Avenue. "But this —" She looked down at the glowing gold in the case. "This is a fake."

"How I wish I could sit at Karyn's table everyday to be nourished sufficiently. I know that eating this way is what provides and prolongs superior health and vitality, but along with that is the fact that it tastes so good. Now I can eat like this at home. Thanks, Karyn."

ANGELA BASSETT, ACADEMY AWARD NOMINEE AND ACTOR

"It's a pleasure and valuable experience to eat at Karyn's on Green. The food is healthy and fulfilling. Every time I visit Chicago, I look forward to going!"

COMMON, HIP-HOP ARTIST AND ACTOR

"I used to think a hamburger in a Range Rover beat a salad in a Prius. Now I crave Karyn's kale salad with Caesar dressing and vegan crab cakes in taxi cabs. I never thought eating vegan and raw food could taste this good, but the real addiction isn't the flavor; it's the way Karyn's food makes you feel."

ORLANDO JONES, ACTOR AND COMEDIAN

"I first decided I loved being vegan when I met Karyn. The things she talked to me about and the food she cooked convinced me I'm never going back to eating meat."

JERMAINE DUPRI, PRODUCER, RAPPER, AND SONGWRITER

"I had the most extraordinary chicken dish at Karyn's Chicago restaurant— and it wasn't even chicken! It was a testament to the breadth of Karyn's talent, the creativity she uses in presenting her food, and the depth of her commitment to superior nutrition for all of us. Bravo!"

DELROY LINDO, ACTOR

SOAK YOUR NUTS

KARYN'S CONSCIOUS COMFORT FOODS

VEGAN FARE

Karyn Calabrese

BOOK PUBLISHING COMPANY
Summertown, Tennessee

Library of Congress Cataloging-in-Publication Data

Calabrese, Karyn.
    Soak your nuts : Karyn's conscious comfort foods : recipes for everyday life / Karyn
Calabrese.
       pages   cm
    Includes index.
    ISBN 978-1-57067-275-0 (pbk.) — ISBN 978-1-57067-907-0 (e-book) (print)
    1. Vegan cooking.   2. Vegetarian foods.   I. Title.
    TX837.C3147 2013
    641.5'636—dc23

                                                              2012038495

Cover and interior design: John Wincek
Cover photo (vegan): D'Andre Michael
Cover photo (raw): Josh Gibson
Interior photos: Christopher Free, Jennifer Girard
Food photos: Lin Eagle, Jamie McKeown
Photography assistant: Xin Xin Hauf
Makeup artist: Rebekah Veen

Book Publishing Company
P.O. Box 99
Summertown, TN 38483
888-260-8458
bookpubco.com

ISBN 13: 978-1-57067-275-0

Printed in Canada

19 18 17 16 15 14 13   9 8 7 6 5 4 3 2

Book Publishing Company is a member of
Green Press Initiative. We chose to print this
title on paper with 100% post consumer
recycled content, processed without chlorine,
which saves the following natural resources:

    48 trees
    1,502 pounds of solid waste
    22.437 gallons of water
    4,137 pounds of greenhouse gases
    21 million BTU of energy

For more information on Green Press Initiative,
visit greenpressinitiative.org.

Environmental impact estimates were made
using the Environmental Defense Fund
Paper Calculator. For more information visit
papercalculator.org.

Printed on recycled paper

contents

dedication

This book is dedicated to my husband, Jerry,

daughter, Nicole, son, Michael,

and my grandchildren, Quinton and Emilio.

They force me to keep it real

and inspire me to motivate people

to eat a plant-based diet.

to Jerry, Nicole, Michael, Quinton & Emilio

acknowledgments

I would like to acknowledge all of the wonderful customers,

clients, and fellow travelers on the path to improving

our planet and our bodies through including

or wholly adopting a plant-based diet.

Thank you all, especially Chicagoans,

for helping me to keep my vision of service alive.

improving our planet and our bodies

foreword

To call Karyn Calabrese's food healthy is beside the point. It is, but more importantly, everything she touches in the kitchen is magically delicious. It's one of the reasons I live 50 feet from one of her restaurants. My wife and I are avid fans not only of her restaurants but also of Karyn's holistic approach to life. Just look at her—enough said, right?

To distill good nutrition and high sensuality into your cuisine is the true definition of culinary artistry. Run—don't wait—to buy this book. Three cheers, Karyn. You are the best.

CHARLIE TROTTER
author and chef-owner, Charlie Trotter's

everything she touches in the kitchen is magically delicious

introduction

Veganism. Seems like everyone is doing it these days. Bill Clinton, Russell Simmons, Ellen DeGeneres, Alicia Silverstone, Woody Harrelson, and Joaquin Phoenix are using their celebrity to promote the cause. Elite athletes like John Salley, Tony Gonzalez, Robert Cheeke, and Brendan Brazier, who once thought they could only build muscle and compete professionally by consuming large meals of steak, chicken, fish, and whey protein, are discovering that their bodies perform better and recover more quickly with a diet of greens, tofu, hempseeds, and all the other "hippie" foods that used to exist only on the fringes of the American diet.

Even doctors are getting on board, touting the benefits of a plant-based diet for their patients. Books like *The China Study* and documentaries like *Forks Over Knives* have presented scientific proof that the human body can heal itself from illnesses both major and minor by eliminating meat, fish, chicken, and dairy products.

But I could have told you that a long time ago—more than forty years ago, actually—back in the dark ages of vegetarianism and veganism when I felt like the only person on the planet juicing wheatgrass and pressing tofu. So how did I get so ahead of the curve? Well, I've always considered myself a trendsetter (you should see my closet), but veganism found me as much as I found it.

My journey started when I was in my twenties and my mother was diagnosed with cancer. She started juicing and eating a cleaner diet as part of her healing process, and I joined her for moral support. To my surprise, I soon saw an improvement in allergies and skin conditions that had plagued me for most of my life. My mother succumbed to illness as her body became too weak to overpower the negative effects of chemotherapy, but her influence forever changed the way I treat my body.

1

Over time, I transitioned from the standard American diet to vegetarianism to veganism and eventually to a raw vegan diet, and I felt better and better along each step of the way. On my journey, I met several influential teachers who taught me the benefits of raw vegan food and detoxification. Soon I realized that my allergies were gone, my skin was clear, my energy was through the roof, and I felt more alive and vibrant at thirty than I did at twenty. Holistic nutrition made such a huge impact on my life and health that I started sharing my knowledge with anyone who would listen. I eventually built a business around vegan food and detoxification.

I feel so fortunate to have been led down this path. Although it certainly hasn't been the path of least resistance, it has kept me out of doctors' offices, hospitals, pharmacies, and drug stores for the past forty years. Now that I'm in my sixties, I am witnessing my peers degenerate and develop diseases as they succumb to the effects of many years of unhealthful eating, smoking, drinking, and chemical overload. For me, aging has been a graceful process; I have gone through menopause with no symptoms, stayed away from Botox and surgery, and look and feel years younger than my age. I promise you, though, I am not special. Better health and natural beauty is within our reach as soon as we realize we have to feed our bodies the right fuel. I am so grateful to know that we never have to look far from nature to heal ourselves, and that we all have the power within us to enjoy optimal health.

For more information on the benefits of a vegan diet, please see Resources (page 78).

MY JOY OF COOKING

Simply put, I love to feed people. I learned to cook at my great-grandmother's knee. Every Sunday afternoon she would prepare a feast for her church friends. We'd spend hours in the kitchen preparing the meal, and I loved every minute of it. There was so much love and joy in that process. We made all sorts of traditional soul food, from chili and fried chicken to greens with ham hocks, biscuits, gravy, pie, you name it. These were the traditional foods I grew up on, and though I've never had formal training as a chef, years of assisting my great-grandmother in her kitchen made me a great cook.

When I got married, I started preparing my great-grandmother's soul food along with my mother-in-law's traditional Italian recipes. I loved being in the kitchen. My first husband gained fifty pounds the first year we were together. At the time, I took pride in my cooking skills, but I would soon come to learn the downside to all this delicious food I was making.

After I changed my diet, I embraced the challenge of eliminating animal products from my cooking, but one thing I never eliminated was the soul. I truly believe that cooking with passion makes food taste better, and I refused to fall into the trap of bland, tasteless vegetarian food. Soggy vegetables and boiled rice? No, thank you. So I adapted many of my great-grandmother's recipes into delicious vegan meals.

With a little bit of guidance and endless creativity, I embraced the challenge of creating delicious, satisfying food without the meat, fish, chicken, and dairy. I have been lucky to share this food with not only my family and friends, but also with thousands of customers and students over the years.

LESSONS IN PERSEVERANCE

Before I opened my businesses, I had never worked a day of my life in a restaurant. I never even had the dream or goal of opening restaurants. But in all honesty, I had never set out to do any of the things I'm doing now. I truly believe this was all in God's plan and that I ended up exactly where I was meant to be.

So how did I find myself the owner of three restaurants? My business began as a true grassroots operation. After creating a vegetarian meet-up group in my home to network with like-minded individuals, I started counseling clients on healthful eating, as well as preparing meals that I would deliver to their homes. As my client base grew, I quickly needed to expand my workspace, so I rented space in a small market in Chicago to sell my food and in a greenhouse in Evanston, Illinois, where I grew sprouts and wheatgrass. At one point, I was the largest distributor of wheatgrass in Chicago, selling to Whole Foods Market and other local businesses. Although there were many naysayers who considered me the crazy lady, over time, more and more people became customers and friends.

Despite the growing customer base, my little hippie operation was not always a profitable business venture, and I eventually lost both spaces. It seemed the next logical thing to do was to take a giant leap and rent my own storefront. So in 1995, I opened Karyn's Fresh Corner on Lincoln Avenue in Chicago, in a neighborhood that at the time was pretty desolate. I created a small menu with a healthful selection of raw food and some of my favorite products for sale. I held a grand opening party and hundreds of people showed up, so on opening day, I hung a big banner outside that read, "Raw Living Food!" and prepared for an onslaught, and . . . tumbleweeds. Yep, those early days were rough.

Hard to believe nowadays, with "raw" and "vegan" as trendy, diet buzzwords on everyone's lips, but in 1995, not everyone was as enlightened or as passionate as I was about "Raw Living Food!" At one point, things got so bad that my husband met with my landlord and came closer than I care to admit to turning Karyn's Fresh Corner into a pizza place. I begged my husband to give me six months to prove I could turn it around. I started a grassroots marketing campaign, promoting my detox program everywhere I could, passing out coupons at health fairs, speaking at schools, hospitals, churches, and anywhere I was invited. As word spread, I managed to attract some media attention and got great reviews in the *Chicago Sun-Times* and the *Chicago Tribune*. I decided I might need a gentler approach to get people in the door, so I changed that banner to read "Good Fresh Food." And turn around it did. So much so that, in 2002, I moved into a 7,000-square-foot building at 1901 N. Halsted St. in Lincoln Park, one of the most popular neighborhoods in Chicago.

My storefront now consists of a sit-down restaurant, café, juice bar, store, classroom, and holistic day spa. Some days when I come to work and see the store packed with people of all ages, races, and religions stocking up on raw food, rejuvelac, and enzymes as if it's the most normal thing on earth, it amazes me to think about where it all started.

Over the years, I have taught my detox program and conducted free information sessions for thousands of people, and one important lesson I teach is that you can't go from A to Z overnight. Like anything in life, finding better health and healing from illness is a process. It's a challenge to go from the Standard American Diet or even a vegetarian diet to eating 100 percent raw without some baby steps in between. I was teaching people about the benefits of a vegan diet—and many seemed willing to give it a try—but it became apparent that there was a huge void in the availability of good, cooked vegan food. I wanted to be able to offer a bridge for people that would ease their transition, or at least encourage them to eat more plant-based meals throughout the week.

So in 2003, I opened Karyn's Cooked, a vegan restaurant serving what I like to call "conscious comfort food." The menu includes ribs, mac and cheese, meat loaf, sloppy joes, steak wraps, and bread pudding, but not an animal product in sight. We have become creative with meat and dairy substitutes, so no one even thinks about what's missing. Just like my first endeavor, there were bumps in the road during the early days of Karyn's Cooked. In the beginning, we weren't always busy, and sometimes I had to worry about making the rent. But thanks to word of mouth, more and more people were willing to give vegan food a try. Our loyal customer base grew tremendously, and we quickly found ourselves running out of room. In 2009, I began to look for larger spaces with the intention of expanding Karyn's Cooked. Eventually, we found a beautiful space at 130 S. Green St., just outside of the Greektown neighborhood in Chicago. (The restaurant that was in the space before us was called, ironically, Butter.) As the project evolved, we decided to keep Karyn's Cooked in its current location and open a new restaurant called Karyn's on Green. We had a beautiful, open, airy space to work with and created an "earthy chic" design. Thanks to the décor, the huge bar, a second-story lounge, and the absolutely delicious food and drinks, Karyn's on Green provided an atmosphere for vegan dining that rivaled the trendiest Chicago restaurants.

I wanted to transform the image of vegan food and vegan restaurants from weird or "granola." I think the best way to convince the average person that it's perfectly normal to eschew meat, fish, chicken, and dairy is to make eating at a vegan restaurant a normal experience. I get asked often why I call things "steak" or "chicken" or "crab" or "cheese." I want to give people a point of reference to what they are used to eating. Rather than using the names of ingredients people would probably not be familiar with, like Grilled Seitan and Textured Vegetable Protein with Soy Cream, I wanted to evoke either the romance of classic dishes—our tag line for Karyn's on Green is "making vegan sexy"——or traditional home-style cooking. We make a fried "chicken" at Karyn's on Green that uses my great-grandmother's breading recipe, and one of the most popular dishes at Karyn's Cooked is my Southern Comfort plate—greens, beans, cornbread, and rice, with enough flavor and soul to make the church ladies proud.

STARTING YOUR VEGAN JOURNEY

Many people I meet act like vegan cooking is equivalent to learning a foreign language, and they are so positive that they will not be able to handle it that they never even try. They refuse to be the Ugly American in a foreign land and choose instead to stay in their comfort zone and stick to what they know.

Unfortunately, it's often what's easy and comfortable that gets us into trouble—a phenomenon I call "dying for convenience." In today's world, it's much more convenient to drive through a fast-food restaurant or microwave a frozen dinner than to prepare home-cooked meals. It's easier to go with the flow and order like everyone else in a restaurant or eat whatever you're served at a dinner party. It's not always easy or comfortable to be different and make a stand for your health and your body. But once you experience the powerful effect of eliminating animal products from your diet, you will begin to re-examine your priorities. Learning to make delicious vegan recipes will mean better health for you, your family, and the planet.

I am here to tell you, to promise you, that this is one of the easiest transitions you will ever make in your life. Vegan cooking simply requires a few minor tweaks to what you're used to. Embrace them. You will be amazed that your food tastes just as good if not better than ever. I have served food that has tricked the most devout carnivore, and I have seen vegan cupcakes win major competitions on national television against their egg-and-dairy counterparts.

I am so excited to share my recipes so you can begin to see how easy and rewarding it can be to prepare vegan food. This book includes just a tiny percentage of the food I've served in my home and in my restaurants over the years. And I have plenty more that are still in my head or filed away in my office. Creating new recipes and veganizing classic dishes is one of my passions in life. Luckily, vegan cuisine has come a long way from when I first started. There are so many great meat and dairy substitutes on the market and more and more vegan and vegan-friendly restaurants opening all over the country. It's a great time to be on this journey, and I'm glad to have you along for the ride!

I hope that you find something in this book that resonates with you, and that my recipes can become part of your daily life and family traditions. My greatest wish is that my forty-plus years of experience on this path can be of help to you on your own journey to better health. Happy eating!

AND A FINAL THOUGHT

One important lesson I've learned from operating restaurants is that you are never going to please all of the people all of the time. I've been criticized that my portions are too big or too small, criticized by the raw-food community for my restaurants that serve cooked food, criticized by people who don't think I should serve meat substitutes at all, and for just about everything in between. It's easy to get discouraged by the criticism, but I always remind myself that if I had listened to the naysayers, I would have been out of business a long time ago. The important thing is, there are thousands of people who have tried and loved vegan food because my restaurants exist.

I've never tried to force my beliefs on anyone or judged anyone for their decisions, because none of us has it all figured out. I think an important lesson for us all is that striving for perfection is the quickest way to fail. It's best to do what feels right, to serve a great product, and to ignore the people who want you to be something you're not. Don't worry about being 100 percent vegan or 100 percent raw or 100 percent anything else except true to yourself. Make yourself number one and you'll be amazed at how much energy you will have for everyone around you. And remember: If you don't take care of your body— the most magnificent machine you'll ever be given—where will you live?

my thoughts about nutrition

I've been a vegan for over forty years and a raw foodist nearly as long. I don't worry about how much protein or calcium I'm getting, and I've never counted a calorie. In these past forty years, I've also never struggled with my weight, taken any medication, or visited a doctor. So what's the secret to my near-perfect health? I eat raw and living foods every day, as nature intended. I also eat intuitively, satisfying my body's needs without stuffing myself (remember your stomach is the size of your fist—that's it!), fasting when I feel the need, and detoxing regularly.

It is my wish that everyone is able to enjoy the same optimal health that I have. I've devoted my life to sharing my knowledge, experience, and delicious healthy food. The biggest lesson I've learned is that people need a bridge from their less-than-ideal diets to the "hard core" world of raw veganism. You don't make converts by introducing people to wheatgrass and sprout salad and telling them to eat it because it's good for them. This is where my cooked recipes come in. I call them "conscious comfort foods," because they offer familiar flavors and textures without the harmful animal products that cause poor health. When you're ready for the next step, my raw-food recipes will blow you away. Not only are they perfectly nutritious, but they're delicious and deeply satisfying as well.

I purposely chose not to include nutritional information for the recipes in this book, because I don't want you to fixate on numbers that may or may not make any sense for you. No two people are alike and neither are their nutritional needs. Who's to say you need so many glasses of water or grams of protein a day without knowing your unique makeup and lifestyle? My goal is for you to work your way towards eating as closely as nature intended; focus on taking out the animal products and adding in more fruit, vegetables, whole grains, and nutritious fats. Most importantly, remember, you can't go from A to Z overnight; any transition is a process and changing your eating habits is one of the most difficult transitions you can make. Whether you need convenience foods to help you juggle a busy schedule or you just want to fit in with friends and family, finding the time and place in your life to eat right can be hard work. Why add more stress by measuring yourself against standards that may or may not make sense for your body? Eat intuitively, eat as nature intended, detox (very important), find the right balance for you, and treat yourself with love and patience—every step of the way.

ingredient guide

As you transition to a plant-based diet or at least try to incorporate more vegan recipes into your repertoire, you'll want to start by giving your pantry and fridge a makeover. In other words, your kitchen needs to detox. Once you start scrutinizing labels more closely, you will be amazed at how many products contain dairy, for example. Another part of your kitchen's makeover should be to include more organic products, fruits, and vegetables.

Some of the ingredients we consider essential in a vegan kitchen may not be very familiar to the average person. This is a guide to some of the ingredients you'll see throughout the book, what they are, how they are used, and what to look out for.

AGAVE NECTAR: A sweetener made from the agave plant (the same plant from which tequila is made), agave is frequently used in vegan and raw desserts as a substitute for honey. It has a milder taste than honey or maple syrup that won't influence the flavor of a recipe as much. You will find light, amber, and dark varieties of agave nectar. The darker the variety, the more intense the flavor will be.

BRAGG LIQUID AMINOS: Bragg Liquid Aminos is a protein concentrate derived from soybeans. It adds flavor and essential amino acids to almost any dish, and can be used as a substitute for soy sauce and tamari.

CAROB: Carob is the fruit from the carob tree. It has a flavor very similar to chocolate and is often used in vegan baking in place of chocolate by people looking to avoid caffeine. Since carob is naturally sweeter than cacao, you may find that it requires less sugar to sweeten recipes made with this ingredient. I make several carob desserts in my restaurants. I think it has a great flavor, but diehard chocolate lovers may not think it quite does the trick. Carob powder and carob chips are available in most natural food stores and in some larger grocery stores.

CHOCOLATE (CACAO): The raw ingredient in all chocolate products is cacao, which is by nature vegan. Chocolate only becomes nonvegan when dairy products are added. When using chocolate to bake or add to recipes, check the ingredients to make sure there is no dairy, or buy chocolate that is labeled vegan.

COCONUT MILK: Coconut milk is made from the meat inside the coconut. The meat is grated, squeezed through cheesecloth, soaked in warm water, and squeezed again. The more it is squeezed and soaked, the thinner the consistency and lighter the fat and calorie content will be. Coconut milk is often used as a base ingredient in sauces and other recipes. It can be used for its unique flavor or as a dairy substitute. Coconut milk has become a popular alternative to soy milk in vegan yogurt and ice cream.

EGG REPLACER: Egg replacer is a powdered vegan egg substitute. Ingredients vary according to brand, but each contains a leavener such as potato starch. Egg replacer is best used as an egg substitute in baked goods. If you are modifying a recipe that utilizes eggs as a binding agent, you also have the option of substituting applesauce, bananas, or flaxseeds. If you are changing a dish that is egg-based, such as a quiche, substitute tofu instead of egg replacer to get the right consistency.

FLAXSEEDS: Rich in fiber, protein, and omega-3 fatty acids, flaxseeds have been shown to help lower cholesterol and may prevent certain types of cancer. Grinding flaxseeds before use improves digestion and increases nutrient absorption. However, some people prefer the crunch and texture from whole flaxseeds. If you are eliminating eggs from a recipe, you can use 1 tablespoon of ground flaxseeds with 3 tablespoons of warm water to replace each egg.

HONEY: Honey is one of the more controversial ingredients I use in my recipes. Many vegans don't eat honey because they consider it an animal product, so if you prefer, substitute another sweetener, such as agave nectar.

MILK SUBSTITUTES: There are many great milk substitutes on the market, including soy milk, rice milk, hempseed milk, almond milk, and coconut milk. In general, these are interchangeable in any recipe that calls for nondairy milk. Milk substitutes are easy to make at home. (Try Nut Milk; see Raw Recipes, page 10.)

NORI: Nori is thin sheets of pressed seaweed ranging in color from dark green to black and used to wrap sushi, or, when cut into very thin strips, used as a garnish or flavoring.

NUTRITIONAL YEAST FLAKES: Nutritional yeast is an inactive yeast that is often used in vegan cooking when a nutty cheese flavor is desired. Some brands are nutritionally fortified, making them a good dietary source of vitamin B_{12} for vegans.

SALT: I believe in using the highest quality ingredients whenever possible, and this is especially important when it comes to salt. I primarily use Himalayan salt, which is a mineral-rich pink salt mined primarily in Pakistan. There are also many great sea salt options out there (my favorite is Celtic), so use whichever you prefer or have access to.

SEITAN: A meat substitute made from wheat gluten, seitan is often used with or in place of soy products such as tofu.

SOY CREAMER: Soy creamer is a soybean-based alternative to dairy cream, used to provide richness and thickening in beverages, soups, and desserts.

SOY FOODS: All soy products are made from soybeans, a legume native to Asia. You will find soy versions of milk, cream, creamer, cream cheese, mayonnaise, sour cream, and just about any other dairy product (see Tofu).

SWEETENERS: Most granulated white sugar is made from cane sugar and, believe it or not, is often processed with animal bone char to remove color and impurities, including nutrients and minerals. This will never be labeled on a package so it's best to look for sugars that are labeled vegan or to use alternatives such as agave nectar, beet sugar, date sugar, dehydrated cane juice, honey, maple syrup, and turbinado. The less processed the sugar, the better.

TAMARI: Tamari is a dark sauce made from soybeans. It is similar to soy sauce but it is thicker and doesn't have the sharp flavor of regular soy sauce. Tamari is used as a condiment or a dipping sauce.

TOFU: Tofu, also known as bean curd, is made from soy milk and is a great source of protein in the vegetarian diet. Tofu has a mild, neutral flavor and will take on the flavor of anything you season it with, making it an ideal meat substitute. Tofu is available in different textures. Silken tofu has the highest moisture content and is generally used for baking and creamy sauces; firm and extra-firm tofu have been drained and pressed and are generally best for meat substitutes.

WATER: I recommend using only filtered, purified water in all of your cooking.

ZA'ATAR: Also spelled zaatar, zahtar, and zattar, and known as za'atar, green za'atar, and za'atar thyme, this is a blend of sesame seeds and herbs, such as dried marjoram, oregano, savory, and thyme. Some versions also include salt or ground sumac. Za'atar lends a mildly tart, herbal, nutty Middle Eastern flavor to a variety of dishes. Look for it in Middle Eastern markets or in the spice or Middle Eastern food aisle of your natural food store or supermarket.

mocktails and cocktails

Blueberry Mint Fizz

See photo between pages 16 and 17.   **YIELD: 1 SERVING**

Fun drinks keep the party alive and kicking. This is a particular favorite for people of all ages.

- **1¾ cups ice cubes**
- **5 or 6 fresh mint leaves**
- **5 or 6 blueberries**
- **2 tablespoons lemon juice**
- **2 tablespoons agave nectar or sweetener of your choice**
- **¼ cup club soda**

Put 1 cup of the ice cubes in a white wine glass. Set aside.

Crush the mint leaves and blueberries with the back of a spoon or a muddler in a cocktail shaker. Add the remaining ¾ cup of ice cubes, lemon juice, and agave nectar. Cover and shake for a couple of seconds. Strain the cocktail into the prepared wine glass. Add the club soda. Stir gently. Serve immediately.

VARIATION: Add ¼ cup of vodka to the shaker with the ice cubes, lemon juice, and agave nectar.

Aloe Kombucha Cooler

YIELD: 1 SERVING

I drink this every day, minus the agave nectar, because I enjoy drinks that are less sweet. My wonderful bartenders made it into a mocktail for everyone to enjoy. You will need kombucha, which can be found at most natural food stores.

- ¾ cup ice cubes
- 2 tablespoons aloe vera juice
- 2 tablespoons açai juice
- 2 tablespoons agave nectar or sweetener of your choice
- 2 tablespoons lemon juice
- ¼ cup kombucha, in the flavor of your choice

Put the ice cubes, aloe juice, açai juice, agave nectar, and lemon juice in a cocktail shaker. Cover and shake for a couple of seconds. Pour into a white wine glass. Add the kombucha. Stir gently. Serve immediately.

El Gallo Bravo

YIELD: 1 SERVING

"El gallo bravo" is Spanish for "the angry rooster," but don't let that scare you. This drink is as refreshing as it is enjoyable.

1 cup sugar

1 cup water

1 cup pineapple juice

¼ cup fresh cilantro

2 to 3 slices jalapeño chile

1¼ cup ice cubes

¼ cup lime juice

2 tablespoons club soda

To make the pineapple simple syrup, cook the sugar and water in a small saucepan on high heat until it starts to boil and the sugar dissolves, stirring constantly. Add the pineapple juice and boil for another minute. Let cool.

Crush the cilantro and jalapeño slices with the back of a spoon or a muddler in a cocktail shaker. Add ¾ cup of the ice cubes, lime juice, and 2 tablespoons of the pineapple simple syrup. Cover and shake for two seconds. Put the remaining ½ cup of the ice cubes in a Collins glass. Strain the cocktail into the prepared glass. Add the club soda. Stir gently. Serve immediately.

NOTE: Stored in a covered container in the refrigerator, the pineapple simple syrup will keep for 6 months.

VARIATION: Add ¼ cup of tequila with the ice cubes, lime juice, and pineapple simple syrup.

Clip On

This coconut drink will make you close your eyes and feel like you are lying on a beautiful beach somewhere.

1 cup sugar

1 cup water

1 cup crushed almonds

½ cup ice cubes

¼ cup coconut water

¼ cup lime juice

1 twist orange peel

To make the almond simple syrup, cook the sugar and water in a small saucepan on high heat until the mixture starts to boil and the sugar dissolves, stirring constantly. Add the almonds and boil for another minute. Stir. Decrease the heat to low and cook for another 20 minutes, stirring often, until brown. (The longer the syrup cooks, the stronger the almond flavor will be.) Let cool. Strain and discard almonds.

Put the ice cubes, coconut water, lime juice, and 2 tablespoons of the almond simple syrup in a cocktail shaker. Cover and shake for two seconds. Strain the cocktail into a martini glass. Garnish with the twist. Serve immediately.

NOTE: Stored in a covered container in the refrigerator, the almond simple syrup will keep for six months.

VARIATION: Add ¼ cup of whiskey with the ice cubes, coconut water, lime juice, and almond simple syrup.

Chairman's Cobbler

YIELD: 1 SERVING

Feel free to substitute your favorite sweetener for the sugar in this recipe. Even agave nectar will work well.

1 cup ginger sugar or sugar of your choice

1 cup water

1 tablespoon chopped fresh ginger

5 or 6 fresh mint leaves

3 or 4 blueberries

3 or 4 raspberries

1½ cups ice cubes

¼ cup lemon juice

¼ cup brewed green tea

2 tablespoons pomegranate juice

3 or 4 goji berries

To make the ginger simple syrup, cook the sugar and water in a small saucepan on high heat until it starts to boil and the sugar dissolves, stirring constantly. Add the ginger and decrease the heat to medium. Cook for about 6 minutes, stirring constantly. Strain into a medium bowl. Let cool.

Crush the mint, blueberries, and raspberries with the back of a spoon or a muddler in a cocktail shaker. Add ¾ cup of the ice cubes, lemon juice, tea, 2 tablespoons of the ginger simple syrup, and the pomegranate juice. Cover and shake for a couple of seconds. Put the remaining ¾ cup of the ice cubes in a large rocks glass. Strain the cocktail into the prepared glass. Garnish with the goji berries. Serve immediately.

NOTE: Stored in a covered container in the refrigerator, the ginger simple syrup will keep for six months.

Karyn's on Green

Karyn's on Green

Blueberry Mint Fizz, *page 12*

Coconut-Squash Soup with Garbanzo Bean Garnish, *page 27*

breakfast and brunch

CHAPTER 2

Tofu Scramble

YIELD: 6 SERVINGS

Breakfast is sometimes one of the hardest meals to keep vegan, yet interesting. Tofu Scramble will satisfy the hungriest. Serve it with corn or flour tortillas. For a buffet-style breakfast, include refried beans, salsa, and guacamole.

2 tablespoons olive oil

1 cup chopped green bell pepper

1 cup chopped onion

1 cup chopped tomato

2 cloves garlic, minced

1 pound firm tofu, drained

1½ teaspoons sea salt

1 teaspoon balsamic vinegar

1 teaspoon ground cumin

Pinch ground turmeric

Heat 1 tablespoon of the oil in a large skillet on medium heat. Add the bell pepper, onion, tomato, and garlic. Cook and stir until the onion is translucent, about 5 minutes. Transfer the onion mixture to a medium bowl. Set aside.

Add the remaining 1 tablespoon of oil to the same skillet. Add the tofu. Mash it with a potato masher or a fork until it resembles scrambled eggs. Add the salt, vinegar, cumin, and turmeric. Return the onion mixture to the skillet and mix well. Cook on medium heat for about 5 minutes. Serve immediately.

Breakfast Potatoes and Onions

YIELD: 4 SERVINGS

Red potatoes differ from white potatoes like night and day. Red potatoes are more flavorful, have a nicer texture, are less starchy, and more nutritious. Try seasoning this dish with ground dried papaya seeds. They add a delicious, subtle flavor and aid in digestion. The whole seeds can be ground in a pepper mill or clean coffee grinder. Dry your own, or buy the seeds at any natural food store.

6 red potatoes, scrubbed

¼ cup olive oil

2 yellow onions, chopped

2 tablespoons ground dried papaya seeds

Sea salt

Put the potatoes in a medium saucepan with enough water to cover. Bring to a boil. Decrease the heat. Simmer for about 15 minutes, or until fork-tender. Drain. Let the potatoes cool. Chop them into bite-sized pieces.

Heat the oil in a medium skillet on medium heat. Add the onions and fry for 5 to 10 minutes, or until the onions start to brown. Stir in the potatoes, papaya seeds, and salt to taste. Mix well. Cook for about 10 minutes, or until the potatoes are crispy. Serve immediately.

Banana Pancakes

YIELD: 10 (6-INCH) PANCAKES; 5 SERVINGS

When introducing someone to healthful foods, always prepare something delicious. Everyone loves pancakes, so what better way to introduce your family to vegan food than with these rich and tempting hotcakes.

2 cups pastry flour or cake flour

½ cup all-purpose flour

1 tablespoon baking powder

¼ teaspoon sea salt

2 cups soy milk

¾ cup brown sugar or coconut sugar or ¾ cup maple syrup

½ cup olive oil or coconut oil

1 tablespoon egg replacer

½ teaspoon vanilla extract

1 tablespoon plus 2 teaspoons vegan buttery spread

2 bananas, sliced

Sift the flours, baking powder, and salt into a large bowl. Pour the soy milk, brown sugar, oil, egg replacer, and vanilla extract into a blender. Process until thoroughly mixed, stopping occasionally to scrape down the blender jar. Gradually pour the soy milk mixture into the flour mixture, whisking constantly, until smooth.

Heat ½ teaspoon of the vegan buttery spread in a small nonstick skillet on medium heat. (The skillet is the correct temperature when a drop of water sizzles in the pan.) Pour about ½ cup of the batter into the skillet. Cook for about 1 minute, or until the center of the pancake begins to bubble. Place a few banana slices on top and turn the pancake over with a spatula. Cook for another minute, or until golden brown. Repeat with the remaining batter and banana slices, adding ½ teaspoon of vegan buttery spread to the skillet before cooking each pancake.

Coconut French Toast

YIELD: 6 SERVINGS

French toast makes for a quick, easy, delicious and filling breakfast. It is also a wonderful way to use up stale bread. This version is made with coconut milk.

½ cup coconut milk

½ cup brown sugar or ¾ cup maple syrup

¼ cup vegetable oil

1 tablespoon egg replacer

1 teaspoon ground cinnamon, plus more for garnish

1 teaspoon coconut extract

1 teaspoon vanilla extract

6 slices vegan bread

Sliced fresh fruit, for garnish

Pour the coconut milk, brown sugar, oil, egg replacer, 1 teaspoon of the cinnamon, coconut extract, and vanilla extract into a blender. Process on high speed for 2 minutes, stopping occasionally to scrape down the blender jar. Pour into a medium bowl.

Lightly coat a medium skillet with cooking spray. Heat on medium heat. Quickly dip 1 slice of the bread in the coconut milk mixture and put it in the skillet. Cook until crispy on the bottom, about 1 to 1½ minutes. Turn the bread over and cook for another 1 to 1½ minutes. Repeat with the remaining bread and coconut milk mixture. To serve, cut each slice diagonally and garnish with fruit and cinnamon if desired.

Deviled Tofu

Deviled tofu is a great treat to bring to any dinner party. Test it out. I'll bet most people will not be able to tell the difference between this and deviled-egg filling.

TOFU MIXTURE

3 pounds firm tofu, drained

2 stalks celery, minced

½ green bell pepper, minced

3 green onions, minced

SAUCE

¾ cup vegan mayonnaise

2 tablespoons Bragg Liquid Aminos

2 tablespoons ketchup

2 tablespoons stone-ground mustard

2 tablespoons sweet pickle relish

2 tablespoons minced pimientos

3 cloves garlic, minced

SEASONINGS

¼ cup nutritional yeast flakes

2 tablespoons dried parsley

Vegetable-salt seasoning to taste

1 teaspoon ground turmeric

½ teaspoon ground coriander

½ teaspoon ground cumin

¼ teaspoon cayenne

Combine all of the tofu mixture ingredients in a large bowl. Combine all of the sauce ingredients in a medium bowl. Combine all of the seasonings in a small bowl.

Add the sauce mixture and seasoning mixture to the tofu mixture. Mix with your hands. Form into 1-inch balls and place them on a serving tray.

Biscuits Gone Vegan

You can serve these wonderful biscuits at all your holiday gatherings, and I guarantee you no one will suspect they are vegan.

2 cups unbleached pastry flour or cake flour

1 tablespoon plus 2 teaspoons baking powder

1 teaspoon sea salt

¼ cup cold vegan buttery spread

¾ cup soy milk

Preheat the oven to 350 degrees F. Mix the flour, baking powder, and salt in a medium bowl with your hands. Work in the vegan buttery spread with your hands until thoroughly combined. Add the soy milk. Knead until the dough is smooth. Do not overknead or the biscuits will be tough.

Roll out the dough ¼ inch thick. Cut out biscuits using a 2-inch biscuit cutter. Place them on a medium baking sheet. Gather up the remaining dough. Repeat until all the dough is cut into biscuits. Bake for 10 to 15 minutes, or until the edges are golden brown.

soups

CHAPTER 3

Creamy Tomato-Basil Soup

This is a great soup for a cold winter day. It is as simple to prepare as it is delicious.

1 tablespoon olive oil

1½ cups chopped celery

1 cup chopped carrots

½ yellow onion, chopped

¼ cup fresh basil leaves

1 teaspoon chopped garlic

1 cup soy milk

1 medium tomato, chopped

¾ cup tomato sauce

1 teaspoon sea salt

½ cup cashews

Heat the oil in a large saucepan on medium heat. Add the celery, carrots, onion, basil, and garlic. Cook for about 10 minutes, stirring frequently, or until the onion is soft and translucent. Stir in the soy milk, tomato, tomato sauce, and salt. Bring to a boil on medium heat.

Immediately transfer the mixture to a blender. Add the cashews. Process on high speed for 2 minutes, or until smooth and creamy, stopping occasionally to scrape down the blender jar.

Creamy Sweet Potato-Cashew Soup

YIELD: 6 TO 8 SERVINGS

Sweet potatoes are an excellent example of healthful food: fat-free, cholesterol-free, nutrient-rich, and delicious.

2 tablespoons olive oil

3 sweet potatoes, peeled and chopped

1/2 cup chopped celery

1/2 cup chopped yellow onion

1 teaspoon chopped garlic

8 cups water

2 cups soy creamer

1/2 cup cashews

Heat the oil in a large saucepan on high heat. Add the sweet potatoes, celery, onion, and garlic. Cook and stir on high heat for 5 minutes, or until the onion is translucent. Stir in the water and soy creamer. Bring to a boil. Cook for about 35 minutes, or until the sweet potatoes are soft.

Transfer the mixture to a blender. Add the cashews. Process on high speed for about 3 minutes, or until creamy, stopping occasionally to scrape down the blender jar.

Coconut-Squash Soup with Garbanzo Bean Garnish

See photo between pages 16 and 17.   **YIELD: 8 SERVINGS**

Top with a drizzle of chile oil, if you like, and feel free to prepare the soup in advance; time only makes it more flavorful.

2 butternut squash

1 tablespoon olive oil

1 cup cooked garbanzo beans, drained and dried

$\frac{1}{2}$ teaspoon paprika

$\frac{1}{2}$ teaspoon sea salt, plus more to taste

$\frac{1}{2}$ teaspoon raw sugar

2 (28-ounce) **cans coconut milk**

Water as needed

Preheat the oven to 350 degrees F. Line a large baking sheet with parchment paper. Set aside.

Slice off the stems of the squash. Cut the squash in half lengthwise. Remove and discard the seeds. Place the squash halves cut-side down on the prepared baking sheet. Roast for $1\frac{1}{2}$ hours, or until the squash is very soft. Let cool to room temperature.

Meanwhile, heat the oil in a medium skillet on medium heat. (The skillet is the correct temperature when a drop of water sizzles in the pan.) Add the garbanzo beans. Cook and stir for about 5 minutes, or until they are browned. Drain the garbanzo beans. Transfer them to a medium bowl with the paprika, $\frac{1}{2}$ teaspoon of the salt, and sugar. Mix well. Set aside.

Peel the squash halves and put them in a large saucepan. Add the coconut milk. Simmer on medium heat for about 20 minutes, stirring frequently. Transfer the squash mixture to a blender. Process on high speed for about 2 minutes, or until smooth, stopping occasionally to scrape down the blender jar. Add 1 to 2 tablespoons of water as needed to thin the soup as desired. Season with more salt to taste. Ladle into serving bowls. Top each serving with some of the garbanzo beans.

Chipotle Tortilla Soup

YIELD: 6 TO 8 SERVINGS

Tortilla soup encompasses everyone's favorite things about Mexican food. If you want to make this a meal and not a starter, you can add your choice of chopped vegetables about 10 minutes before the soup is ready.

6 medium tomatoes, chopped

3¼ cups tomato sauce

2 tablespoons chopped chipotle chiles

1 tablespoon chopped fresh epazote

¼ cup olive oil

½ cup diced yellow onion

2 cloves garlic, crushed

Sea salt

2 (6-inch) corn tortillas

Put the tomatoes, tomato sauce, chiles, and epazote in a blender. Process until well blended, stopping occasionally to scrape down the blender jar.

Heat 3 tablespoons of the oil in a large soup pot on medium heat. Add the onion and garlic. Cook and stir for about 5 minutes, or until the onion is translucent. Pour in the tomato mixture. Increase the heat to high. Season with salt to taste. Bring to a boil. Cook for 10 to 15 minutes.

Meanwhile, line a plate with paper towels. Slice the tortillas into long, narrow strips. Heat the remaining 1 tablespoon of oil in a small skillet on medium heat. Add the tortilla strips. Fry until crispy. Drain on the prepared plate. To serve, divide the tortilla strips among the serving bowls. Ladle the soup over the tortilla strips.

Sprouted Black Bean Soup

YIELD: 6 TO 8 SERVINGS

The key to the rich flavors in this soup is to cook each of the vegetables before adding them to your soup pot. For instructions on sprouting beans, see How to Sprout (Raw Recipes, page 12).

2 quarts water

2 cups dried black beans, sprouted

¼ cup plus 1 tablespoon extra-virgin olive oil

2 bay leaves

2 cloves garlic

½ yellow onion, chopped

½ green bell pepper, chopped

½ red bell pepper, chopped

2 Roma tomatoes, chopped

1 stalk celery, chopped

2 tablespoons chili powder

2 tablespoons ground cumin

Sea salt

Pour the water, beans, ¼ cup of the oil, bay leaves, and garlic in a large soup pot on high heat. Bring to a boil. Immediately decrease the heat. Simmer while preparing the remaining ingredients.

Heat the remaining 1 tablespoon of oil in a large saucepan on medium heat. Add the onion, bell peppers, tomatoes, celery, chili powder, and cumin. Cook and stir for about 7 minutes, or until the onion is translucent. Transfer the bell pepper mixture to the soup pot. Bring the soup to a boil. Cook for about 30 minutes, or until the vegetables are soft. Season with salt to taste.

Potato-Vegetable Soup

YIELD: 6 TO 8 SERVINGS

There is nothing more comforting than a bowl of steaming vegetable soup. Thicken this one by mashing some of the potatoes.

8 cups water

6 white potatoes, peeled and quartered

1 teaspoon sea salt, plus more to taste

1/2 cup corn kernels

1/2 cup green peas

1/3 green bell pepper, chopped

1/3 red bell pepper, chopped

1/3 white onion, chopped

1 stalk celery, chopped

1 teaspoon red pepper flakes

1/2 teaspoon celery seeds

1/2 sprig thyme, leaves only

1/2 cup broccoli florets

1/2 cup cauliflower florets

1 cup shredded soy cheese, for garnish

Bring the water, potatoes, and 1 teaspoon of the salt to a boil in a large soup pot on high heat. Cook for about 15 minutes, or until the potatoes start to soften. Break up some of the potatoes with a potato masher.

Add the corn, peas, bell peppers, onion, celery, pepper flakes, celery seeds, and thyme. Bring to a boil. Immediately decrease the heat to medium. Simmer for 20 minutes. Add the broccoli, cauliflower, and salt to taste. Simmer for another 5 minutes. Ladle into serving bowls and garnish with soy cheese if desired.

NOTE: Soy cheese should be used only as a garnish. The soup will keep longer if you do not add it to the soup pot.

French Onion Soup

It is very hard to find a place that serves vegan or vegetarian French onion soup because most restaurants use beef broth as a base. Here's one you don't have to worry about.

1 baguette

½ cup shredded vegan mozzarella cheese

¼ cup olive oil

6 yellow onions, sliced

8 sups homemade or prepared mushroom stock

Sea salt

Freshly ground pepper

1 cup dry red wine

Preheat the oven to 350 degrees F. Slice the baguette into 12 to 16 (1-inch-thick) slices. Place them on a baking sheet. Top each slice with about 1 teaspoon of the vegan mozzarella. Bake for 5 minutes, or until the cheese has melted. Set aside. Let cool.

Heat the oil in a soup pot on low heat. Add the onions. Cook for about 25 minutes, or until the onions are dark brown, stirring occasionally. Add 1 or 2 tablespoons of mushroom stock as needed to prevent the onions from burning. Season the onions with salt and pepper.

Increase the heat to medium. Add the wine. Cook and stir for 2 minutes. Add the remaining mushroom stock. Simmer for 25 minutes.

Preheat the broiler. Pour the soup into serving bowls. Place 2 slices of the toasted baguette in each bowl. Top each serving with an additional teaspoon of the vegan mozzarella. Broil for 2 minutes, or until the cheese has melted and browned.

Split Pea Soup

YIELD: 6 SERVINGS

Nothing says comfort like split pea soup.

- **3 cups dried split peas**
- **8 cups water**
- **½ cup olive oil**
- **½ yellow onion, chopped**
- **1 carrot, chopped**
- **1 stalk celery, chopped**
- **3 cloves garlic, chopped**
- **Sea salt**

Rinse the split peas in a fine-mesh strainer under running water until the water runs clear. Transfer them to a large saucepan. Add the water, oil, onion, carrot, celery, and garlic. Bring to a boil on high heat. Boil for about 30 minutes, or until the split peas are soft. Season with salt to taste. Boil for another 3 minutes.

entrées

CHAPTER 4

BBQ Seitan Sandwich

Serve this barbecue seitan sandwich at your next cookout.

SPICE MIX

1 teaspoon Cajun seasoning

1 teaspoon chili powder

1 teaspoon ground cumin

1 teaspoon garlic powder

1 teaspoon hickory smoke powder

1 teaspoon onion powder

1 teaspoon sea salt

SEITAN STEAK

1/2 pound firm tofu, drained

1 cup water, plus more for baking

2 tablespoons olive oil

1 cup high-gluten flour or bread flour

BBQ SAUCE

1 tablespoon olive oil

1 yellow onion, chopped

2 cloves garlic, chopped

1 (28-ounce) can Roma tomatoes

1 cup brown sugar, packed

2/3 cup cider vinegar

MARINADE

3 tablespoons olive oil

1 teaspoon chopped fresh basil leaves

1 teaspoon chopped garlic

Pinch sea salt

TOPPINGS

12 slices yellow onion

1 1/2 green bell peppers, sliced into thin strips

1 1/2 red bell peppers, sliced into thin strips

6 whole wheat kaiser rolls

6 leaves lettuce

Preheat the oven to 350 degrees F.

Combine all the spice mix ingredients in a small bowl.

To make the seitan steak, put the tofu, 1 cup of the water, oil, and 2 tablespoons of the spice mix in a food processor. Process for about 2 minutes, or until creamy, stopping occasionally to scrape down the work bowl. Add the flour. Process for another 2 minutes, or until a dough forms.

Transfer the dough to the countertop. Knead the dough for about 3 minutes, or until it becomes stretchy. Put it on a large rimmed baking sheet. Flatten the dough with your hands until it is no more than 1 inch thick. Leave about 1 inch of space between the edge of the dough and the sides of the baking sheet.

Pour water into the space between the edge of the dough and the sides of the baking sheet until the water almost reaches the same level as the dough. Cover with aluminum foil. Bake for 35 minutes. (The water level should not go lower than half the height of the dough. Add water as needed while the crust is baking.) Turn the baking sheet and bake for another 35 minutes, or until the seitan is firm, not spongy. Let cool. Cut the seitan into 48 thin strips. Set aside.

To make the BBQ Sauce, heat the oil in a large skillet on medium heat. Add the onion and garlic. Decrease the heat to low. Cook for about 25 minutes, or until the onion is dark brown, stirring occasionally. Stir in the tomatoes, brown sugar, and vinegar. Simmer for 40 minutes. Transfer the mixture to a blender. Process until smooth, stopping occasionally to scrape down the blender jar.

To make the marinade, put the oil, basil, garlic, and salt in a blender. Process until well mixed. Brush the marinade over the seitan steak strips. Cook the strips in a large skillet on high heat for 3 minutes, turning often to keep them from burning.

To make the toppings, brown or grill the onion and bell pepper strips in a skillet or on a grill for about 1 minute. Slice the rolls in half and place them cut-side down in a skillet on low heat or on the grill until warm or toasted.

To serve, place the bottom half of a roll on a plate. Place a few seitan steak strips on the roll. Top with some bell pepper strips, 2 slices of the onion, a lettuce leaf, and the top half of the roll. Dip the sandwiches into the BBQ Sauce.

Vegan Meat Loaf

YIELD: 16 SERVINGS

If you prefer not to chop vegetables by hand, using a food processor is a great, fast alternative. This meat loaf can be time-consuming from start to finish but well worth the time and effort. It's a hearty meal for a family dinner or a holiday gathering.

2 tablespoons olive oil

1 yellow onion, diced

2 stalks celery, diced

2 carrots, diced

4 cloves garlic, minced

2 cups cooked brown rice

6 ounces firm tofu, drained and chopped

1 recipe Seitan Steak, chopped (page 34)

¼ cup chili powder

¼ cup paprika

1 tablespoon ground cumin

1 tablespoon sea salt

2 sprigs thyme, minced

6 slices whole wheat bread

2 cups water

¼ cup olive oil

1 tablespoon egg replacer

Preheat the oven to 350 degrees F. Coat a 16 x 4 x 4½-inch loaf pan with olive oil cooking spray. Set aside.

Heat the oil in a medium skillet on medium heat. Add the onion, celery, carrots, and garlic. Cook and stir for about 5 minutes, or until the onion is translucent. Transfer the onion mixture to a large bowl. Set aside.

Put the rice and tofu in a food processor. Process about 3 minutes, or until smooth, stopping occasionally to scrape down the work bowl. Transfer it to the bowl with the onion mixture. Add the seitan, chili powder, paprika, cumin, salt, and thyme. Mix well.

Wash and dry the work bowl and blade. Put the bread in the food processor. Process to coarse crumbs. Transfer the bread crumbs to the bowl with the seitan mixture. Add the water, oil, and egg replacer. Mix well. The consistency should be like mashed potatoes.

Transfer the seitan mixture to the prepared pan. Smooth the top with the back of a spoon. Cover with aluminum foil. Place it in a larger pan. Pour water into the larger pan until it reaches the level of the seitan loaf. Bake for 45 minutes. Remove the foil and bake for another 15 minutes, or until well browned. Let cool.

To serve, unmold the loaf onto a serving platter and slice.

Two-Sauce Taco Wraps

YIELD: 8 SERVINGS

This is a great homemade, fast food. If you're a family on the go, you can prepare the taco "meat" in advance and keep it refrigerated until you are ready to put the wraps together.

TOMATO SAUCE

1/2 cup sugar

1/4 yellow onion, chopped

1/4 cup fresh basil leaves, chopped

3 cloves garlic, chopped

1 (15-ounce) can tomato sauce

1/2 cup olive oil

1 tablespoon ground anise

1 tablespoon dried oregano

1 tablespoon za'atar

CHIPOTLE SAUCE

2 cups soy milk

1/4 cup vegetable oil

2 or 3 chipotle chiles

1 teaspoon sea salt

1 small clove garlic

VEGAN TACO MEAT

1/4 cup olive oil

1/4 cup chopped yellow onion

1 clove garlic

2 cups textured soy protein

1 1/2 cups Tomato Sauce (above)

1 1/2 cups water

1/4 cup chili powder

2 tablespoons ground cumin

1 tablespoon sea salt

1 tablespoon za'atar

TACO WRAPS

8 (10-inch) flour tortillas

CONDIMENTS

2 cups chopped romaine lettuce

1 cup chopped tomatoes

1/2 cup BBQ Sauce (page 34; optional)

To make the tomato sauce, put the sugar, onion, basil, and garlic in a food processor. Process until well mixed, stopping occasionally to scrape down the work bowl. Transfer to a large saucepan. Add the tomato sauce, oil, anise, oregano, and za'atar. Bring to a boil on high heat. Decrease the heat to medium and simmer for 30 minutes. Remove from the heat. Let cool.

To make the chipotle sauce, put all the ingredients in a blender. Process until smooth. Set aside.

To make the vegan taco meat, heat the oil in a medium saucepan on medium heat. Add the onion and garlic. Cook for about 3 minutes, or until the onion is translucent. Add the soy protein, 1 cup of the tomato sauce, 1 cup of the water, the chili powder, cumin, salt, and za'atar. Cook for about 10 minutes. Stir in ½ cup of the tomato sauce and ½ cup of water. Simmer for about 10 minutes.

To serve, place 1 tortilla on a plate. Put about ¾ cup of the vegan taco meat in the middle of the tortilla. Top with about ¼ cup of the romaine, 2 tablespoons tomatoes, and 2 tablespoons of the optional BBQ Sauce. Fold the sides of the tortilla over the filling. Fold the bottom of the tortilla over the filling and roll up into a wrap. Repeat with the remaining tortillas, vegan taco meat, lettuce, tomato, and optional BBQ Sauce. Serve with the remaining tomato sauce and the chipotle sauce for dipping.

Veggie-Potato Potpies

See photo on facing page.

YIELD: 6 POTPIES

Potpies in our home were the result of my great-grandparents having weathered The Great Depression and living by the adage, "waste not, want not." We cooked Monday through Thursday, and Friday was Potpie Day, a combination of the week's meat and vegetable leftovers baked in a yummy crust. Dig in to your fridge and get creative.

Vegan buttery spread

¼ cup plus 2 tablespoons olive oil

2 (16-ounce) bags mixed frozen vegetables, such as green beans, carrots, corn, and peas

Sea salt

¼ cup chopped garlic

2 tablespoons red miso

3 cups cold water

3 tablespoons cornstarch

8 cups cooked and mashed potatoes

1 (10-inch) pie crust

Preheat the oven to 400 degrees F. Coat 6 (4-inch) ramekins with the vegan buttery spread. Set aside.

Heat the oil in a large saucepan on medium heat. Add the frozen vegetables and salt to taste. Cook and stir for about 5 minutes, or until the vegetables are tender. Add the garlic and miso.

Meanwhile, combine the water and cornstarch in a bowl until smooth. Stir it into the vegetables. Form the mashed potatoes into 1½-inch balls and add them to the saucepan with the vegetable mixture. Cover and remove from the heat.

Cut the pie crust into circles to fit the tops of the ramekins, gathering up the scraps and rolling out to cut more circles. Divide the vegetable mixture among the ramekins. Top each with a pie crust. Poke 4 slits in each crust with a sharp knife. Bake for 30 minutes, or until the crusts are golden brown.

Prize-Winning Chili, *on facing page*

Prize-Winning Chili

See photo on facing page.   **YIELD: 6 TO 8 SERVINGS**

This award-winning chili has proudly beaten the meat-filled variety in Chicago. It's also been up against the Chicago Fire Department's version and held its own. The beans need to soak overnight, so plan ahead.

2 cups dried red kidney beans

2 tablespoons olive oil

½ green bell pepper, minced

¼ red bell pepper, minced

¼ yellow onion, minced

2 cloves garlic, minced

1 (14-ounce) can crushed tomatoes

¼ cup chili powder

¼ cup ground cumin

2 tablespoons za'atar

1 tablespoon Cajun seasoning

1 tablespoon red pepper flakes

2 cups textured soy protein

Sea salt

Soak the beans in enough water to cover for 24 hours. Drain and rinse. Bring the beans and 8 cups of fresh water to a boil in a large saucepan on high heat. Boil for about 30 minutes, or until soft. Set aside.

Heat the oil in a large saucepan on high heat. Add the bell peppers, onion, and garlic. Cook and stir for about 7 minutes, or until the onion is translucent. Decrease the heat to medium and add the tomatoes, chili powder, cumin, za'atar, Cajun seasoning, and pepper flakes.

Add the beans, the reserved cooking water, and the soy protein. Mix well and cook for another 10 minutes. Season with salt to taste. Add more water if the soy protein absorbs too much.

Not-so-Classic Lasagne

YIELD: 12 SERVINGS

No one turns down lasagne, and, with this recipe, your guests will ask for seconds.

1½ pounds extra-firm tofu, drained

1½ teaspoons nutritional yeast flakes

1½ teaspoons ground cumin

½ cup olive oil

½ green bell pepper, chopped

½ red bell pepper, chopped

½ yellow onion, chopped

1 tablespoon chopped garlic

2 pounds frozen spinach, thawed and squeezed dry

2 tablespoons tamari (optional)

12 to 15 whole wheat lasagna noodles

1 tablespoon olive oil

4 cups Tomato Sauce (page 38)

½ cup shredded soy mozzarella cheese

Preheat the oven to 350 degrees F.

Crumble the tofu into a medium bowl with your hands. Sprinkle with the nutritional yeast and cumin. Mix well. Set aside.

Heat the oil in a large skillet on medium heat. Add the bell peppers, onion, and garlic. Cook and stir for 5 minutes, or until the onion is translucent. Add the tofu mixture. Cook and stir for another 10 minutes, or until golden brown. Set aside.

Cook the spinach and tamari in a medium saucepan on medium heat just until heated through. Set aside.

Cook the lasagna according to package directions until al dente. Drain. Set aside.

Pour 1½ cups of the Tomato Sauce into a 13 x 9-inch baking pan. Layer 4 or 5 noodles in the pan. Spread the tofu mixture onto the noodles. Layer another 4 or 5 noodles on top of the tofu mixture. Pour 1 cup of the Tomato Sauce over the noodles. Spoon the spinach mixture evenly over the Tomato Sauce. Layer the remaining 4 or 5 noodles over the spinach mixture. Pour the remaining 1½ cups of the Tomato Sauce over the noodles. Sprinkle the soy cheese over the top. Cover the lasagne with aluminum foil. Bake for 30 minutes. Let sit for 15 to 30 minutes before serving.

Curry-Cashew Pasta

YIELD: 6 TO 8 SERVINGS

Curry is a great complement to the delicate flavor of cashews.

1 (14½-ounce) **package whole wheat pasta of your choice**
¼ cup cider vinegar
¼ cup olive oil
2 tablespoons honey
1 teaspoon cayenne
1 teaspoon ground coriander
1 teaspoon ground cumin
1 teaspoon curry powder
1 teaspoon ground turmeric
1 clove garlic
½ teaspoon sea salt
¼ teaspoon ground pepper
1 cup chopped cauliflower, blanched
½ cup roasted cashews
½ cup sliced red onion
1 carrot, julienned
¼ cup chopped red bell pepper
1 green onion, chopped
¼ cup sliced black olives

Cook the pasta according to package directions in a soup pot until it is al dente. Drain and return the pasta to the pot.

Pour the vinegar, oil, honey, cayenne, coriander, cumin, curry, turmeric, garlic, salt, and pepper in a blender. Process on high speed until creamy. Transfer it to the pot with the pasta. Mix well. Bring to a boil on high heat. Immediately decrease the heat to low. Add the cauliflower, cashews, red onion, carrot, bell pepper, green onion, and olives. Mix well. Simmer for 15 minutes.

Slab o' Tofu Ribs

YIELD: 4 SERVINGS

Serve these ribs with a side of coleslaw and mashed potatoes, or make them into a sandwich with your favorite whole wheat buns.

SEASONING MIX

2 tablespoons Cajun seasoning

2 tablespoons chili powder

2 tablespoons ground cumin

2 tablespoons garlic powder

2 tablespoons hickory smoke powder

2 tablespoons onion powder

2 tablespoons sea salt

TOFU RIBS

½ pound firm tofu, drained

1 cup water

2 tablespoons olive oil

1 cup high-gluten flour or bread flour

SAUCE

2 cups BBQ Sauce (page 34) **or prepared barbecue sauce**

½ cup apple juice

Combine all the seasoning mix ingredients in a small bowl.

To make the tofu ribs, put the tofu, water, oil, and 2 tablespoons of the seasoning mix in a food processor. Process for 2 minutes, or until creamy, stopping occasionally to scrape down the work bowl. Add the flour. Process for another 2 minutes, or until a dough forms.

Transfer the dough to the countertop. Knead the dough for about 3 minutes, or until it becomes stretchy. Put it on a large rimmed baking sheet. Flatten the dough with your hands until it is no more than 1 inch thick. Leave about 1 inch of space between the edge of the dough and the sides of the baking sheet.

Pour water into the space between the edge of the dough and the sides of the baking sheet until the water almost reaches the same level as the dough. Cover with aluminum foil. Bake for 35 minutes. (The water level should not go lower than half the height of the dough. Add water as needed while the crust is baking.) Turn the baking sheet and bake for another 35 minutes, or until the dough is firm, not spongy. Let cool. Cut the dough into 1-inch strips. Heat a grill pan on medium-high heat. Cook the strips just until grill marks form. Turn and cook the other side.

Combine the BBQ Sauce and apple juice in a small saucepan on high heat. Cook just until heated through, stirring frequently. Place the ribs in a large saucepan. Pour the sauce over the ribs. Cook on medium heat for 3 minutes. Serve immediately.

Sloppy Soy Joes

When is the last time you had a sloppy joe? This vegan version will have you eating it regularly.

¼ cup olive oil

¼ cup chopped yellow onion

1 clove garlic, chopped

2 cups textured soy protein

3 cups **Tomato Sauce** (page 38)

1½ cups water

¼ cup chili powder

2 tablespoons ground cumin

1 tablespoon za'atar

Sea salt

8 whole wheat hamburger buns

1 cup **Saucy Soy Cheese** (page 57) **or prepared vegan cheese**

Heat the oil in a large saucepan on medium heat. Add the onion and garlic and cook until the onion is translucent. Add the soy protein, 1 cup of the Tomato Sauce, 1 cup of the water, chili powder, cumin, and za'atar. Mix well. Cook on low heat for about 10 minutes.

Add another ½ cup of the Tomato Sauce and the remaining ½ cup of water. Simmer for about 5 minutes, or until the soy protein is soft.

Add the remaining 1½ cups of Tomato Sauce. Bring to a simmer on medium heat if necessary to heat through. Season with salt to taste. Grill the buns if desired. Serve the filling on the buns topped with some of the Saucy Soy Cheese.

Mushroom-Pinto Burgers

YIELD: 6 SERVINGS

If you use the right ingredients and spices when cooking mushrooms, they can very much resemble meat in both taste and texture. Even people who normally don't like mushrooms are surprised by this tasty burger.

2 tablespoons olive oil

1 yellow onion, diced

1 clove garlic, minced

¾ cup diced mushrooms

3 green onions, thinly sliced

½ teaspoon ground cumin

2 cups cooked pinto beans,
  or 1 (15-ounce can) **pinto beans,**
  drained and rinsed

1 teaspoon chopped parsley

Sea salt

Freshly ground pepper

2 tablespoons grapeseed oil

6 whole wheat hamburger buns

Heat the olive oil in a medium skillet on medium heat. Add the yellow onion and garlic. Cook and stir for 5 minutes, or until the onion is soft. Add the mushrooms, green onions, and cumin. Cook for another 5 minutes. Set aside.

Mash the beans in a medium bowl with a fork or a potato masher. Add the mushroom mixture, parsley, and salt and pepper to taste. Mix well.

Shape the mixture into 6 (3-inch) patties. Heat the grapeseed oil in a medium skillet on medium heat. Add the patties. Cook for 1½ to 2 minutes, or until crispy. Turn and cook the other side until crispy. Serve on hamburger buns with the traditional condiments, such as ketchup, mustard, and hot peppers.

Shepherd's Pie with Red Wine Gravy

This shepherd's pie recipe will satisfy even the most skeptical of meat eaters.

SEITAN STEW

½ cup peeled diced carrots

½ cup peeled diced parsnips

¼ cup diced celery

¼ cup diced red onion

1 teaspoon minced garlic

4 ounces crumbled Italian sausage-style seitan

1 tablespoon tomato paste

1 teaspoon ground pepper

½ teaspoon chopped fresh oregano leaves

½ teaspoon chopped fresh thyme

Water

Sea salt

RED WINE GRAVY

1 tablespoon olive oil

1 tablespoon unbleached white flour

1 cup dry red wine

1 teaspoon minced fresh rosemary

Water

Sea salt

POTATO CAKES

2 small Yukon gold potatoes, peeled

¼ cup soy milk

1 tablespoon unbleached white flour

1 tablespoon minced fresh chives

2 teaspoons grated fresh horseradish

Sea salt

1 tablespoon olive oil

To make the seitan stew, combine the carrots, parsnips, celery, onion, and garlic in a large skillet on high heat. Cook for 7 to 10 minutes, or until the onion is translucent and the carrots are tender, stirring occasionally. Add the seitan, tomato paste, pepper, oregano, and thyme. Add just enough water to thin the mixture to a stew-like consistency. Decrease the heat and simmer for 15 minutes. Pour the stew into a medium casserole. Season with salt to taste.

To make the red wine gravy, heat the oil in a medium skillet on medium heat. Add the flour and whisk until smooth. Gradually add the wine, whisking constantly. Whisk in the rosemary. Add just enough water to thin to a gravy consistency. Season with salt to taste. Pour the gravy over the stew. Keep warm.

To make the potato cakes, bring the potatoes to a boil in a medium saucepan in enough water to cover until tender. Drain and transfer to a medium bowl. Mash the potatoes with a fork, gradually beating in the soy milk and flour. Stir in the chives, horseradish, and salt to taste. Form the potato mixture into 3-inch patties with your hands. Heat the oil in a medium skillet on medium heat. Cook the patties for about 5 minutes, or until browned. Turn and cook the other side until browned. To serve, place the potato cakes on top of the stew.

Rainbow Avocado Sandwich

YIELD: 4 SERVINGS

To make this sandwich soy-free, leave out the vegan mayo. If you avoid gluten, make a sandwich with gluten-free bread, or substitute a lettuce or cabbage leaf for the pita bread.

2 avocados

¼ cup vegan mayonnaise

2 teaspoons thinly sliced jalapeño chiles (optional)

1 clove garlic, minced

½ shallot, minced

Sea salt

Freshly ground pepper

2 whole wheat pita breads

½ cup alfalfa sprouts

½ cup cucumber slices

½ cup diced yellow onion

½ cup Roma tomato slices

To make the avocado spread, break the avocados into large chunks in a large bowl with a potato masher. Mix in the vegan mayonnaise, jalapeños, garlic, shallot, and salt and pepper to taste.

Heat a pita in a toaster for 2 minutes or in a small skillet on medium heat for 30 seconds on each side. Slice the pita in half. Put ¼ cup of the avocado spread inside the pita. Top with some sprouts, cucumber slices, onion, and tomato slices. Repeat with the remaining ingredients.

Polenta Fiesta

If you are not familiar with polenta, you will be very glad you stopped on this page. Although usually a side dish, this one features soy cheese and vegetables and is hearty enough for the main course.

2 tablespoons olive oil

1 green bell pepper, chopped

1 red bell pepper, chopped

1 small red onion, minced

½ cup sliced black olives

7 cloves garlic, minced

8 cups water

4 cups cornmeal

4 cups Saucy Soy Cheese (page 57) **or prepared vegan cheese**

Sea salt

Line a large rimmed baking sheet with a piece of plastic wrap that hangs over the edges of the pan by about 2 inches. Set aside.

Heat the oil in a large saucepan on medium heat. Add the bell peppers, onion, olives, and garlic. Cook and stir for 7 to 10 minutes, or until the onion is translucent. Add the water and bring to a boil. Gradually stir in the cornmeal, Saucy Soy Cheese, and salt to taste. Cook for about 20 minutes, or until thickened to a dough-like consistency. Pour the polenta onto the prepared baking sheet. Spread it out evenly with a spatula. Refrigerate until the polenta is thoroughly chilled and firm.

Pull up the edges of the plastic wrap to remove the polenta from the baking sheet. Place the polenta on a cutting board and slice it into 10 equal-size triangles. Heat a grill pan on medium-high heat. Cook the triangles just until grill marks form. Turn and cook the other side.

Jerry's Pizza

YIELD: 1 (12-INCH) PIZZA; 8 SERVINGS

This is the perfect pizza for the secret vegan in every meat lover. Any leftover vegetables also make great toppings, as would seitan sausage, crumbled veggie burgers, and other meat substitutes.

1 tablespoon olive oil

½ cup sliced shiitake and oyster mushrooms

1 clove garlic, chopped

2 (12-inch) flour tortillas

1 tablespoon olive oil

¾ cup Tomato Sauce (page 38) **or prepared marinara sauce**

2 teaspoons thinly sliced fresh basil leaves

1 cup shredded vegan mozzarella cheese

Preheat the oven to 400 degrees F.

Heat the vegetable oil in a small skillet on high heat. Add the mushrooms and garlic. Cook, stirring constantly, for 1 minute. Remove from the heat.

Put 1 tortilla on a small baking sheet. Brush the tortilla with some of the olive oil. Place the other tortilla on top. Spread the Tomato Sauce on the top tortilla. Top with the mushroom mixture and basil. Sprinkle with the vegan mozzarella. Bake for 5 to 7 minutes, or until the cheese has melted.

Falafel with Tahini Sauce

YIELD: 12 SERVINGS

The tahini sauce also makes a delicious salad dressing.

FALAFEL

4 cups cooked garbanzo beans

1 bunch cilantro, chopped

½ yellow onion, chopped

¼ cup olive oil, plus 2 to 3 cups more for frying falafel

1 tablespoon plus 1½ teaspoons ground coriander

1 tablespoon plus 1½ teaspoons ground cumin

1 tablespoon chopped garlic

Sea salt

TAHINI SAUCE

1 cup tahini

½ cup olive oil

Juice of 3 lemons

3 cloves garlic, chopped

Sea salt

CONDIMENTS

12 pita breads

3 cups chopped romaine lettuce

¾ cup chopped cucumber

¾ cup chopped tomato

Line a platter with paper towels. Set aside.

To make the falafel, put the garbanzo beans, cilantro, onion, ¼ cup of the olive oil, coriander, cumin, garlic, and salt to taste in a food processor. Process until well mixed and fairly smooth, stopping occasionally to scrape down the work bowl.

Heat the remaining 2 to 3 cups of olive oil in a large skillet on high heat until hot. (There should be 2 inches of oil in the skillet.) Form the bean mixture into balls, 2 tablespoons at a time. Drop the balls into the hot oil. Cook for 5 minutes, or until the falafel floats to the top. Drain on the prepared platter.

To make the Tahini Sauce, put the tahini, oil, lemon juice, garlic, and salt to taste in a blender. Process on low speed until smooth and creamy. If the sauce is too thick, add 1 tablespoon of water and process again until it reaches desired consistency.

To serve, slice each pita in half. Place 3 falafels in each half. Top with romaine, cucumber, and tomato. Drizzle with Tahini Sauce.

Jerk Tofu Wraps

YIELD: 3 SANDWICHES

I recommend this for anyone transitioning to a plant-based diet. It will dispel all myths that vegan food is bland food.

JERK SAUCE

2 tablespoons BBQ Sauce (page 34) **or prepared barbecue sauce**

2 tablespoons Caribbean jerk seasoning mix

1½ tablespoons water

GARLIC SAUCE

½ cup soy milk

2 tablespoons vegetable oil

1 tablespoon dried parsley

1 tablespoon sugar

2 teaspoons cider vinegar

1 teaspoon chopped garlic

TOFU WRAPS

1 pound extra-firm tofu, drained and cut into 6 slices

3 (12-inch) **flour tortillas**

1 cup chopped romaine lettuce

2 Roma tomatoes, sliced

Combine the jerk sauce ingredients in a small bowl.

Put all the garlic sauce ingredients in a blender. Process until creamy.

To make the tofu wraps, coat a large skillet with olive oil cooking spray. Cook the tofu slices in the skillet on medium heat for 3 minutes per side or until lightly browned.

To serve, place 1 tortilla on each of three plates. Place 2 slices of tofu in the middle of each tortilla. Top with equal amounts of romaine and tomato slices, 1 teaspoon of the jerk sauce or to taste, and 2 tablespoons of the garlic sauce. Fold the sides of the tortilla over the filling. Fold the bottom of the tortilla over the filling and roll up into a wrap. Slice each wrap in half diagonally.

side dishes and snacks

Caesar Salad with Herbed Croutons

YIELD: 4 SERVINGS

This Caesar salad is one that even Caesar Cardini would approve of.

CAESAR DRESSING

¼ cup shredded vegan
    mozzarella cheese

½ sheet nori

1 small clove garlic, minced

½ teaspoon Dijon mustard

½ teaspoon tamari (optional)

½ teaspoon rice wine vinegar

½ cup extra-virgin olive oil

CROUTONS

1 baguette, cut into cubes

2 cups chopped parsley

¼ cup extra-virgin olive oil

3 cloves garlic, minced

SALAD

1 head romaine lettuce, chopped

Sea salt

Freshly ground pepper

Preheat the oven to 350 degrees F.

To make the Caesar dressing, put the vegan mozzarella in a blender. Process until it becomes a smooth paste. Add the nori, garlic, mustard, the optional tamari, and vinegar. Process again until thoroughly mixed, stopping occasionally to scrape down the blender jar. With the blender running, gradually add the oil and process until smooth. Set aside.

Combine all the crouton ingredients in a medium bowl. Toss until the bread is well coated. Put the bread cubes in a single layer on a large rimmed baking sheet. Bake for about 10 minutes, or until lightly browned.

In a medium bowl, combine the romaine and croutons. Serve with the Caesar dressing. Season with salt and pepper to taste.

Saucy Soy Cheese

YIELD: 6½ CUPS

You will want to make sure you always keep some of this cheese in your fridge. You'll find lots of uses for it, such as on chili and pizza or as a dip.

4 cups soy milk

1½ cups vegetable oil

1 cup nutritional yeast flakes

1 tablespoon chopped garlic

1 tablespoon sea salt

Put all the ingredients in a blender. Process until thick, stopping occasionally to scrape down the blender jar. Stored in a covered container in the refrigerator, Saucy Soy Cheese will keep for 5 days.

Vegan Buttery Popcorn

YIELD: 10 SERVINGS

It isn't Movie Night without the popcorn.

1 cup high-quality white or black kernel popcorn

¼ cup grapeseed oil

¼ cup olive oil

Sea salt (optional)

Pop the popcorn in the grapeseed oil until fluffy. Drizzle with the olive oil and season with salt to taste.

VARIATIONS: Try flavoring your popcorn with nutritional yeast flakes, dulse flakes, Karyn's Powdered Enzymes (see karynraw.com, p. 78), sea salt, or raw vegan Parmesan. Have a sweet tooth? Turn your Vegan Buttery Popcorn into kettle corn or caramel corn by sprinkling it with coconut sugar.

Caramelized Brussels Sprouts with Mustard Vinaigrette

YIELD: 6 SERVINGS

Most people will scrunch their noses at the thought of eating Brussels sprouts, but with this recipe, they will be asking for seconds.

1 teaspoon sea salt, plus more to taste

1 pound Brussels sprouts, trimmed and cut into quarters

1 tablespoon olive oil

½ cup Mustard Vinaigrette (see Raw Recipes, page 37) **or prepared mustard dressing**

Freshly ground pepper

Bring a large pot of water to a boil. Add 1 teaspoon of the salt and the Brussels sprouts. Boil for 5 minutes. Meanwhile, prepare a large bowl of iced water. Drain the Brussels sprouts and transfer them to the bowl of iced water. When the sprouts are cold, drain and dry them with paper towels.

Heat the oil in a large skillet on high heat. Add the Brussels sprouts and cook, cut-sides down, for 1 to 2 minutes, or until golden brown, stirring occasionally. Transfer to a serving bowl. Add the Mustard Vinaigrette and toss well. Season with salt and pepper to taste.

Potatoes au Gratin

YIELD: 4 TO 6 SERVINGS

Is there such a thing as "bad" potatoes au gratin? I really don't think so.

4 white potatoes, peeled and sliced

4 cups Saucy Soy Cheese (page 57)

1 cup whole wheat bread crumbs

Sea salt

Preheat the oven to 350 degrees F. Coat a 9 x 9-inch baking dish with olive oil. Set aside.

Bring the potatoes to a boil in a medium saucepan in enough water to cover. Boil for about 15 minutes, or until the potatoes are soft. Drain. Transfer the potatoes to the prepared dish. Pour the Saucy Soy Cheese over the potatoes and top with the bread crumbs and salt to taste. Cover with aluminum foil. Bake for 20 minutes. Remove the foil and bake for another 10 minutes, or until golden brown.

Southern-Style Greens

YIELD: 4 SERVINGS

2½ bunches (1 pound) **collard greens, stemmed and chopped**

½ cup olive oil

¼ yellow onion, chopped

1 tablespoon plus 1½ teaspoons nutritional yeast flakes

1 teaspoon hickory smoke powder

Sea salt

Bring a large pot of water to a boil on high heat. Add the collard greens, oil, onion, nutritional yeast, and hickory smoke powder. Stir and cover. Cook for 45 to 60 minutes, or until the collard greens are soft. Drain. Season with salt to taste.

Cornbread Stuffing with Mushrooms, Corn, and Black-eyed Peas

YIELD: 10 TO 12 SERVINGS

You don't have to wait for Thanksgiving to enjoy stuffing, and you certainly do not have to serve it with turkey.

CORNBREAD

2 cups unbleached white flour

2 cups yellow cornmeal

¾ cup corn flour

½ cup dehydrated cane juice

¼ cup plus 2 tablespoons water

¼ cup brown sugar firmly packed

2 tablespoons baking powder

1½ cups soy milk

1 cup frozen corn kernels

½ cup olive oil

¼ cup agave nectar (preferably light)

1 teaspoon sea salt

STUFFING

1 tablespoon olive oil

1½ bunches celery, sliced with leaves

3 cloves garlic, minced

1 shallot, minced

2 or 3 fresh sage leaves

1 pound mushrooms (such as beech, maitake, or oyster), **chopped**

1 cup cooked black-eyed peas

1 cup frozen corn kernels

4 cups vegetable broth

Sea salt

Freshly ground pepper

To make the cornbread, preheat the oven to 375 degrees F. Coat a 13 x 9-inch baking pan with olive oil and set aside.

Sift the all-purpose flour into a medium bowl. Add the cornmeal, corn flour, dehydrated cane juice, water, brown sugar, and baking powder. Mix well.

In a large bowl, combine the soy milk, corn, oil, agave nectar, and salt. Add the cornmeal mixture to the soy milk mixture. Whisk until the dry ingredients are well combined. Pour into the prepared pan. Bake for 15 minutes, or until the top begins to brown. Let cool completely.

To make the stuffing, increase the oven temperature to 400 degrees F.

Heat the oil in a large skillet on medium heat. Add the celery, garlic, shallot, and sage leaves. Cook for 3 minutes, stirring frequently, until the shallot is translucent. Add the mushrooms, black-eyed peas, and corn. Cook for 5 to 6 minutes, stirring frequently, until the vegetables are browned.

Heat the broth in a small saucepan on medium heat until hot. Stir it into the mushroom mixture. Decrease the heat to low. Simmer for 10 minutes, or until all the liquid has evaporated. Remove and discard the sage.

Crumble the cornbread into a deep 13 x 9-inch baking pan or large roasting pan. Pour the mushroom mixture over the cornbread and mix thoroughly. Season with salt and pepper. Bake for 12 minutes, or until the stuffing is firm and golden brown.

Red Beans for Greens

YIELD: 6 SERVINGS

These red beans will complement your favorite greens. The beans need to soak overnight, so plan ahead.

2 cups dried red kidney beans

¼ cup olive oil

1 stalk celery, finely chopped

¼ yellow onion, finely chopped

¼ red bell pepper, finely chopped

2 cloves garlic, chopped

1 cup coconut milk

1½ teaspoons celery seeds

1½ teaspoons cumin seeds

1½ teaspoons garam masala

1½ teaspoons ground ginger

5 sprigs fresh thyme

1 tablespoon chopped fresh cilantro

Sea salt

Soak the beans in enough water to cover for 24 hours. Drain and rinse. Bring the beans and 8 cups of fresh water to a boil in a large saucepan on high heat. Boil for about 30 minutes, or until soft. Drain. Set aside.

Heat the oil in a large skillet on medium heat. Cook and stir the celery, onion, bell pepper, and garlic for about 7 minutes, or until the onion is translucent and the vegetables are soft. Stir in the beans, coconut milk, celery seeds, cumin seeds, garam masala, ginger, and thyme. Cook for another 5 minutes. Remove thyme sprigs and stir in cilantro just before serving. Season with salt to taste.

Blueberry Pie, *page 72*

Carrot-Raisin Cake, *page 76*

No-Bake Coconut Snowballs, *page 75*

from Karyn's Cooked

Mac and Cheese

YIELD: 6 SERVINGS

Try this recipe on kids. They won't be able to tell the difference between this version and the stuff in that blue box.

4 cups macaroni

4 cups soy milk

1 cup vegetable oil

½ cup nutritional yeast flakes

1 stalk celery, chopped

½ red bell pepper, chopped

4 cloves garlic, minced

Sea salt

Paprika, for garnish

Preheat the oven to 350 degrees F. Coat a 9 x 9-inch baking dish with olive oil. Set aside.

Cook the macaroni according to package directions until al dente. Drain.

Mix the soy milk, oil, nutritional yeast, celery, bell pepper, and garlic in a large bowl. Combine the macaroni with the soy milk mixture. Season with salt to taste. Transfer to the prepared baking dish. Sprinkle with the paprika if desired. Bake for 30 minutes, or until the top is golden and crispy.

Party Pasta Salad

This is a great pasta salad to bring to dinner parties. It tastes even better if you let it marinate for a day or two. For instructions on sprouting beans, see How to Sprout (Raw Recipes, page 12).

2 cups sun-dried tomatoes (not oil-packed)

1 (12-ounce) **package rotini**

1 cup **extra-virgin olive oil**

2 cups **chopped kalamata olives**

2 cups **chopped baby spinach**

1 cup **dried cannellini beans, sprouted**

1 cup **dried garbanzo beans, sprouted**

½ cup **chopped garlic**

½ cup **honey or agave nectar**

Sea salt

Soak the tomatoes in enough water to cover for 1 hour. Drain. Chop the tomatoes and set aside.

Meanwhile, cook the rotini according to package directions until al dente. Drain. Transfer the rotini to a large bowl. Add ½ cup of the oil and toss well. Add the olives, spinach, tomatoes, beans, garlic, and honey. Mix well. Add the remaining ½ cup of the olive oil and toss again. Season with salt to taste.

CHAPTER 6

desserts

No-Bake Chocolate-Peanut Butter Pie

Pie is good any time of the day, especially if the pie is a delicious, hassle-free, no-bake one.

CRUST

1 (16-ounce) bag pretzels

¼ cup agave nectar

FILLING

2 cups semisweet chocolate chips

12 ounces silken tofu

1½ cups smooth peanut butter

¾ cup soy milk

COCONUT CREAM TOPPING

1 cup cashews, soaked, drained, and rinsed
(see Soak Your Nuts, page 69)

¼ cup water

¼ cup light agave nectar

1 teaspoon vanilla extract

⅔ cup coconut oil

To make the crust, put the pretzels and agave nectar in a food processor. Process until the pretzels are ground and sticking together. Transfer to a 10-inch spring-form pan. Using the bottom of a glass, press the pretzel mixture evenly into the bottom and up the sides of the pan. Wash and dry the food processor work bowl and blade.

To make the filling, melt the chocolate chips in the top of a double boiler. Put the tofu, peanut butter, and soy milk in the food processor. Process until smooth, stopping occasionally to scrape down the work bowl. Pour in the melted chocolate. Process again until well blended. Pour the filling into the crust. Refrigerate for 2 hours, or until firm.

To make the coconut cream topping, put the cashews and water in a blender. Process until creamy. Add the agave nectar and vanilla extract. Process on low speed. With the blender running, gradually add the coconut oil until incorporated. Serve a dollop with each slice of pie.

Soak Your Nuts

Nuts contain natural compounds that prevent them from sprouting prematurely. Soaking breaks down these compounds and begins the sprouting process, which I believe makes nuts easier to digest. An added bonus is that it may increase the absorption of their nutrients. I feel satisfied more quickly and am likely to eat fewer nuts if I've soaked them first. This applies to seeds, grains, and legumes as well.

I always have several jars of soaked nuts in my refrigerator ready for a quick snack or to use in a recipe. Nuts can be dried at room temperature or in a dehydrator to return them to their presoaked crunchiness.

Soak nuts in a bowl in enough water to cover and follow recipe instructions. If you have time, soak them overnight, or use this general guide.

NUT OR SEED	SOAK TIME
Almonds	8 hours or overnight
Brazil nuts	1 to 2 hours
Cashews	1 to 2 hours
Pecans	2 to 4 hours
Sesame seeds	30 minutes
Sunflower seeds	30 minutes
Walnuts	2 to 4 hours

Some recipes also will call for some soaked grains, such as quinoa, rice, and wheat. This requires a little more prep work, but it's an easy process and the rewards are well worth it. (Just follow recipe instructions.) I actually find it pretty amazing that a little water and a few days' time can bring these grains to life.

Gluten-Free Berry Cobbler

YIELD: 6 SERVINGS

This is a recipe with soul for everyone to enjoy, especially those on a gluten-free diet.

- 1⅓ cups plus 2 tablespoons gluten-free flour
- ¾ cup turbinado sugar
- ½ cup plus 3 tablespoons soy milk
- ¼ cup plus 1 tablespoon vegan buttery spread
- 1½ teaspoons baking powder
- ½ teaspoon sea salt
- 4 to 5 cups frozen berries of your choice, thawed
- 1 teaspoon lemon zest

Preheat the oven to 350 degrees F.

Put 1⅓ cups of the flour, 3 tablespoons of the sugar, ½ cup of the soy milk, the vegan buttery spread, baking powder, and salt in the bowl of an electric mixer. Mix at medium speed until thoroughly combined and a dough forms.

Combine the berries, the remaining 2 tablespoons of flour, ½ cup of the sugar, and lemon zest. Spread the mixture evenly into a 15½ x 10-inch rimmed baking sheet. With a spatula, spread the dough on top of the berry mixture. Brush the dough with the remaining 3 tablespoons of the soy milk and sprinkle it with the remaining 1 tablespoon of sugar.

Bake for 45 minutes. Let cool before serving.

Pecan Pie

This will win everyone over at your next holiday party.

1¼ cups cashew butter

½ cup turbinado sugar

¼ cup cider vinegar

½ cup soy creamer

¼ cup vegetable oil

1 tablespoon cornstarch

1½ teaspoons egg replacer

5 cups raw pecans

1 (8-inch) **graham cracker pie crust**

Preheat the oven to 350 degrees F.

Put ½ cup of the cashew butter, sugar, and vinegar in a food processor. Process for 1 minute, stopping occasionally to scrape down the work bowl. Add the creamer, oil, cornstarch, and egg replacer. Process for 8 minutes, or until it reaches a pudding consistency. Transfer to a large bowl. Mix in 4 cups of the pecans. Pour the mixture into the pie crust and smooth the top with a spatula. Garnish the perimeter of the pie with the remaining 1 cup of pecans. Cover with aluminum foil.

Poke a few holes in the foil with the tip of a knife. Place the pie on a baking sheet. Bake for 30 minutes, or until the pecans on top of the pie begin to brown.

Blueberry Pie

See photo facing page 64.

YIELD: 12 SERVINGS

Garnish this pie with a fresh fruit other than blueberries. Your decoration will really pop against the dark color of the blueberries. Substitute almost any seasonal fruit for the blueberries.

PIE

1 pound extra-firm tofu, drained

1 cup turbinado sugar

1/2 cup vegan sour cream

1 cup frozen blueberries, thawed

1 teaspoon cider vinegar

1 (10-inch) pie crust

TOPPING

1 cup frozen blueberries, thawed

1/2 cup turbinado sugar

1 teaspoon cornstarch

Preheat the oven to 350 degrees F.

To make the filling, put the tofu in the food processor. Process until smooth. Add the sugar and vegan sour cream. Process again until smooth, stopping occasionally to scrape down the work bowl. Add the blueberries and vinegar. Process again until smooth, stopping occasionally to scrape down the work bowl.

Pour the tofu mixture into the pie crust. Bake for 30 minutes or until the pie has risen. Let cool completely.

To make the topping, cook the blueberries in a small saucepan on low heat just until they have released liquid and started to boil. Add the sugar and cornstarch and stir until the sugar dissolves. Pour the blueberry mixture into a blender. Process until smooth. Pour the topping over the pie and smooth the top with a spatula.

Sweet Potato Pie

YIELD: 8 SERVINGS

Sweet potatoes are deceptively good for you, so don't feel guilty if you want to indulge.

2 sweet potatoes

1 cup frozen mango, thawed and chopped

½ cup honey or agave nectar

½ teaspoon ground cinnamon

1 (8-inch) pie crust

Preheat the oven to 350 degrees F.

Bake the sweet potatoes for 20 to 30 minutes, or until soft. Let cool. Peel the potatoes and put them in a food processor with the mango, honey, and cinnamon. Process until smooth, stopping occasionally to scrape down the work bowl.

Pour the filling into the pie crust. Bake for 30 minutes, or until the top starts to brown.

Ginger Molasses Cookies

YIELD: 3 DOZEN COOKIES

The holidays seem warmer when the smell of sweet ginger is wafting through your home.

3 cups unbleached white flour

¼ cup plus 1 tablespoon ground ginger

1½ teaspoons baking powder

1 tablespoon sea salt

2 teaspoons ground cinnamon

1 teaspoon ground cloves

1 cup vegan buttery spread

1 cup molasses

½ cup agave nectar or honey

¼ cup soy milk

1 tablespoon egg replacer

Preheat the oven to 350 degrees F.

Sift the flour, ginger, baking powder, salt, cinnamon, and cloves into a medium bowl.

Combine the vegan buttery spread, molasses, agave nectar, soy milk, and egg replacer in a separate medium bowl with an electric hand mixer. Gradually add the flour mixture to the molasses mixture, stirring after each addition. Mix well.

Place tablespoonfuls of dough 2 to 3 inches apart on a baking sheet. Bake for about 10 minutes, or until golden brown.

No-Bake Coconut Snowballs

See photo between pages 64 and 65.   **YIELD: 3 DOZEN SNOWBALLS**

A no-bake dessert. Need I say more?

2 cups sweetened shredded dried coconut

$2\frac{2}{3}$ cups honey

2 cups smooth peanut butter or almond butter

$1\frac{1}{2}$ cups carob powder

$1\frac{1}{2}$ cups chopped pecans

$1\frac{1}{2}$ cups chopped walnuts

2 tablespoons peppermint extract

2 cups sesame seeds

Put the coconut in a shallow bowl.

Combine the honey, peanut butter, carob, pecans, walnuts, and peppermint extract in a medium bowl. Mix in the sesame seeds.

Form the mixture into 2-inch balls with your hands, roll them in the coconut, and place them in paper baking cups. Serve at room temperature, or refrigerate and serve chilled.

Carrot-Raisin Cake

See photo between pages 64 and 65.

YIELD: 20 SERVINGS

Everyone you serve this to will want the recipe for this moist and delicious cake.

CAKE

2 cups pastry or cake flour

½ cup unbleached white flour

1½ teaspoons baking powder

1 teaspoon ground cinnamon

½ teaspoon baking soda

½ teaspoon sea salt

Pinch ground cloves

¾ cup shredded carrot

¼ cup golden raisins

1⅛ cups soy milk

1 cup soy creamer

1 cup raw sugar

¾ cup vegetable oil

1 scant tablespoon egg replacer

2 teaspoons orange extract

1 teaspoon vanilla extract

FROSTING

1 pound extra-firm tofu, drained

1 pound vegan buttery spread

1¾ cups turbinado sugar

2 tablespoons cornstarch

1 tablespoon egg replacer

Preheat the oven to 350 degrees F. Coat a 12-inch cake pan with cooking spray. Set aside.

To make the cake, sift the flours, baking powder, cinnamon, baking soda, salt, and cloves into a large bowl. Stir in the carrot and raisins.

Pour the soy milk, soy creamer, sugar, oil, egg replacer, orange extract, and vanilla extract in a blender. Process until smooth. Add the soy milk mixture to the carrot mixture. Stir until well combined. Pour the cake batter into the prepared pan. Bake for 30 minutes, or until a wooden pick inserted in the center comes out clean. Let the cake cool completely.

To make the frosting, put all the ingredients in a food processor. Process until smooth and creamy, stopping occasionally to scrape down the work bowl. Refrigerate the frosting until thoroughly chilled.

Unmold the cake from the pan. Frost the top and sides. Or, slice the cake in half and make a double-layer cake.

Bread Pudding with Coconut Cream Sauce

YIELD: 12 SERVINGS

BREAD PUDDING

8 toasted or day-old whole wheat kaiser rolls

2 cups turbinado sugar

1 cup sweetened shredded dried coconut

¾ cup golden raisins

1 tablespoon plus 1½ teaspoons egg replacer

1 teaspoon baking powder

1 teaspoon salt

½ teaspoon ground cinnamon

3 (14-ounce) cans coconut milk

1½ cups grapeseed oil

1 teaspoon coconut extract

1 teaspoon vanilla extract

COCONUT CREAM SAUCE

3 (14-ounce) cans coconut milk

½ cup raw sugar

2 tablespoons coconut extract

2 tablespoons cornstarch

Preheat the oven to 350 degrees F. Coat a 13 x 9-inch baking pan with cooking spray. Set aside.

To make the bread pudding, break the rolls into pieces and put them in a food processor. Process into crumbs. Transfer them to a large bowl with the sugar, coconut, raisins, egg replacer, baking powder, salt, and cinnamon. Mix well.

Pour the coconut milk, oil, coconut extract, and vanilla extract in a blender. Process until smooth. Pour it over the bread crumb mixture. Mix well. Transfer to the prepared pan. Bake for 30 minutes, or until the top is golden brown and the pudding is soft but not dry. Let cool for at least 1 hour.

To make the coconut cream sauce, mix all the ingredients well in a large saucepan. Bring to a boil on medium heat, stirring constantly to prevent the mixture from burning. Boil for 3 minutes, or until the sauce thickens. Serve warm over the bread pudding.

resources

VISIT US

Karyn's Fresh Corner and Inner Beauty Center
1901 N. Halsted St.
Chicago, IL 60614

312-255-1590

Karyn's Cooked
738 N. Wells St.
Chicago, IL 60654

312-587-1050

Karyn's on Green
130 S. Green St.
Chicago, IL 60607

312-226-6155

VISIT US ON THE WEB

karynraw.com

Visit our website for our entire line of products, upcoming events, specials, and more information on Karyn's Inner Beauty Center, Karyn's Fresh Corner, Karyn's Raw Bistro, and Karyn's Cooked.

karynsongreen.com

Visit our website for pictures, hours of operation, drink and food menus, reservations, and more information on booking your next event at Karyn's on Green.

youtube.com/karynraw

Visit our YouTube Channel for food demos, Karyn's free information seminars, information on Karyn's Detox class, and other video blogs.

Like us on Facebook

Search Karyn's Raw Café and Inner Beauty Center, Karyn's on Green, Cleansing with Karyn, and/or Karyn Calabrese for up-to-date news.

Twitter

Follow us @KarynsRawBeauty, @karynsongreen, and/or @KarynCalabrese for the latest news.

RECOMMENDED BOOKS

Becoming Vegan, by Brenda Davis and Vesanto Melina (Book Publishing Company, 2000)

Eating Animals, by Jonathon Safran Foer (Back Bay Books, 2010)

Soak Your Nuts, by Karyn Calabrese (Book Publishing Company, 2011)

The China Study, by T. Colin Campbell (BenBella Books, 2011)

Thrive, by Brendan Brazier (Da Capo Lifelong Books, 2008)

RECOMMENDED MOVIES

Food, Inc.

Forks Over Knives

Peaceable Kingdom

RECOMMENDED WEBSITES

Mercyforanimals.org

Farmsanctuary.org

Vegan.org

index

Karyn Calabrese is a successful entrepreneur and popular holistic health expert based in Chicago. For the past 30 years, Karyn has been committed to taking care of her body and helping others to do the same.

Karyn started on her journey to health after suffering from a host of allergies and ailments as a child. In her 20s, she turned to a natural approach and a plant-based diet to improve her health, gradually transitioning from a vegetarian to a vegan to a raw diet. Her journey not only resulted in lifelong personal health and fitness, but also in a mini empire of four natural food restaurants, holistic health and teaching programs, a cleansing and detoxification therapy center, a line of all-natural foods and supplements, and home care, skin care, and cosmetic products.

As a student of Dr. Ann Wigmore and Viktoras Kulvinskas, Karyn used raw food and detoxification to heal her illness, fatigue, and allergies. With two children to raise, she began growing and distributing wheatgrass, the first step in opening Karyn's Fresh Corner. It became a thriving success, and to this day is the longest-standing raw-food restaurant in the country. In addition, she developed a detoxification program that she teaches to hundreds of people each year in Chicago. That led to her debut book, *Soak Your Nuts: Cleansing with Karyn*. To facilitate this process of cleansing, she opened a holistic therapy center, Karyn's Inner Beauty Center.

Karyn has enjoyed huge success as a health expert in the local and national media, including two appearances on The Oprah Winfrey Show. She was awarded the first annual Raw and Living Foods Golden Branch Award in 2002 for introducing raw and living foods to the greatest number of people in the mainstream public.

Now 65, Karyn has helped thousands of people on their own health journeys. *Soak Your Nuts: Karyn's Conscious Comfort Foods* is her second book.

Soak Your Nuts
Cleansing with Karyn
978-1-57067-264-4
$16.95